One
Summer
Day

Emi Yusa
(The Hero, Emilia Justina)

Mommy! I wish she'd stop fighting with Daddy so much! We're always together! I love her!

Sadao Maou
(Devil King Satan)

Daddy! He works real, real hard all the time! We're always together! I love him!

...aki

...th

...,

...my ...her, too.

*Dramatization.
May not
actually
happen
in the
story.

Alas Ramus's Character Intro

I'll do my best!!

Suzuno Kamazuki

(Crestia Bell, Reconciliation Panel Cleric)

Suzu-Sis! She dresses soooo pretty. And she cooks a lot, too! I love her!

**Han:
Urush**

(Demor
Lue

Looshifer! W
beat mean
Stop picki
love him!

THE DEVIL IS A PART-TIMER

4

SATOSHI
WAGAHARA
ILLUSTRATION BY
029 (ONIKU)

OROCHIMIN C

CONTENTS

SATOSHI WAGAHARA

ILLUSTRATED BY 029 (ONIKU)

4

YEN ON

NEW YORK

THE DEVIL IS A PART-TIMER!, Volume 4
SATOSHI WAGAHARA, ILLUSTRATION BY 029 (ONIKU)

Translation by Kevin Gifford

HATARAKU MAOUSAMA!, Volume 4
©SATOSHI WAGAHARA 2012
All rights reserved.
First published in 2012 by KADOKAWA CORPORATION, Tokyo.

English translation rights arranged with KADOKAWA CORPORATION, Tokyo, through Tuttle-Mori Agency, Inc., Tokyo.

Yen On
1290 Avenue of the Americas
New York, NY 10104
www.yenpress.com

Yen On is an imprint of Yen Press, LLC.
The Yen On name and logo are trademarks of Yen Press, LLC.

The publisher is not responsible for websites (or their content) that are not owned by the publisher.

First Yen On Edition: April 2016

Library of Congress Cataloging-in-Publication Data
Names: Wagahara, Satoshi. | 029 (Light novel illustrator) illustrator. | Gifford, Kevin, translator.
Title: The devil is a part-timer! / Satoshi Wagahara ; illustration by 029 (Oniku) ; translation by Kevin Gifford.
Other titles: Hataraku Maousama!. English
Description: First Yen On edition. | New York, NY : Yen On, 2015–
Identifiers: LCCN 2015028390| ISBN 9780316383127 (v. 1 : pbk.) | ISBN 9780316385015 (v. 2 : pbk.) | ISBN 9780316385022 (v. 3 : pbk.) | ISBN 9780316385039 (v. 4 : pbk.)
Subjects: | CYAC: Fantasy.
Classification: LCC PZ7.1.W34 Ha 2015 | DDC [Fic]—dc23 LC record available at http://lccn.loc.gov/2015028390

10 9 8 7 6 5 4 3 2

RRD-C

Printed in the United States of America

PROLOGUE

Emeralda Etuva felt she was already short enough, even without the stress weighing her down.

While serving as Court Alchemist for the Holy Empire of Saint Aile, even as the Hero's companion, she had become a household name. Emeralda now found herself one of the most influential people in all the Western Island.

The role of court alchemist was traditionally an academic one, with some government advisory work mixed in as necessary. Before the previous wholesale invasion of Ente Isla by ransacking demon hordes, she had been in little position to speak up on political or diplomatic affairs.

But thanks to the role she played in the Hero's quest, the people of this island now hung on every word she spoke publicly—and beside them, the Federated Order of the Five Continents, the group tasked with the rebuilding of the world.

As a result, compared to her duties before the Demon King's ultimate demise, her unexpected new role as advisor to the Federation's top generals had the effect of dramatically increasing her workload.

This rise in the political ladder made her the envy of Saint Aile's power brokers. Beneath the surface, it made the Church—whose relationship with her took a major blow after the whole Olba Meiyer affair—view her with hostility. It all led to a dangerous amount of stress, enough to make her vent at her former traveling partner Albert:

"Once the Central Continent is rebuilt, I think I'm gonna defect, you knooooow?"

Her only solace was that her official post in the Federated Order of the Five Continents was overseeing the armies tasked with wiping up the demons that remained in the land.

These hordes were nothing to sweat about, particularly. They certainly didn't call for Emeralda herself to ride for the battlefield.

But the job of annihilating the demons that remained in the Central Continent still required the efforts of warriors from every nation, united under the common banner of protecting the weak and helpless. Beholding this spontaneous show of brotherhood was enough to make Emeralda believe there was still some hope for this world yet.

But Emeralda, and Albert as well, knew the truth.

The battle between the Hero and Devil King still raged on. Far away. In another world.

And though barely two years had passed since the Devil King's forces fell, the people of Ente Isla, unaware of this, were quickly ferrying the name of the Hero Emilia away into the oblivion of legend.

At first, Emeralda and Albert worked fervently to restore Emilia's good name, so badly besmirched by Olba's would-be altering of history.

But even at this early point, the world situation no longer required Emilia. It needed a decent bureaucrat or two, not a semi-heavenly savior.

Whether she was alive or dead hardly mattered. To most of the people who lived and breathed here, the name Emilia Justina meant little more than "this lady with a sword who lived somewhere or other."

Only a small clutch of people, the ones who knew Emilia personally, could associate that name with an actual human being any longer.

And any attempt to restore Emilia's reputation would require revealing Olba and the Church's high crimes to the public—costing the organization its power, its authority, its whole reason for existing.

Justice, wrought by the connected and powerful in the name of righteous anger, could damage far more than it could heal. If Saint Aile and the Church—the two most powerful presences on the

Western Island—were to formally clash with each other, the entire subcontinent would be split in two, the decline of the entire region no doubt in the offing.

Emeralda found herself lost.

The other four lands that comprised Ente Isla were devoting their collected strength to rebuilding the world. The Western Island couldn't afford *not* to keep a unified front. She had to keep that from unraveling; keep their power from being wasted on internal strife.

Thus, Emeralda Etuva made a politician's decision: She put her country's future ahead of her friend's honor.

Emeralda was no heartless powermonger, though. Her decision was supported by another factor:

Crestia Bell, cleric on the Reconciliation Panel.

Once feared as the "Scythe of Death," the leader of the Council of Inquisitors, Crestia was now a loyal companion to Emilia.

A Church cleric, one in a position to advise the Archbishops in their Sanctuary, was working to restore Emilia's honor and reaffirm the noble name of the Church. The news came as music to Emeralda's ears.

The fact that she once directly reported to Olba was also enormous.

If Crestia, an outsider to politics, could take Emeralda's place in exposing the corruption that threatened to topple the Church—although news of such heinous apostasy would no doubt roil the public—it would help the Church "heal thyself," as it were. Faith in it would remain strong, and with it, stability. Wasteful infighting and disorder among the masses would be kept at a minimum.

Emeralda, meanwhile, was pinned in place by her very public name. If she clashed directly with the Church, the resulting shock waves would throw the people into panic and agitation.

It vexed her not to raise the flag for Emilia, considering she was her first real friend in life. But if she wanted to both restore Emilia's name and keep the peace nationwide, Emeralda concluded it wiser to allow Crestia to take action in her place.

And someday, there would come a time when Crestia's name took a rightful role alongside her own as a fighter for the Hero's cause.

Maybe.

"It'd be niiiiice…but, ooooh, maybe not so niiiiice…"

Emeralda murmured to herself as she read through a weighty stack of reports on the desk in her office, a gift from the Federated Order's headquarters.

"But…I don't knoooow…maybe Emilia shouldn't come back home at alllll…"

Japan. That alien world. That blissfully bountiful, peaceful land.

Emilia might be better off living a quiet life over there. It was her second home now.

The thought refused to banish itself from Emeralda's mind as she shot a glance at the alchemic audio transmitter—Emilia referred to it as a "cell phone"—on one corner of her desk.

"Hey! Eme! Listen to this!"

The voice that had spoken through it not long ago was agitated, but somehow still light and airy.

"He's been volunteering with the neighborhood cleanup crews! Him! The Devil King! That horrible monster! Doesn't that make you laugh like a maniac?"

Once, not long ago, she was a knight in the Church's service. A woman whose entire life was devoted to one thing: revenge for her father, earned by blood.

"Can you believe this, Eme? I'm going nuts here! The Devil King is killing me! Why is changing a diaper so goddamn hard?!"

But now, like any woman her age, she laughed, cried, and raged in equal doses.

Her report about a "girl who popped out of a giant apple" a while ago, followed by the revelation of the child's true identity, was enough to stun even Emeralda. But instead of this girl's origin, the people on the other side seemed more preoccupied about the fact that she saw Emilia and the Devil King as her parents. Things like Heaven and the Sephirah, both far more pressing topics of discussion, were somehow by-and-large glossed over.

"I want to restore my father's wheat fields."

That had been Emilia's dream.

But if she returned to Ente Isla, she was Emilia Justina, The Hero Who Saved the World. If they could repair her reputation, the people would lovingly sing her praises as they adopted her as a symbol of justice for all time. But it would keep her from those fields, likely forever.

To Emeralda, it wouldn't mark the end of Emilia being solely her friend. But it would make access far more difficult.

Besides, she was already deep into the political game, a position she accepted without asking for Emilia's feedback.

"Things never go as one expects, dooo they?"

Emeralda heaved an exaggerated sigh, letting the stress out before it diminished her any further. Emilia had already accomplished her main mission in life. What happened to her next, she was free to decide on her own.

Whether she returned to Ente Isla or not, it was Emeralda's role to prepare a world for her that was as bright and shiny as possible. She saw this as her responsibility, the result of plucking a simple girl out from the village and transforming her into a myth.

Then Emeralda realized it: This entire line of thinking hinged on the assumption that the Devil King, too, was staying put in Japan.

She knew why that was so easy to take for granted. The Devil King, to his credit, was no longer the Devil King she and Ente Isla once knew and loathed.

Satan, lord of all demons, was now hard at work in the human world, living an honest, sober life among them and even attempting to raise that girl from the apple. Like a human parent would. Emilia herself admitted to it.

"So is that all it takes for peeeace? Without any of these other questions answered? Or should we seek to *find* those answers, even if it leads to certain...saaacrifices? A tough nut to crack, indeeeed."

Emilia Etuva, friend of Emilia, struggled against the Saint Aile court alchemist within her.

"Hmmm...?"

Distracted by these intertwining emotions, Emeralda's hand stopped as she more closely examined the documents she was stamping.

For the past half month, she had noticed that the demon hordes seemed to be, oddly enough, growing. The number of demons eyewitnessed during a typical patrol was slowly, yet clearly, on an upward trend.

"Oooh, I don't like thaaat…"

Last month, there was even a day or two with zero demons put down. The rise was very slight from day to day, but through the previous two weeks, this gradual rise was starting to add up, with no sign of a decline.

The rise in potential demon targets also led to an accompanying rise in Federated Order casualties. Emeralda frowned.

If this kept up, she might have need to set off herself to investigate.

It was just as she began to write her recommendations along those lines in a supplementary report that a shrill voice rang out.

"Lady Etuva!!"

It belonged to a knight's assistant from the North Island, who all but sprinted into the office with a clatter.

"What is it?"

The young squire's face was white as a ghost as he gasped for breath, eyes darting to and fro nervously.

It indicated before she even asked that there was no good news to come.

THE
DEVIL
FINDS
HIMSELF
JOBLESS,
THEN
HOMELESS

Her flowing silver hair shone beautifully, like the Milky Way gracing the night sky.

The pair of eyes bobbing in this heavenly waterway emitted a quiet, powerful poise, presenting a sublime light brighter than even those twin rulers of the skies, the sun and the moon.

"She's so pretty…"

His frail whisper, as if his soul had been torn from his body, dissipated into the air before it could reach anyone's ear.

A turn of the eye, and then he was enraptured by the figure's powerful, bounding arms and legs: life personified, at the peak of kinetic activity.

The innocent frame was gifted with seemingly limitless possibility, the rest of its life awaiting it with open arms, reaching the pinnacle of beauty in a way that surpassed any work of art that came before it.

She was as dexterous and nimble as a bounding gazelle, but her legs were as supple and delicate as the petals of a lily.

Her beauty had an airy, almost lyrical quality to it, like the wings of an angel, but her arms were as bewitching and beguiling as a jaguar on the prowl.

But above anything else, her face—more beautiful and fluid than a kaleidoscope, more colorful than a rose, more graceful than a peony in full bloom, more fleeting than a cherry blossom—was sheer bliss, far beyond what a thousand songs and poems could hope to capture in sound and word.

"Mwa-ha-ha-ha-ha…"

The sight snatched his heart away. And although he was alone, nobody could have chided him for losing himself in the mesmerizing sight.

"Um…Maou?"

"Ah-hah-hah-hah…"

After all, from the moment he awoke to the moment his eyes closed, he was forever caught in her siren-like attraction.

"Maou, you should really keep your voice down…"

"Bwah-hah-hah-hah-hah!"

Heart and soul, he was her prisoner, his very life a mere plaything in her hands.

"Maou, come *on*!"

"Gahh! Wh-What, Chi?!"

Sadao Maou, feeling someone shake him by the shoulder, flashed a creepy smile to himself before returning to his senses.

Turning around, he saw his coworker, the only girl he fully trusted in Japan (and the only native Japanese woman to know his true identity), puffing up her cheeks as she put her hands to her hips.

Inside the staff break room at the MgRonald in front of Hatagaya rail station, the world-conquering Devil King was being scolded by a teenage girl.

"We can hear you laughing all the way over in the kitchen. And it's kind of freaking *me* out, too!"

"Oh. Uh? *Ohhh*. Sorry. Guess I kinda lost control."

Chiho Sasaki, face reddened as she looked up at the taller Maou, glanced down and frowned at the cheap cardboard photo album in his hand, the kind most camera shops give out for free with purchases.

"Ugh… You're looking at those pictures of Alas Ramus again, aren't you?"

"Sure was! Hey, take a look at this one a sec."

Shaking off Chiho's accusation, Maou thrust the album in her face, fully forgetting what she'd told him three seconds ago.

"…Another new one?"

The photo he showed off depicted a silver-haired toddler frolicking around somebody's lawn, arms wide open in the air as she breathlessly ran forward.

"Y'know, this isn't really a photo, though. It's a…uh, what do you call it? A screen capture? One of those. From a video. I had them print it out for me!"

"……"

"That bastard Emi hardly brings her over at all, you know, so it's like, *jeez*, having to wait for the big day practically drives me nuts! I shot this when I took Alas Ramus to the sports gym in Hatagaya the other day, but man, she pretty much ran around the whole day! She's an animal!"

"…That's *great*."

Chiho couldn't find any other response.

"Hey, did you need any of these, though? I got a lot of new pictures of her!"

"…I'm fine for now, thanks. I got a lot to look through already."

Despite her attraction to Maou and her honest love for Alas Ramus, his output was proving difficult to keep up with. She gently returned the photo.

In the past two weeks, once Emi brought Alas Ramus back to Maou after the girl was feared lost forever, Maou's behavior around the child had tiptoed past mere devotion and was now fully ensconced in the land of overprotectiveness.

The all-consuming love was enough to drive Maou, who'd never purchased anything beyond the bare necessities for himself during his entire time in Japan, to buy an outdated digital camera and photo printer. It was clear how much of a terminal case this was.

He had Hanzou Urushihara, the deadbeat fallen angel who now had nothing to boast of apart from his past glories and Web-surfing skills, process the photos and videos on their computer, allowing Maou to view what he had shot while Alas Ramus wasn't around to soothe his soul. However, the purchase of these not-so-bare necessities was far from a welcome sight for Shirou Ashiya, the demon who served as guardian of the Devil's Castle coffers.

The running costs associated with the ink alone was nothing at all to sniff at. Urushihara also had the habit of leaving the printer on after processing Maou's photos, a colossal waste of electricity. To Ashiya, whose fervent dream was to make the demon realm's official slogan "A penny saved is a penny earned," it was yet another everyday stress to tangle with.

"I mean, you're free to use your break time any way you want, but…Ms. Kisaki's gonna come back pretty soon, so could you, uh, try to get it together a little more?"

"No problemo! I flip the switch in my brain, and *bam*, it's back on the clock!"

The shift supervisor/Devil King's avowal, delivered in the wake of being admonished by a teenage girl, turned up lacking in the way of convincing force considering the simpering, half-mad grin he accented it with.

Granted the right to dote on Alas Ramus from Emi Yusa—her other "parent" and his own sworn enemy—on the several occasions per month she brought her along on a visit, Maou acted exactly like a father who'd lost custody of his child after a long, bitter divorce.

To Chiho, fully aware of Maou's goals and his former cloven-hoofed self, it wasn't a cause of exasperation so much as honest concern. She left the staff room, having said her fill.

"I hope Maou's all right, going on about Alas Ramus all day and night like that. I guess he could afford the camera and printer, so he must have some spare cash…but then again, I don't think he works anywhere else…"

She took a glance at the calendar on a side wall as she whispered furtively to herself.

"We're closing up shop tomorrow, too…"

✳

Sadao Maou: Better known elsewhere as the Devil King Satan, an all-powerful scoundrel from the demon realms who all but had Ente Isla wrapped around one clawed finger. Emi Yusa: Better known elsewhere as Emilia the Hero, the savior who rescued Ente Isla from a fate worse than death.

Thanks to the child called Alas Ramus claiming both of them as her parents, the Hero and Devil King were now struggling with a life of child-rearing that neither were particularly used to. It was only with extreme reluctance that they worked together on the effort.

The confrontation against the archangel Gabriel over the fate of this child had ended in a narrow victory for these "parents," if only thanks to a very unlikely chain of completely unpredictable events.

It was really more of a forfeit than a victory, but with Gabriel unable to fulfill his mission, Alas Ramus was now free to live where she wanted to be.

What made things tricky was that Alas Ramus had fused herself with the Better Half, the holy sword that Emi wielded in battle.

The sword, and Alas Ramus herself, was created from shards of Yesod, one of the world-creating Sephirah jewels that grew on the Tree of Sephirot.

Gabriel's goal was to snatch away the child and Emi's sword, connecting the Yesod fragments together to restore the Sephirah to its original state.

Despite leaving these fragments unattended for what would seem like eons to a regular person, Gabriel seemed to be in a terrible rush to glue, as it were, the Yesod back together. His sudden frantic haste was difficult to understand.

But thanks to Alas Ramus merging with the holy sword that proved doggedly nonremovable from Emi's body, Gabriel had no way of returning home anything but empty-handed.

Thanks to that, Alas Ramus was forced to move from her previous domain—the Devil's Castle located in room 201 of the sixty-year-old Villa Rosa Sasazuka apartments in Sasazuka, Shibuya ward, Tokyo—to Emi's place, a condominium in the Eifukucho area of Tokyo's Suginami ward.

This created assorted issues.

One: Alas Ramus was hopelessly devoted to Maou, her "daddy."

Emi, as a Hero, could never let herself ignore common sense and allow Alas Ramus to live near the Devil King, someone who'd not only stunt her educational growth but also quite possibly eradicate humanity from the face of the Earth.

But now that Alas Ramus was a literal holy sword with the power to take human form, she had a tendency to cry out in Emi's mind whenever she felt lonely.

The crying of a young infant, as anyone who's been around one knows, has more destructive force than the roar of a savage beast.

Emi had sworn to herself after the fusion to keep Alas Ramus away from Maou's apartment as much as possible. That resolve crumbled to dust in three days.

Alas Ramus's mental outlook on life remained the same whether she was in baby or sword form, it seemed. She didn't care whether Emi was at work, or sleeping, or doing anything else. When she wanted to see Daddy, she turned up the volume.

So, in order to avoid the morbid tragedy of being kept up all night by plaintive sobbing only she could hear, Emi's visits to Devil's Castle came even more often than before.

Two: Even if it weren't for that, there was the matter of all the care the Devil's Castle residents practically tore their hair out giving to the child. Food. Teeth brushing. Diaper changes. Now Emi was traveling down that same road, and in her weakened mental state, their support was like an inviting beacon, a surefire way out of life's annoyances.

Alas Ramus generally listened to what Emi told her, rarely erupting into a temper tantrum if things didn't go her way. But her life cycle continued unabated, sword or not. Emi returning home after work, only to find Alas Ramus materializing before her with a disturbingly full diaper, was a catastrophe that happened more than a few times.

This didn't mean she could just toss the child over to Devil's Castle, though. That would be too easy. Alas Ramus could run around in child form independent of Emi, but deep down, she was still deeply connected—fused, really—to Emi.

If the toddler ever ventured too far away from her, she would dematerialize and force her way back into Emi's body. The Hero confirmed this for herself with some experimentation.

All in all, Alas Ramus could remain physically separate from Emi as long as she stayed within roughly the length of one stop on the Keio train line.

The only woman who could understand Emi's current state of anguish was Crestia Bell, cleric for the Church's Reconciliation Panel, currently living next door to Devil's Castle under the name Suzuno Kamazuki.

Chiho, upon learning of this, had been less than sympathetic.

"Wow! So you don't have to worry about her getting lost or anything?"

She had it dead-on, of course, but what it spelled for Emi was the humiliating thought of constant paternity visits to Devil's Castle. At least, Emi rationalized to herself, Maou liked getting to see her more often. Hopefully that would thin out any evil urges in his blood. The thought was the only thing Emi had to keep herself together.

※

As crackerjack MgRonald store manager Mayumi Kisaki frequently reminded her thoroughly cowed employees at the franchise near Hatagaya station, she never told a joke unless she wanted people to laugh.

She was feared by the part-time crew, who called her the "demon of sales" under their breath in their hushed conversations behind the counter, but she was always sincere with her customers and evenhanded with her staff.

There was no guile behind that attitude, no two-faced treachery at all, but the matter-of-fact remark she had just tossed in Sadao Maou's direction was something he couldn't unravel at all.

Kisaki never told lies. Or unfunny jokes. That's what made it so unbelievable.

"Okaaaay, shutdown's tomorrow, people!"

She uttered those foreboding words at four in the afternoon, a relatively quiet time customer-wise, just as Maou, Chiho, and the rest of the afternoon shift were wrapping up.

At that moment, all sound disappeared from Maou's ears.

To him, it was like Kisaki cast a magic spell—demonic, holy, it didn't matter—that froze everything in the space around her. It was an instant locked in infinity, like the nanosecond before the Big Bang.

"M-Maou?"

"Npghh!"

If Chiho hadn't called for him, hand brushing against his arm, Maou might have embarked on a boundless journey across space and time he could never return from.

Recovering from the science-fiction dreamscape, Maou's brain was pounded by a torrent of conflicting information.

Within this region of the corporate map, the Hatagaya-station MgRonald was a poster boy for superb management, posting rising sales on a constant year-to-year basis.

It wasn't a very large location by square footage, but its combination of flexible service, sincere customer relations, and painstaking standard of cleanliness earned it a commendation after every quarterly regional contest.

That Hatagaya store was being closed?!

It verged on the absurd.

But Maou appeared to be the only one the declaration took by surprise. Chiho and the rest of the crew betrayed no sign of anger or shock.

The only emotion being shown at all was the concern in Chiho's eyes as she watched Maou all but melt into a puddle of goo.

"I suppose we'll be going our separate ways for now, but I hope you all won't forget what you learned here, wherever you wind up. Keep up the good work! That's all."

"Ah, uh, uh, uh, Ms. Kisaki?!"

"Hmm? Got a question, Marko?"

"Q-Question...? I mean, like...?"

The ignition system powering up Maou's thought process was having trouble finding a spark to work with. Where could he begin? Wait—before that, what did she mean by "wherever you wind up"?

And why wasn't anyone else going nuts over this? Maou didn't know who to turn to any longer.

"The place is…shutting down?"

Kisaki's eyebrows plunged downward at the few words he finally managed to squeak out.

"We talked about this two or so weeks ago, didn't we?"

"Uhh…"

This reminded Maou of absolutely nothing. Two weeks ago would've marked the more-or-less endpoint of the cross-world struggle over Alas Ramus.

"Um…Maou…?"

From behind, Chiho whispered into his ear.

"I think it might've been the time you thought Alas Ramus was gone…"

"Uhhh…"

With another dimwitted drone, Maou pressed deeper into his memory, dragging out the events of half a month ago to the forefront.

Right after he asked Kisaki for more shifts in order to provide for Alas Ramus, Gabriel showed up and wreaked havoc on his life.

For the next two days, Maou thought that Gabriel took Alas Ramus away to heaven-or-wherever. It admittedly depressed him. In fact, it was one of the worst eras of his employment with MgRonald, one where he repeatedly made the kind of mistakes a newbie on his first shift would make. But Kisaki let it slide. She was a bit concerned about Maou's health, but…

"Oh. Wait…back then…?"

"Don't tell me…you weren't listening?"

The disbelieving tone to Kisaki's voice made the rest of the crew instinctively tense up.

She was always fair when evaluating work performance, but when it came to carelessness or laziness, she was a slave driver.

"…Well, nobody else has a problem with this, right?"

"No, ma'am!!"

Everyone except Maou shouted in practiced unison, like a well-trained military choir.

"You heard 'em, Marko. Why don't we go to the office?"

The blood drained from Maou's face as he sheepishly followed Kisaki.

Despite it being the middle of summer, the air around them stung blisteringly cold as Chiho and the crew watched them go in blood-curdling silence.

Kisaki sat at her desk, leaving Maou standing, and silently began tapping at her computer.

Maou, bolt upright, couldn't see anything apart from her turned back.

After a moment, a printer even older than the Alas Ramus one buzzed loudly while it spat out a form.

Picking up the first page, Kisaki finally turned around and brusquely presented it to Maou.

"If this can't help you, I'm afraid there's not much else I can do."

"Uh...mm...? What's this?"

"It's a list of MgRonalds you can pick up shifts at right now."

"A list of Mags...? So this location's really closing down?"

Kisaki averted her face from the ashen-faced Maou, one finger on her temple.

"Wow. You really weren't listening at all, were you? You just kind of stared into space and mumbled 'okay' to me back then, but I figured you must have noticed the calendar and the bulletin board by now. I mean, there's even a notice to customers on the door out front. You've been kinda mailing it in lately, Marko. Didn't the shift schedule look weird to you at all?"

Kisaki's "mailing it in" observation was half wrong, half right.

Since Alas Ramus showed up, Maou devoted himself to working more shifts than ever before. In an attempt to gain a more stable paycheck, he tried to pick up one shift per day as supervisor. This meant he now started and ended work on the same times daily, which made him pay far less attention to the shift schedule than before.

Alas Ramus might be living at Emi's apartment, but since Maou all but declared that he was responsible for the child's upbringing, he was always on the lookout for an opportunity to give Emi some money for child-rearing expenses.

It hadn't quite happened yet—Emi steadfastly refused all offers so far—but Maou kept on working, figuring that it'd help prop up his own budget if worse came to worst.

Reflecting on these past events, Maou turned his eyes toward the printout Kisaki had given him.

"Why would one of the best-performing locations in the west Shibuya region have to shut down, Marko? This is temporary. We're remodeling the place to convert it to a new category. It'll open back up in mid-August, after the Obon holiday wraps up. Most of the offices nearby are on summer break right now anyway."

"New category?"

The explanation wiped away a decent percentage of the disquiet in Maou's soul. Just learning that it wasn't a permanent closing lightened his heart tremendously.

Not every MgRonald was the same, of course. There were suburban locations with large indoor playgrounds, smaller "Mini-Mag"-themed storefronts inside shopping centers, and drive-through MgRonalds by major highways.

Along those lines, the Hatagaya MgRonald was now being converted to a "MagCafé" that offered a premium breakfast-café menu in addition to the standard offerings.

MagCafés had to handle a larger variety of dishes and ingredients, so the new menu veered toward the more costly side compared to the regular fare.

To compensate for that, MagCafé dining spaces were designed for more comfort and a more refined atmosphere. This required a top-to-bottom remodel of the store space, though, and that required time.

The interior would be completely different, from the lighting and ceilings to the walls and floors, and the kitchen would also need a litany of refurbishments to handle the new menu selections.

"But...we're building a MagCafé in *this* space?"

That was the other rub, the niggling concern that kept him uneasy.

Currently, there were no MagCafé-exclusive locations in Japan. MagCafé was a subset of a typical MgRonald setup, but due to the square footage required to execute the concept, all MagCafés were in fairly large spaces, whether in the city or out in a freestanding building.

The Hatagaya MgRonald set up shop in the ground floor of a commercial building facing a shopping area. But it was small. They couldn't even fit fifty seats in there.

Maou could picture the new MgRonald/MagCafé combo essentially forcing the customers out of the place, what with all the remodeling and new equipment. Kisaki, however, pointed upward in response.

"We're taking over the second floor."

"Whaaa?!"

"No way could we pull this plan off otherwise. Not in *this* tiny space. The company upstairs is pulling out at the end of July, and we managed to snap it up from them. It happened pretty quick, so this conversion's kind of on a breakneck schedule, but we're planning to have the regular setup downstairs, MagCafé upstairs, and ninety seats total."

Maou wondered aloud why they didn't just remodel the second floor, then, and keep a smaller operation running downstairs.

"That wouldn't work. There's just too much construction to do. A location's exterior and product lineup is kind of like a businessman's suit. If your shirt isn't tucked in and your jacket has moth holes in it, that'll turn off your customers. You need to have the full package ready, or else you'll be scraping for dimes in the gutter."

The way Kisaki put it, despite the suddenness of this conversion, it was a pretty involved project. A common water system would need to be installed across both floors, and the POS register system required a complete upgrade. Trying to stay open in the midst of all that, the higher-ups decided, would scare customers away. Hence the decision to close for remodeling.

"So for the time being, we're sending the staff out to nearby locations in a support role...but I guess you didn't get the memo, huh? I probably could've found somewhere pretty close for you if you'd noticed sooner."

Kisaki shrugged a "my hands are tied" shrug.

The available MgRonalds in the list Kisaki handed him were all either an impractically long commute from Sasazuka or didn't have much to offer shiftwise. It being the middle of summer break, the employee rolls at most MgRonalds were fairly well saturated with students and other part-timers.

Maou, having risen to the point where he boasted a regular shift-supervisor gig, no longer had the chance to see Kisaki in person as much as before. Being the general manager, she didn't need to be around when Maou was.

That was another indirect cause of this current disaster.

"All of the crew's jobs are guaranteed. It's the company closing this location on its own volition, after all. But, I'm sad to say, a lot of this is your fault. You weren't checking up on our important notices. I like you, Maou, and I want you to work in the best possible environment I can find for you. But at this point, this is about all I got."

Kisaki stood up and placed a hand on Maou's shoulder.

"If you want to help support any of those locations, let me know by tomorrow evening."

Maou could feel his vision blacking out.

Chiho, still looking worried, was there to greet Maou as he shambled out of the staff room like a horror-film extra.

"So you didn't notice at all?"

"N-No... No. Uh, are you gonna work some other location, Chi?"

"Nah, I'm gonna take some time off until we reopen, but... I dunno. I'm sorry."

Chiho, her head lowered in apology, baffled Maou.

"I haven't had too many shifts lately 'cause I've been busy with school club trips and so on...and you've been so busy with Alas Ramus, too. You probably would've noticed sooner if we had a chance to talk a little more..."

Apparently Chiho felt some odd sense of responsibility for Maou's error. She turned her head back upward, eyes welled up a little. Maou briskly shook his head, fully aware that she bore exactly zero of the blame for this.

"N-No! No no no no! It's not your fault, Chi! And, I mean, Alas Ramus is over at Emi's place now, so it's my fault for spacing out so much, you know? Heh-heh! Guess I can't switch my brain on and off like I thought I could, huh? But…uh, hey, you wanna come over to my place today, Chi?"

"Huh?"

Chiho's eyebrows shot upward at the sudden invite.

"Suzuno told me this morning that Emi's gonna come over to eat dinner with us. Alas Ramus would *love* to see you and all, and… well, like I give two craps about Emi, but the more, the merrier when it comes to dinner, right? So, you know…"

Maou gave Chiho a pat on the shoulder.

"I…I mean, I'm okay, so cheer up a little, huh?"

"A-all right…"

Chiho's face turned a light shade of pink as she shallowly nodded.

"Yo! I'm back!"

"Um, hello, guys…"

Thanks to today's morning start, Maou found himself back home by seven PM. It was still sunny out, but lights shone through the windows of nearby houses as the people inside prepared for dinner.

"Daddyyyy!"

Returning to Villa Rosa Sasazuka, an apartment building that was new back when Elvis was considered "up and coming," Maou and Chiho were greeted by the warm, angelic smile of Alas Ramus, enough to instantly calm the frazzled Maou's mind and body.

This would normally be Alas Ramus's cue to jog around the low table in the center of the room to hug Maou. This time, though, the child executed some nimble cornering to collide straight-on with Chiho instead.

"Chi-Sis!"

"Wow, Alas Ramus! Somebody's sure excited, huh?"

Chiho deftly scooped Alas Ramus up mid-bullrush, boosting her into the air and away from the disappointed Maou, his hands still aloft in anticipation of being imminently full of toddler.

Emi Yusa, her "mommy" and greatest threat to the continued existence of Devil's Castle now that she dropped by after work, grinned wryly to herself.

"Glad to see *someone's* making the right decision."

"Shut up! Yeah, hit a man while he's down, huh? Hey, Alas Ramus, I'm here, too, y'know!"

"Chi-Sis!"

She was oblivious.

"Welcome to your domain, Your Demonic Highness. Please, take this hot towel."

The sensible Ashiya, stepping up to soothe his supreme leader's bruised ego, whisked over an *oshibori* towel he had just warmed up in the microwave. The king of all demons wiped the sweat he worked up on the way home, scrunching his face in an attempt to shake away his fatigue.

"Ooooooo, that feels good…"

"And welcome to you, too, Ms. Sasaki. Please, take a seat right here."

The ever-thoughtful gentleman of the house passed a cloth to Chiho, Alas Ramus still in her arms, before inviting her to a corner of the center table. She nodded a greeting at Ashiya and Emi.

"Sorry I kind of came uninvited."

"Oh, I don't care. Not like I really have a say in it, but it's fine. You're making *her* happy, too."

A refined female voice emerged across from Ashiya.

"You may always consider yourself welcome, Chiho. But…"

She flashed a scornful look at the two demons, both far taller than herself, as she brought a bowl and set of chopsticks for Chiho.

"I had no objections to you tossing those silly hot towels around, but I beg of you, please stop rubbing it against your face and neck while grunting like some horrid beast. You *are* the Devil King, remember. You have a reputation to uphold."

Suzuno Kamazuki, decked out in her trademark apron and triangular hair cover, was unreserved as ever in her complaining. She was, after all, just as much Maou's enemy as Emi was, a full-fledged cleric aligned with the Ente Isla Church.

"Why should I care about my reputation around you freaks at *this* point?"

Maou's reply was defiant as he tossed the hot towel back to Ashiya, enough so to make Suzuno heave a mighty sigh as she crept back to the kitchen to mix a bubbling pot of miso soup.

"You do realize that Alas Ramus is learning her table manners from you, yes?"

Suzuno's snide observation came just before Chiho's harried voice re-entered the picture.

"Agh! Wait a minute, Alas Ramus! You're supposed to use your hands!"

The group turned to see Alas Ramus snatch away Chiho's towel and vigorously rub her own face with it, in a perfect imitation of Maou's classic "dad" move.

"Ooooo! Goooooood!"

"Alas Ramus! You will *not* act like some middle-aged lout around this house! That's Chiho's!"

Emi snatched the towel away from the pudgy fingers of the triumphant-looking Alas Ramus.

"All right, Alas Ramus. Let's get your hands nice and neat, okay?"

The towel back in her hands, Chiho softly took up Alas Ramus's little hands as she sat in Chiho's lap, and calmly wiped them clean.

"Pfft."

Suzuno, her concern now a reality, let an ironic smile cross her lips. Maou's own face darkened as he awkwardly turned his back to the table, enlisting Ashiya's help in changing the topic.

"Uhh, so where's Urushihara?"

Ashiya's face darkened for its own reasons.

"Playing around on that silly computer again, no doubt, over in Devil's Castle. Bell refuses to let him bring it in here."

Suzuno, tray tucked under her arm, chimed in.

"And why would I? I tell you, if we left that fool alone, he would be glued in front of that screen from dawn 'til dusk—and far beyond, too! I fear for your electric bill, but more than that, the mere sight of him...*irks* me."

Bucking his usual habit, Maou had fully avoided visiting his Devil's Castle, room 201 in the Villa Rosa Sasazuka building, after work.

This was room 202, currently occupied by Suzuno Kamazuki.

After the battle against Gabriel, the Devil's Castle decor was largely dominated by a gigantic hole in the wall. It honestly surprised Maou that nobody thought to call the police about it. Maybe his neighbors thought it was an improvement.

As an emergency measure, the demons linked together a set of cheap waterproof bicycle covers purchased on clearance at the local home-improvement store to craft an extremely makeshift cover. But they couldn't live with that forever. As remodels went, it wasn't really up to code.

So they trudged back to their real estate agent, the one who stuck them in there in the first place and refused to let them install an AC unit. He placated them with a promise that he'd try to contact Miki Shiba, the landlord.

By today, the hole had become a familiar, semipermanent fixture. It didn't present any critical obstacle, thankfully—they still had gas, electricity, and water, at least. Over the past sixty years, the building had survived typhoons, assassinations, even the '80s. It could survive a bit of a puncture wound.

Or so the demons hoped. But there was no telling what the force of the blast could have done to their apartment's structural integrity behind the walls. Another misstep inside Devil's Castle could compromise God-knew-what underneath the floorboards.

So, on the basis that any further accidents could literally wipe their demonic domain off the map, Maou and his demon generals grew accustomed to the habit of inviting themselves to their Church-cleric neighbor for meals. Open flames and heavy electrical use was something they wanted to avoid for the time being at their place.

Which explained why, to Suzuno and Devil's Castle itself, the greatest threat to life and limb was very much Urushihara, sitting there browsing God-knew-what on his computer all day.

If there was any silver lining to the cloud looming over the wholly-holey Devil's Castle, it was that the past few days had been blessedly rain-free.

But that couldn't continue for long. Maou took his place at the table next to Chiho, contemplating another futile trip to the real estate agent first thing in the morning.

"Daddyyy!"

Alas Ramus, still on Chiho's knee, reached out toward Maou with stubby arms.

That act, and that smile, was enough to make the day's exhaustion and apprehension fly away.

"Ooh, you wanna move over to Daddy, huh? …Is that okay?"

Noticing the rapt anticipation on Maou's face, Chiho positioned the child over his leg, turning her head to check Emi's response. She replied with a reluctant nod.

Emi, as a rule, went pretty easy on Alas Ramus.

Settled into position on Maou's lap, the girl lunged for the chopsticks in front of her with both hands and began jabbing a drumbeat into the table.

"Whoa there, Alas Ramus. That's not what you use 'em for. You have to be polite around here, okay?"

"Oooo."

Alas Ramus, for her part, tended to listen to and follow Maou's and Emi's admonishments, although rarely with heaping spoonfuls of enthusiasm.

Frowning as she returned the chopsticks to where they were (albeit with each of them facing opposite directions), Alas Ramus was rewarded with a rub on the head.

"Therrrre you go. Good girl! Can you sit tight for a little bit until your big sis Suzuno's done serving your food?"

"Okie!"

Suzuno winced for a moment as she ladled rice into each bowl on the table.

"…I wonder why. Every time I hear 'big sis Suzuno' from you, it makes the hairs stand up on my neck."

"Yeah, yeah, yeah. I'm *really* sorry about *that*."

"Ehh, ehh, ehh!"

Alas Ramus joyfully recited Maou's mantra, rewarding the demon with more dirty looks from Emi and Suzuno. He fell silent, returning the chopsticks to their correct position. When it came to his girl, at least, he didn't want to screw things up.

But it was time, he admitted to himself, that he thought a little more seriously about her future. He would need to discuss financials with Ashiya. Then he'd either brave the commute to one of the locations Kisaki showed him, or he'd do…something else.

But there was no need to blurt it out yet. It'd just put him in a weaker position in Emi's eyes. He could imagine her grinning ear to ear: "Guess what, Alas Ramus? Your daddy is unemployed! Can *you* say 'unemployed'? Good! I knew you could!" It was hard to imagine life around the child after that.

"You. Alciel!"

Suzuno, almost done with dinner, barked at Ashiya as she removed her apron.

"Can you please fetch Lucifer for me? You know what a hue and cry he will raise otherwise. Tell him he will miss dinner if he dawdles any further."

"…Very well."

Suzuno, being human, and Ashiya, being demonic, were generally polar opposites of each other. But lately, with both of them manning the kitchen most evenings, they had started to reach a certain sort of détente, at least when it came to Urushihara and home chores.

Ashiya was expressionless as he heeded Suzuno's command, removing and neatly folding his apron before leaving the room.

"That's gotta suck, huh? Having to make an extra portion for *him*, too."

Suzuno blithely untied her head cloth.

"The Devil King is paying his food bill. That, and there are certain monetary savings involved with cooking for many, over cooking for one. It makes menu planning easier."

"You better be careful, though. Keep saying that, and they're gonna leech off of you forever."

"Hmm?"

Suzuno flashed a confused look at Emi's rejoinder, but decided to abandon the topic, folding her legs primly underneath her as she sat across from Maou.

"Daddy, can we eat? Can we eat yet?"

"Just a little bit longer, okay? You're a good girl. We're all gonna eat together, all right?"

"Looshifer, hurry *up!*"

Alas Ramus fully understood the cause of the delay.

Emi fixed her eyes on Alas Ramus, making sure Maou never entered her sight.

"By the way, what're you gonna do with all the stuff in here? I mean, you still got a lot."

"Yes…well, given our current circumstances, I had my real estate agent refer me to a storage site. I intend to send it all there tomorrow."

"What about the stuff in the fridge?"

"I used everything left inside today."

"Ooh."

Maou, idly listening in on the two women's conversation, turned his eyes to the table once again.

"Y'know, I was just thinking this looked a lot fancier than usual. Didja need to clean the fridge or something? You only just bought it."

A brimming plate of sautéed vegetables sat next to a bowl of miso soup infused with onions, eggplant, tofu, and *wakame* seaweed. Another bowl of deep-fried, marinated chicken steamed nearby a stack of minced-beef cutlets. A gaggle of pork dumplings was accompanied by a selection of *nerimono* fish cakes. There was even enough chopped salad for everyone.

A menu like this, borrowing something from almost every aisle in the supermarket, was a change of pace from Suzuno's colorful, more seasonally oriented spreads.

Even with Chiho stopping in unannounced, it was a toss-up whether they'd be stuck with leftovers or not.

Emi's and Suzuno's eyebrows arched upward in unison at Maou's question.

"Uh, what're you talking about?"

"I'm not sure this is any time to be fretting over me. What about you? Have you demons trundled away all your furniture yet?"

"Huh? Whaddaya mean?"

Returning that kind of a question with another question was never a good sign.

It was just as Emi and Suzuno gave a quizzical look to each other that Maou felt something cold rush down his spine.

"Dah! That's freezing!"

No streak of sudden dread, this: Only Alas Ramus, who had climbed off his lap somewhere along the line and was now sticking a bottle of chilled mineral water against his back, the condensation seeping through his shirt.

"That's all wet, Alas Ramus. Can I have it?"

"Ahnn! Nooo!"

The toddler tried her very, very best to keep the bottle in hand as Chiho waged a calm, composed battle to the death for it.

"You *realize*, myself and all of you will have to vacate this apartment for a while beginning tomorrow."

"Hey! Alas Ramus! You gotta listen to Chi for a bit, all right? Hang on, vacating the..
.............................*what'd* you say just now?"

Maou snapped to attention. The moment he did, he felt his body temperature plummet, his face attaining the pallor of a Noh mask as he turned to Suzuno.

"Vacate...the apartment?"

"Oh, for...heaven's *sake*, Devil King..."

The envelope Suzuno produced from her pocket looked familiar.

That opulent lacework on the borders. The smooth, silken paper.

"This arrived right after you ran off to the real estate agent! A notification from our landlord!"

"Huhhh?!"

Maou's chin fell halfway to the floor. The display made Alas Ramus drop the bottle she was cradling with both hands.

"Daddy, don't shout like that! You scaaaary!"

But even Alas Ramus's voice couldn't reach Maou's ears.

He practically ripped the envelope away from Suzuno's hand, ever-so-slowly removing its contents in fear of another grotesque photograph.

It contained a rarity by Shiba standards—a copy of a notification typed up on a computer, and some kind of contract, filled with small, densely-spaced writing.

"To the Residents of Villa Rosa Sasazuka," it began. Maou noticed the date on top. Just about two weeks ago. Then he began reading.

"This...has to be a joke..."

This time, the earth really did flip out from under him. He fell unconscious.

"M-Maou?!"

"Would you look *out*?! You're gonna hit your head on that thing!"

"Daddy?!"

"Did someone just trip, or... M-My liege?!"

"Daaamn, I'm hungry! ...Ooh, hey, Chiho Sasaki! Man, check out this spread today!"

Ashiya's eyes boggled as he was greeted by the sight of a lifeless master past the doorway. Urushihara wasn't quite so moved.

"Al-cell. Daddy went nappies!"

Alas Ramus picked up the paper and handed it to Ashiya.

"Ah, thank you. Hmm? A letter from our landlord to Bell...?"

Emi and Suzuno couldn't stop him in time. He ran his eyes across the notice.

"............Hoooohhh..."

Then he crumpled to the ground, as if breathing his last.

"Hmm? Hey, what's up with you and Maou?"

Without bothering to help his roommates, and without bothering to ask for permission, Urushihara found Emi, Chiho, and Suzuno ruefully glaring at him as he popped a piece of fried chicken into his mouth.

Suzuno plucked the letter from Ashiya's hand, then all but jammed it up Urushihara's nose.

"*Read* this, you walking personification of greed."

"Mngh! Wh-What, dude...? Huh? 'To the Residents'...?"

Urushihara continued to chew with his mouth open as he took in the letter.

"Huh. 'Due to refurbishment work to be done on the main

apartment building, all residents will be compensated during the period of temporary eviction from...' What, *what*? We're getting booted out?! The hell?!"

It was enough to make even him panic. He threw his chopsticks aside as he read on.

To sum up, the structural damage Maou had informed the real estate agent of two weeks ago had, indeed, made its way to the owner.

The size of the hole in room 201 was no laughing matter. A simple patch-up job could destabilize the entire building.

All the age their apartment wore so modestly also led to landlord concerns about the water, gas, and electric systems. In her eyes, the only move to make was a full building renovation.

"...Uh, so, like, I never heard anything about this..."

"I suppose so. If it was enough to make Alciel and the Devil King keel over like a timid goat, I somehow doubt *you* were any less in the dark."

"Bell's gonna be staying at my place until they're done with the repairs, but... Seriously? You guys haven't done anything at all?"

Urushihara listlessly shook his head, then stared blankly at Emi for a moment.

"If you're expecting me to invite you guys in 'cause I'm somehow nostalgic about living in a multifamily household, forget it."

"...Yeah. Guess not."

Not even Urushihara would dare it.

Glancing at the sighing demon, Alas Ramus, unable to comprehend her guardians' harried conversation, toddled up to her fallen housemates.

"Daddy? Al-cell? What's wrong?"

"Uhhhh... I think they're just tired, you know? Here, could you try waking them up for us, Alas Ramus?"

Chiho, the only one in the room aware of Maou's painful experience at work earlier, found herself in a panic. The job was one thing—now he might lose his *place*, even?

"Mm. Daddyyyy! Allll-celllll! Wakey wakey! Dinnewwww!"

Tugged and pulled by Alas Ramus's tiny hands, the pair finally sat up, looking like they just woke up from some incomprehensible dream.

"...I feel like I just saw some kind of mirage."

"...As do I, my liege. ...Wait. No. More of a nightmare, perhaps."

Not even during their life-or-death final battle with the Hero did the Devil King and Great Demon General act so detached from reality.

"Oh...yeah. Ashiya..."

"Y-Yes, Your Demonic Highness?"

Maou's head wobbled as he whispered something to him. Ashiya's wobbled back in response.

".."

"Un...'ployed?"

The throat-clenching silence was broken by Alas Ramus repeating the unfamiliar word she just overheard.

"Uuuufff...!"

Then, making a sound like someone poking a hole in an already half-deflated balloon, Ashiya fainted.

"Aggghhh! Ashiya! He's turning white as a sheet!!"

"Whoa, is he even breathing? Bell! Get some water over here!"

"Mommy! Minnial warter!"

"Ooh, good, Alas Ramus! Lemme borrow that!"

"Will that make him come to? Should we be performing CPR, or—?!"

"...Dude, what's up with Ashiya?"

Only Maou failed to comprehend the blast radius of the dynamite he'd just lit in the room.

✳

"......"

"......"

"......"

Only a light breeze between the cracks in their hole cover cooled the three mighty demons as they sat in a ring around a small package, each face glumly sizing the other up.

The package, about the size of a large padded envelope, was inexplicably wrapped in layers of both clear and duct tape, DO NOT OPEN written in large, shaky lettering on the front.

"What're you waiting for? Open it," Emi sighed in frustration at the frozen trio.

"Well...not much point now, so..."

"Yeah..."

"True..."

Emi, never a patient woman even in the best of times, pushed the indecisive denizens of the dark away, grabbing the package and tearing it apart with her bare hands.

"Whoaaaaa! What the hell're you doing?!"

"Shut *up*! Don't just sit there and *wish* it away! Just *open* it!"

"D-Damn you! You'll pay for this!!"

"No! Nooooo!!"

Ignoring the wailing demons, Emi ripped the rest of the package to shreds.

"...What's this? A video?" she asked.

They were greeted with a single, labelless VHS tape.

"Aw, crap! That video's cursed! It's so totally got to be cursed!!"

Maou desperately raked his hands through his hair.

"It's p-p-probably got some kind of...horrible, *hideous* video on it!"

Ashiya pinned his body against the wall, his face the color of eggshells.

"Her photos were destructive enough as it is! I can't even *think* about her in a *video*!!"

"Can you guys just *stop* already? ...I mean, your landlord sent this to you, right? Why'd you put that tape all over it?"

"It's a freakin' video message from our landlord, dude! You've met her before!"

"So? You're not making any sense to me. Just play it and see what's inside, all right?"

Right after Maou's now-fateful inquiry with the real estate agent, a delivery winged its way to the Devil's Castle as well.

This was no frilly letter smelling vaguely of perfume, though. It was a package, one the demons immediately grew wary of. On the one hand, it probably wasn't anything very important. On the other, it might contain something just as mind-meltingly terrifying as…*That Photo.*

At one point, a tongue-lashing from Suzuno did finally convince the demons to open up the package.

But there was no label or letter inside. Just a plain, black videotape. And after paying a dear price at the Great Landlord Cheesecake Pin-Up Photo Disaster of Earlier This Year, who could possibly blame the demons for their trepidation at bringing the tape anywhere near a VCR?

Assuming there was even a VCR bumping around the Devil's Castle in the first place. That, of course, was not the case.

Ultimately, it was decided that entombing the tape and pretending it never existed was the best course of action. It was buried deep within one of the prefab shelving units in the corner, but now, that tape was the only chance the denizens of Devil's Castle had of somehow avoiding their impending homelessness.

And yet, even now, the trauma of That Photo weighed all too heavily in their hearts.

"So be it! If you don't believe us, I'll be more than happy to unleash the fury of That Photo upon you, Hero!!"

"N-No, my liege! That Photo is a taboo that must never be summoned in our lifetimes! Even the gods themselves may never lay hands upon it!"

"Silence! If we don't wield it now, then when?!"

"Dahhh! I can feel my memory being subverted by that…That Photo! The end of the world is nigh!"

"Our Devil's Castle is crumbling, Your Demonic Highness! Please! No more of this!!"

Completely ignoring the demons' ranting over some photograph— it meant nothing to her anyway—Emi's eyes stopped on Urushihara's computer.

"If we got a cheap video deck somewhere, do you think we could use that thing to watch it?"

With DVD and Blu-ray the current standard worldwide, devices that converted old analog formats to digital media were a common sight at the big-box stores.

All three demons knew that. But why would they flush their valuable money down the toilet for the sake of undoing the seal placed on this false, fetid idol of disgust?

"L-Look, Emi, there's nothing in the world that can play this thing. Let's just, uh, forget about it, okay? Like, we can figure out something by ourselves! Totally!"

Just as Emi landed a kick on the simpering Maou, Suzuno came in carrying Alas Ramus.

"I heard quite a clamor, Emilia. Have you solved this issue yet?"

Emi shook her head, pointed a thumb at the panic-stricken demonic rulers, and shrugged as she explained the videotape.

"Um...in that case..."

Chiho hesitantly spoke up from Suzuno's side.

"I think we still have a working VCR at home... We could go watch it there, if you like?"

"Hey, Mom, I'm—*wagh*!"

"Oh, myyyyy, hello, hello! You must be that Maou person, *arrrren't* you?"

The moment Chiho opened the front door, she was almost sent flying by the sonic force of a shrill, high-pitched voice.

Maou had a phone conversation with that voice, not too long ago. It belonged to Riho Sasaki, Chiho's fortysomething mother, resplendent in her perfectly applied makeup and wardrobe as she greeted Maou and his companions.

"Um, thanks. I'm sorry for stopping by so late."

Maou felt the beads of nervous sweat run down his back as he tactfully bowed.

"Emi Yusa. Good to meet you."

Behind him, Emi kept it deliberately short.

"Um...this isn't anything fancy, but...you know, Chiho's been a huge help to me this whole time, so..."

Stammering out the words in an awkward attempt at politeness, Maou presented the small cake that Ashiya forced him to bring along.

"Oh, my goodness! Such a thoughtful young man! Thank you *so* much. Please, come right in! *So* sorry for bothering you over the phone earlier. Right over to the living room with you! I'll be happy to make some tea. Chiho, can you lead them over?"

"Um, okay..." Chiho started. "It's right this way, uh...Mr. Maou. Oh, and Ms. Yusa."

"T-Thanks."

"Thank you."

The Sasaki residence was a fairly typical house, nestled in a neighborhood across the Koshu-Kaido road from Sasazuka station, right on the other side of the highway from Devil's Castle.

This was the gang's sole choice if they wanted to check the contents of that video as soon as possible. But it also meant Maou and the rest of the visitors were completely dependent on the whims of the Sasaki family matriarch.

Ashiya rushed right out on Dullahan II in order to buy a suitable gift, but a single faux pas inside this house could ruin all the trust Chiho placed on them. To Maou, this was an all-or-nothing crusade.

Even worse, they were being chaperoned by Emi.

Ashiya should have been with them. But if they both left alone, Emi feared, they would likely toss the tape in a lonely Dumpster somewhere.

To keep the head count low, everyone except for Maou and Emi opted to stay at Villa Rosa Sasazuka, keeping Alas Ramus entertained as they hoped against hope for good news.

But what about Emi? Considering her breezy habit of verbally wishing for the Devil King and his crew's grisly deaths at her bloodied hands, she seemed strangely passionate about finding a solution for Maou's crisis.

"...Mom, you always try too hard..."

Chiho's head drooped down the moment she entered the living room.

Not a single speck of dust was present. A vase filled with colorful flowers was perched atop a brand-new tablecloth in the middle of the room.

The light floral scent that prefaced the area suggested either an aroma candle or more than a few pinches of potpourri.

The cushions on the chairs were thick, fluffy, and clearly not meant for daily use. It was evident, much to Chiho's apparent chagrin, that Maou and Emi were being given an extremely warm welcome.

"Ummm...um, sorry, I guess you can sit down? Oh! Maou, your video..."

Chiho seemed to pick her words carefully as she accepted the tape, kneeling in front of the LCD screen in a corner of the room.

Maou and Emi looked at each other, then gingerly sat down. The crinkle of a brand-new set of cushions could clearly be heard.

"Here we go! I've got some refreshing iced tea, right here for you!"

Then Riho, as high-intensity as before, came barreling in. Maou and Emi flinched slightly in surprise, but Riho paid it no mind as she set a pair of glasses in front of her guests, the tea smelling faintly of citrus fruit. Emi took a sip.

"Thank you... It smells nice. Are these rose hips I'm smelling? It must be some kind of herbal tea."

Riho's eyes sparkled.

"Oooh, very observant! I should have known someone as sophisticated and savvy as *you* both would tell it right off! And thank you *so* much for taking such good care of Chiho for me! She tells me all *kinds* of things about you. And let me tell you, Chiho and my husband just have the *worst* time telling different types of tea apart!"

"I...see."

"Mommm! You don't have to tell them everything!"

The tape safely in the VCR, the red-faced Chiho focused her efforts on shooing her mother out of the room. Riho didn't budge.

"Oh, just play that video before you kick me out! The future of Mr. Maou's housing situation *rides* on this, doesn't it?"

With that, she helped herself to a seat across from Maou and Emi. Chiho had provided the bare minimum of an explanation in order to gain access to the VCR, but now two concerns raced across Maou's head: *What if my landlord does something weird?* And: *What if the sight of my landlord causes Chiho and Riho to lose all semblance of their sanity?*

"Ughh...! All right, all right. Are you ready, Mr. Maou?"

"Uh, sure. Go ahead."

They couldn't toss Riho out of her own house. His mind filled with assorted anxieties, Maou looked on as Chiho pressed the PLAY button, then took an uncomfortable seat next to her mother.

A black screen flashed on for just a moment. Then an image flickered to life.

Underneath a blue sky, amid a gold-colored landscape, a row of pyramid-shaped buildings loomed in the air. One hundred people out of a hundred would have instinctively identified the sight as Egypt.

"Uh, is this on...? Ah-*hem!*"

The landlord's voice boomed out of the speaker. Maou clenched his fists in terror.

"Well! It's been quite a while, Mr. Maou and Mr. Ashiya. Today I'm broadcasting to you from in front of the three great pyramids of Giza!"

She was in the middle of a bright, spotlessly clear desert.

The mere sight of Miki Shiba—their landlord, her high-cut dress and short-sleeved top with the sleeves tattered and almost falling apart, the fancy hat on her head providing only token protection from the sun, her outfit revealing a robust amount of sagging real estate around her arms and legs—was enough to make Maou's pulse surge and face whiten.

Still, compared to her swimsuit pin-up shot, this was still more of a warning salvo than a head-on blast. He didn't have to avert his eyes, at least. Maou couldn't let himself cower in her presence forever.

What was even more surprising to Maou, already in a cold sweat, was that the other three people in the room didn't react at all, eyes sharply focused upon the murderous landlord onscreen.

"During my travels, I received word that you came across some manner of disaster in your apartment. As your landlord, I really do feel I need to apologize for this."

It was hardly the landlord's fault Maou had a hole blown in his wall by some alien toddler punching a renegade archangel through it. But to Maou, being stricken by the accursed sight of the voluminous valley between her two ample breasts as she bowed deeply to apologize was something he felt deserved an apology in and of itself.

"I'm just happy that neither of you were injured. And it goes without saying that I will gladly cover all of the repair costs for your apartment, so there's no need to worry about that. I promise you that this won't affect your rent, either. However, since these will likely be some rather large-scale repairs we're talking about, I'm afraid that chances are you'll both need to vacate the apartment for a period of time."

Now she was all business, her speech largely echoing the content of Suzuno's letter.

Finally growing used to the awesome presence staring into the camera, Maou now had the time to silently lash out at Shiba. Seriously, why did she go through the trouble of filming this just for the Devil's Castle? This all could have been handled a lot quicker if she'd just written them a letter, too.

The video continued on after Shiba wrapped up her explanation.

"Oh! And by the way, Mr. Maou, Mr. Ashiya, I do have one little request for you both. I'm not sure if I told you this, but I actually have a niece, you see."

Maou and Emi exchanged glances.

The landlord's *niece*?! They had never imagined this woman had parents, or siblings, or nieces or nephews, or anything else a normal family would have. Were there *more* of her?

"Now, this niece of mine runs a little restaurant and sundry shop on the beachside over in Chiba."

The keywords *landlord* and *beach* brought back vivid memories of the Great Swimsuit Pin-Up Massacre. This video would be baring its fangs soon. Maou found himself fending off the urge to smash the stop button.

41

"If you like, I was wondering if you'd like to help my niece run the place for a little bit."

Maou stopped.

"It's on a beach in the northeastern corner of Chiba prefecture. A bit far away from you, I know, but considering the state of your apartment, I think you'd likely be staying there for the time being instead of attempting to commute. My niece's house should be free for at least some of that time, so how would you like to stay there from…say, the first half of August or so?"

A free place to live? And work from the start of August until past the end of the Obon holiday?

The sheer perfectness of the timing had to be a put-on. *She's just buttering me up—or herself up, perhaps literally—before she strikes the final blow, isn't she?*

"Northeastern Chiba… The town of Choshi, maybe?"

Chiho nodded to herself as she tried to recall her local geography.

"And you know, having a man there to help out during the busy season would do so much to put my mind at ease. I'm sure you have your own work to worry about, of course, so I won't force you or anything, but I'd love if you gave it some thought, anyway. So if you think you're interested, just call this phone number…"

Shiba pointed a finger downward as a cell-phone number scrolled across the bottom of the screen. Maou stared blankly at the display for a moment.

"Wow, Dev… Maou, that's great! Hurry up and give her a call!"

Maou choked on his own spit after Emi suddenly slapped him on the back.

"*Kheff kheff*…!! Wh-What're you doing, Emi?!"

"She had to have sent this a long time ago. You better call her right now. If she hires someone else, it'll be too late!"

"B-But, Ms. Yusa, it's kind of far from here to some beachfront shop in Chiba…"

Chiho, wary of Emi's unexpected reaction, found herself cut off by her mother.

"No, she's right, Mr. Maou! What a marvelous offer this is! A home, a steady job... All of your problems, solved in one fell swoop! Go ahead! You can call her right in here!"

Riho's reaction was to be expected from a nosy middle-aged mother, but Emi's was all but inexplicable. She sounded almost happy for Maou's reversal of fortune.

Despite all the misgivings he felt at this dual-pronged mystery, Maou nonetheless typed the number into his phone as he gestured the room to be quiet for a moment.

With one final nod to Riho, he took a deep breath and pressed the "call" button.

His assessment of the situation was nowhere near as rosy as Emi's or Riho's. Everything was falling into place a little too neatly for his tastes.

Plus, remember, this was a beachfront place run by *that woman*'s relative. There was no telling what kind of snake pit or lair of spittle-spewing monsters it could be. Commuting to some faraway MgRonald could be far less of an emotional burden on him when all was said and done.

Chiho looked on with similar trepidation, occasionally shooting a glance at Emi. The Hero's erratic behavior must have confused her, too.

They waited, faces tensed up. Several rings passed, and then, a simple greeting:

"Yello?"

A woman's voice.

Which was expected, given it was her niece, but Maou was prepared for anything up to, and including, a flesh-eating ghoul of the night. Being greeted by a seemingly normal human being seemed almost disappointing.

"Oh, uh, hello. Sorry if I'm calling you late."

"No, no."

"Umm, so, Ms. Shiba told me about some possible work available at your beachside restaurant, so I thought I would call you about it, sooo..."

"Shiba... Ahhhh!"

Maou's voice tapered off just in time for his eardrum to be blasted by the girl's bellow.

"Are you the guy living in that apartment building my aunt Mikitty runs in Tokyo?!"

"Mikitty… Oh! Y-Yes, I am. My name is Maou."

He recalled the landlord all but demanding that Emi call her "Mikitty" in the past.

"Oh, yes yes yes yes! She told me all about you! I almost gave up, you know! We're almost at the end of July, but you hadn't called yet, so…"

The woman on the other end of the line couldn't have sounded brighter and bubblier.

Her manner of speech indicated she was likely to be slightly older than Emi or Suzuno, but he couldn't pick up any of the eerie, inscrutable, enigmatic presence Shiba always infused into her speech.

"Yeah, sorry about that. She and I kind of got our wires crossed."

There was no way Maou could confess to being so frightened by the video that he encased it in an entire roll of duct tape.

"Oh, yeah, I know how my aunt likes to go hopping around the world all the time. I usually get a New Year's greeting card from her around February or so, if you know what I mean."

"Hohh. Really?"

If that's how she treated her own kin, it was almost a miracle that she sent word to Maou and Suzuno so promptly.

As he mulled over this, the woman suddenly shifted gears.

"So…Maou, right? You comin', or…?"

Obviously the type of woman who didn't waste time with formalities. Maou had to stop himself from reflexively agreeing.

To Maou, a beachside snack bar and supply shop run by a lone woman was uncharted territory.

They had yet to discuss the nature of his job, for one. For that matter, the presumptive niece of Maou's landlord had yet to give her name.

There was a phrase Maou learned early on in life: Know thy enemy, know thyself, and thou shalt not fear a hundred battles. It was his credo ever since he began his struggle to unite the demon realms, so long ago. He chose his words carefully, seeking to extract the information he needed.

"Um, well, I haven't really heard anything about the job, except that it's at your restaurant in Chiba…"

His conversational partner chimed in on cue.

"Oh, no? Yeah, Aunt Mikitty's never too fussy about details like that, I guess."

Her voice indicated she had nothing to hide.

"But anyway, we're pretty much on the edge of Chiba, in the town of Choshi. Do you know where Kimigahama is, maybe?"

"No…"

From the side, Riho handed Maou a pen and paper. Maou nodded at her as he accepted them.

Hurriedly, he wrote "Choshi" on the paper, hearing a slight, surprised gasp from Chiho behind him.

"Yeah, you probably wouldn't. I guess Inuboh or Toyama would be more recognizable place names up here, huh? Unless you're on an island or a mountain or something, you can see the morning sunrise on the Kimigahama shoreline before anyone else in the Kanto region can."

"Um…"

None of what the woman said sounded familiar. She must have picked up on it.

"Well, just picture the easternmost edge of Chiba, and that's close enough. Just a *liiiittle* bit removed from downtown Tokyo, you know?"

And with that offhand remark, Shiba's niece wrapped up her description of the place.

There was no point whining about it, though. Maou wrote down the unfamiliar names on the paper and pressed onward.

"Oh, and sorry to cut to the chase, but I can't really pay you a fortune or anything, either. I'm thinking a thousand yen an hour per person, but how 'bout it?"

"A th-thousand yen?!"

The figure took Maou aback. It was far from what he anticipated. But what did "per person" mean? Did she want him to bring a busload of friends along?

If Ashiya joined Maou up there, simple math indicated the Devil's Castle would be raking in 2,000 yen an hour.

"Yeah, well, my dad ran this place, like, half as a hobby. Pretty much clueless about how to make money off it, you know? But we still wind up busy during the season, so we're hurting for some help right now. Oh, you can stay here for free, too. And I'll feed you. And at no extra charge, you'll get to swim in the ocean after work all you want 'til it gets dark!"

Free food, free board, a thousand yen an hour. The swimming thing was unimportant—Maou couldn't have asked for a more ideal work situation.

"So...are you looking for multiple people?"

This question was a gamble in some ways. Three people called Devil's Castle home, after all, not two, and the third was the utterly work ethic–less Urushihara.

Judging by Shiba's invite and the way her niece sounded, it seemed to Maou that Ashiya's ticket was already punched. The three of them, though? If her father was that "clueless," the labor costs involved could make it out of the question.

That, and even if Maou asked nicely, there was no guarantee that Person No. 3 would so much as pour a soda for anybody.

But the woman's response surpassed all expectations.

"Oh, what, you got a gang you wanna bring along?"

"Um. Well, with me and my roommates, it'd be three people."

"Huh? Three?"

"Huh? Three?"

It came from Chiba and Emi simultaneously. Maou paid them no mind.

"Well, sure! Bring 'em on over! We're never gonna have too much help here, trust me on that one. It's pretty hard work, apparently, so even if it isn't full-time, you guys could probably take shifts or something if you like."

It was almost like she knew Maou personally.

He still didn't know what kind of work it was, but they could always leave the easy stuff to Urushihara for whatever fifteen minutes of the day he felt like working. Then Maou and Ashiya could pull full-time shifts—and if Urushihara picked up even a gnat's crotch hair worth of inspiration along the way, it'd be an unexpected bounty for all three of them.

"...Would it be okay if the three of us came over, then?"

The woman laughed out loud. Chiho winced across the table.

"Well, sure! When can you show up?"

"Well, we need to get some things sorted out tomorrow, so if it's all right with you, we could make it the next day, August 1."

"Whoa! Better get you guys' room ready quick, huh? Thanks a lot, though. The faster the better! The way my dad puts it, we'll pretty much be slammed starting in August, so it'll be *suuuuper* appreciated."

Something that bothered Maou was how this woman was learning all this information from someone else. The work's "apparently" pretty hard. "Her dad said" it'd be crowded. Maou dared to ask about it.

"Oh, that? Well, I dunno if Aunt Mikitty told you or anything, but my dad runs this place. I help him out usually, but just when we started to gear up for the season, he went on vacation and palmed the whole place off on me. Which, I dunno, I don't mind taking over for him sooner or later, but I kinda have my own job myself, you know? And a girl can't really run this joint alone. *And* I'm just as clueless on how to keep the lights on as my dad is. *And*, you know, I'm kind of about to hit the prime of my life soon, you know what I mean? So this is kind of dangerous for me!"

Exactly what "the prime of my life" meant, and how running a beach stand would be "dangerous" for it, made Maou seriously wonder if this restaurant had any future. The question made it all the way to his lips before he stopped himself.

"But, yeah, if my aunt knows you, then you're all invited. Thanks!"

"Oh, uh, no, thank you... But where should we go, exactly?"

"Oh! Yeah, guess I have to give you *that* little nugget of knowledge sooner or later, huh? Do you have a car, or are you taking the train? Flying, maybe?"

"F-Flying? No, it'd be the train."

No matter where they went, Maou and his cohorts were restricted to public transportation.

"Well, it's gonna be a pretty long trip. From downtown, you'll take the Sobu line to the end in Chiba, then transfer to the JR Sobu Main Line to *that* end station, which is Choshi. From there, there's something called the Choshi Electric Railway. You'll get on that and take it to Inuboh, which is one station away from the end. There's a station called Kimigahara just before that, but Inuboh's actually closer to where we're at. That's gonna be about a three-hour trip overall, but—hey—it'll be like a vacation, right?"

Three of those rail lines, and two of those endpoints, were wholly unfamiliar to Maou. This was farther away than he thought.

Ever since Maou and Ashiya found themselves marooned in Japan, their financial situation all but precluded them from venturing beyond the twenty-three wards of central Tokyo. This would be their first trip to another prefecture, and just as she put it, it sounded like quite the little journey.

Even to a Devil King who'd waged a bloody war of conquest across hundreds of miles of barren wasteland, three hours on a train was three hours on a train.

"I can pick you guys up from Inuboh station, so give me a ring once you arrive, okay?"

"Sure thing. Before you hang up, though, can you tell me what the place is called, and...um...what *you're* called?"

An odd question to ask after making all these arrangements, but one that remained unresolved. The woman burst out in laughter again, loud enough to make Maou almost take his ear off the phone.

"Ahh-hah-hah-hah! Oh, I'm sorry! Jeez, what am I *doing*, not even giving you my *name* or anything?"

Maou honestly wanted to ask her.

"Well, my name is Amane Ohguro. I'm Mikitty's niece, and I run this tiny little place we like to call Ohguro-ya."

"Ohguro... Well, great. What time should we be there, two days from now?"

Another classic part-time job interviewee question. The answer Amane Ohguro gave was a world first for him.

"Oh, uh, anytime's fine, really."

"Uhm?"

"Just show up when you can! I'll pick up you whenever."

"R-Really...? Um, do I need to bring anything for the job, or...?"

"Some muscle?"

An extremely brief answer, and one that missed the point of Maou's query.

"Well, as long as you bring some clothes and a toothbrush and stuff, that's about all, I think. You can pick up anything you need here, so..."

Didn't he need any other tools for the job? This wasn't some summer trip to Grandma's house.

"...Oh! But definitely bring a beach towel, okay? The kind where you can close the corners with Velcro instead of just wrapping it around you. Otherwise you might trip on the sand or fling one of your sandals into the sea or something. You definitely don't wanna work barefoot, 'cuz you might cut yourself on a can or pebble or shell or something in the sand."

"Beach sandals. All right. I'll find some that fit me."

Now *this* was the kind of info he needed. But the rundown of work duties ended almost as it began.

"Well, don't stop at the sandals, you know? You're gonna be by the beach! Get some goggles and swim trunks, too. And if you wanna light some fireworks, we got a whole shelf full over here! We're not allowed to have any that shoot into the air or anything, but if you light one of those Sudden Death sparklers—*man!* The sea breeze makes that thing burn like TNT!"

It was probably best not to approach this job like urban fast-food work after all. There was no telling what direction Amane would zoom off to next with this conversation. Was this how everyone on the beach acted, or was Ohguro-ya an outlier in more than just location?

"Oh! But there *is* one thing I better warn you about."

"What's that?"

Amane never sounded more serious than during this one moment. Maou's face grew stern as he awaited the next sentence.

"This place, you know, it's really nothing fancy or anything. We get customers and all, but they're all pretty chill. It's not really a party beach, I guess you could say."

"Sure."

"We *do* get pretty busy sometimes, too. I know I said you can swim all you want, but you're probably gonna have to keep it to the evenings and early mornings. So..."

A pause, and then she continued, her voice heavy with concern.

"Don't go in expecting to pick up bikini chicks all day, all right? You might get in trouble if you start propositioning girls like that."

"*That's* what you were leading up to?!"

"Huh? Well, what else would it be? I mean, that kinda thing's important if you're a guy, right?"

"No! I mean, um, we *are* gonna be working there, right?!"

Maou was quickly reverting back to his previous "hidden-camera prank TV show" theory.

"Oooh, I see! You already got someone special in your life, huh, Maou?"

"No, I don't!!!"

Out the corner of his eye, he noticed Chiho, Emi, and Riho rear back in surprise as he almost shouted into the phone.

All of his job-application phone calls before now were a lot more... businesslike. Tense. He wanted more from a job than a paycheck and a pat on the head, of course, but this complete lack of tension seemed an issue in itself.

Thanks to Kisaki's positive attitude, life at the MgRonald in front of Hatagaya station never felt stiff or rigid. But working for a large corporation still meant a lot of operational manuals, workplace manners, and unwritten social rules.

For someone like Maou, who found solace in such bureaucracy, Ohguro-ya now felt like a complete unknown.

He let out a raspy sigh as Amane paused, as if in thought.

"Okay, well, that's totally cool, too, if you're really *that* uninterested or whatever. It's just kind of unexpected, you know? The way Aunt Mikitty described you, I thought you were kinda more of a *wild* man."

What kind of description of Maou and Ashiya had Shiba given Amane down at Ohguro-ya? And what kind of mental image did Amane construct from it?

All this time, Maou prided himself on the fact that no demon in all of history was as diligent, as faithful, as scrupulous, in carrying out his by-the-hour quick-service career / global conquest.

Once he arrived, he would take action. All these false preconceptions making themselves known over the phone couldn't be allowed to last.

"Okay, well, anyway, I'll get there the day after tomorrow as soon as I can!"

"Great! I'll be expecting you."

Despite the anticlimactic end to the call, Maou found himself oddly exhausted.

"What were you guys *talking* about?"

Emi was the first to ask. From their incomplete perspective, it sounded very little like a job interview.

"I'm not too sure myself."

It was an unknown job, with an unknown woman, in an unknown place. There was no other way to put it.

"But how'd it go? Do you think you can do it?"

The ice in Riho's tea clinked as she spoke. Maou put away his cell phone and bowed deeply.

"Ms. Sasaki, I really need to thank you for letting me use your VCR. It looks like I've got someplace to go after all. In two days we're all headed off to Chiba to work by the beach."

"Oh, wonderful!"

Riho nodded and smiled.

The nervousness seemed to loosen from Chiho's face as well, before a sudden thought came to her.

"When you said 'three people,' did you mean Urushihara, too? Are you sure about that? Can he even go outside or anything? Can he have a normal conversation?"

She must have had the same thought as Maou. She seemed anxious, all but assuming that the ex-archangel was sure to screw everything up.

"Mm? What do you mean? Is this Urushihara one of those ADHD cases?"

Riho seemed to read her mind, although her terminology was a tad misguided.

"Something like that, I guess...but me and our other roommate are gonna cover for him as much as we can."

"Hmmm..."

This time, Riho's nod was a distracted one as she shot a look askance. Her daughter, processing things in her mind, had her eyes on Maou instead.

"Oh, thanks for the pen and paper."

Emi peeked at the jotted place names as he handed the paper back.

"Now will you promise me you'll actually open whatever your landlord sends you next time?" she demanded.

"Oof..." Maou complained. "I, uh, I'll try."

Of course Emi could say that—she hadn't see That Photo. But Miki Shiba had just rescued them from the brink of poverty. She deserved some thanks.

Then Maou realized the tape was still running. He turned toward the screen to stop it...and then *it* appeared.

"By the way, did you know that they offer free belly dancing classes to the tourists in Egypt?"

His landlord had been rambling on about her trip this whole time in the background.

Somewhere along the line, the pyramid background transformed into a large, open space inside an ornate palace.

"There's a tribe here in the desert that devotes itself to music and dance, and they said I was a first-class student! I'm going to be in a dance competition here in a few days. Care for a sneak preview? Here we go!"

"Oh, my, what a lovely outfit."

The landlord flashed a sidelong glance at the camera. Her new outfit daringly revealed her full shoulders, the top covering that inscrutable boundary between her hips and stomach decked in a dazzling array of jewels and silver pieces. A sheer veil and crimson-red satin skirt completed the picture, turning Shiba into something resembling a huge, man-eating Venus flytrap monster.

Maou moved like lightning.

This video couldn't be allowed to continue. If it did, these innocent bystanders would be traumatized for life!

But before Maou's finger could reach the STOP button, some kind of Oriental instrument began to play, and Shiba began to mercilessly jiggle her arms, stomach, neck, and every other part of her ample frame. Then, in what could be called an insult to the mystical dance that so captivated the cultural tastemakers of nineteenth-century Europe, her belly began to gyrate.

Maou had no recollection after that until the following morning.

"You're getting too excited, Mom," Chiho complained as they saw Emi and the unconscious Maou off, Ashiya having sped over to pick up his friend's limp body.

She could understand her mother's feelings, but a high-tension act like that was enough to make any teenager think twice about bringing her friends around again.

"Oh, it's just fine, Chiho! I already knew that this Maou gentleman was a hard worker, but it's hard to get a gauge on his personality without an opportunity like this."

Chiho's eyes opened wide as her mother cleared the tea set from the living-room table.

"You knew...? Mom, have you been going to that MgRonald?!"

"What are you talking about? Of course I have."

"I *told* you not to do that! This is so embarrassing..."

"I was on my very best behavior, Chiho. I didn't introduce myself to anybody behind the counter. You know, though..."

Riho's eyes rested on the notepad Maou had just used.

"He's a nice person, isn't he? This Maou."

"Huh?"

"I suppose I can't blame you for falling for him like that."

"Mommmm!!"

Chiho raised her voice, a rarity for her. Her mother was fully prepared for it.

"He works hard. He's perfectly polite around people. For a man, his penmanship is perfectly acceptable. He doesn't look like he stays out all night, and I didn't smell any cigarette smoke on him. Judging by his cell phone, he must be living awfully frugally, isn't he? And that man who picked him up... Ashiya? Such a simple, honest man. You don't see his kind too often these days."

"Simple and honest" didn't quite fit. "Nobly poor" would have been more apt.

"Your father certainly put in *his* time as a poor college student, once upon a time. Maybe it's in the genes, hmm?"

Having one's mother accuse her of having the same taste in men as she did would undoubtedly lead to some awkward dinner conversations later.

"But, my, such dedicated people! What an uncommon sight in these modern times. I don't think you have that much to worry about, do you?"

"...Worry?"

Chiho's eyes darted toward her mother's.

"Oh, did you think you could hide it from your own mother? When you heard he'd be working in Chiba, and when you were talking about that Urushihara character... The wrinkles were all over your face!"

Her daughter's face began to unconsciously redden as she brought a hand to her forehead.

"I...I just..."

Chiho squirmed in place as she spoke, right hand on her temple and left hand playing with the hemline of her skirt.

"I mean, yes, Maou and Ashiya work really hard and stuff, but

Urushihara's a lot more selfish and lazy and sleazy and addicted to the Internet, so it really *worries* me, if they get run ragged trying to cover for him in an unfamiliar place, and what if he acts up so much on the job that they all get fired, and they have to go back to Sasazuka and stuff...maybe..."

After that fluent, fast-paced assessment of Urushihara's character, Chiho suddenly ran out of words.

Until now, she saw Maou's sudden loss of work as affecting his food supply and living environment. Now she realized it was much more than that.

Simply missing out on half a month's wages was potentially enough to cost the demons their home. Sasazuka could be a pricey place to live.

And wherever they went, their pursuers—Emi and Suzuno—were bound to follow.

Which was bad enough. But in the worst-case scenario, what if Maou and his friends became homeless and were forced back to Ente Isla? What if they had to finish the "final battle" with the Hero, left unresolved all that time ago?

"I mean...I wouldn't like that."

"Chiho?"

Chiho turned her back to the wall of her house and sighed.

"If this job doesn't turn out okay for them, Maou and his friends might go somewhere really far away... And Yusa, too, and Suzuno..."

She couldn't fight like Emi or Suzuno or Alas Ramus, but when it came to work, Chiho had what it took to help Maou. But that depended on him having a workplace somewhere around Sasazuka.

I'm just a girl in high school. Fully dependent on my parents. Not out there all alone, like they are.

She hung her head sullenly downward.

For a few moments, the only sound was Riho washing the dishes.

"Not to burst your bubble, but if you tell me you want to follow Maou and his friends over there, I don't think I can say yes to that."

"...I know."

Her mother was only speaking common sense. No matter how

much she trusted this man, no parent would allow their teenaged daughter to join some guy on his live-in job by the beach.

There's nothing I can do to help Maou.

"By the way…"

"Huh?"

"I could apply pretty much everything I said about Maou to Ms. Yusa, too."

This was a sudden change of topic.

"So young, but she's always ready with one of those witty comebacks. You don't see many young people like *her* these days, either."

Even a non–Ente Islan like Chiho could surmise that her attitude was more a product of her traumatic past than any supposed quality missing in modern Japanese women.

But before Maou fainted, it hadn't seemed to her that Emi and her mother spoke much. Did they have some kind of involved conversation just before she left?

Chiho found herself bewildered, unable to grasp what her mother was hinting at.

"And you're old enough to make money by yourself. So take the road you have to. And as long as you don't do anything to embarrass yourself or your family, I'm not going to say anything."

"Mom…?"

The washing completed, Riho dried her hands, gave a mischievous wink, and patted her daughter on the head.

✻

"Dude! What happened to you? You look even worse than when you left!"

"Daddy, what's wrong?"

"Ah. You're back. What on earth happened to give you a fainting spell at Chiho's house?"

Urushihara, Alas Ramus, and Suzuno greeted the returning Emi, Ashiya, and Maou in their own ways.

Emi was shocked to find Urushihara giving Alas Ramus a piggy-back ride around the room—and Alas Ramus actually enjoying it.

Maybe the kid was starting to feel some sympathy for him.

"...I can't really say, but I guess it was too much for the Devil King to take in."

"Whoa, it really *was* a cursed video?!"

Emi's offhand reply was enough to make Urushihara almost as pallid as the ghostlike Maou.

Unwilling to drag the unconscious Devil King all the way back to his domain, Emi had called Suzuno and told her to have Ashiya pick him up.

Hefting the limp rag doll on Ashiya's back, she apologized for the uproar, left the Sasaki residence, and made the trek back here.

She watched calmly as Maou staggered like a ghoul in clattering chains across the doorway before collapsing in the darkness.

"Cursed, my ass. It wasn't anything *that* crazy. What kind of guy faints because of some girl dancing? That's just rude."

"D-Dance..."

That verb from Emi was enough to conjure something in Urushihara's imagination. His face began to twitch.

"You guys are acting like it's the end of the world! Chiho and her mom were totally normal, too."

"Whaaaat?! No waaaaay!!"

"Looshifer, Mommy never lies!"

Alas Ramus, still riding on his back, gave him an admonishing bop on the head.

But Emi's testimony was the unvarnished truth.

Riho was honest when she complimented Shiba's outfit, and outside of the landlord's well-nourished frame, Chiho found little to be surprised about, either.

"Well, look, the day after tomorrow, all of you are taking the train to Chiba, all right? At some beach restaurant run by your landlord's relatives until the end of Obon."

"Oh? A job with room and board? Well! A dream come true, indeed!"

Suzuno chimed in with her authentic admiration. Alas Ramus stuck her head out from behind Urushihara's shoulder.

"Mommy go to Chiba, too?"

Emi grinned to herself and shook her head as she plucked the girl off her ride.

"Mommy's gonna be with *you*, Alas Ramus!"

"Yehh!"

Emi lifted Alas Ramus into her arms, distracting her in classic motherly fashion from making the inevitable "I wanna go to Chiba with Daddy!" demand as Urushihara rubbed his tired wrists.

"Whew! Dude, she's starting to get pretty big. Chiba, though, huh? Hmmm. Well, sounds good to me."

Emi didn't let his distracted mutterings go unnoticed.

This fallen angel didn't think *he* was part of the work equation.

"I'm glad you thought enough to take care of Alas Ramus tonight, but what do you think you're getting here? It's hard, running one of those beachfront joints. It'll be a nice opportunity to free yourself from that downward spiral of unemployment you're wallowing in, though."

"What? Dude, *I'm* working, too?!"

Urushihara was shocked in two different ways. Once at this revelation, and again that Emi actually thanked him for something.

"Well, that's what they're assuming for you, at least. I mean, what, you were expecting to hole up in there and not work at all?"

"No, but, I mean… Seriously?"

Urushihara played with a tendril of hair.

"A beach house? In *this* jungle heat? Who the hell would ever *want* to go and work in a sweatbox like that…? And, dude, they didn't confer with me at *all*?"

"You fail to understand your footing."

Suzuno silenced the griping Urushihara from the side.

"Nothing constructive would ever stem from asking for your input in this affair. As Emilia noted, this is a golden opportunity. Think of it as a halfway house on your way to becoming a gainful member of society!"

"I don't wanna! That's a stupid analogy anyway! B-Besides, I'd just get in the way there! I don't know how to work or anything! I'm not even supposed to be seen in public anyway, right? Not as long as the cops have Olba over here."

Urushihara's stifling attempts at weaseling his way out of duty were met by cold, merciless stares from the women.

"How long do you intend to dodge your social duty with those idiotic excuses?"

"Considering how much you are obligated to stay undercover, you seem quite content with showing your face to the Sasuke Express driver who keeps delivering all that Jungle.com claptrap to your door. Am I wrong?"

"Like, has anything even happened in the nearly three months since Olba got caught? You've been going to the public bath, right? Have you ever felt like you were in danger at *all* so far?!"

"B-But, but that's exactly why I can't let my guard down right now! Just because nothing happened today doesn't mean it won't tomorrow! I'm just trying to atone for my own crimes in here, you know…"

"Perhaps I would believe that if you lived an ascetic's life, reflecting upon your sins. But you simply fritter away your time in abject idleness, tugging upon the sleeves of your kin! What right do *you* have to say such things? I would call it endearing, at least, if you *tried* to hatch some world-conquest scheme with the Devil King or somesuch! But no!"

"Nn…rrghh…!!"

The sheer, overpowering logic to the women's counterattack made tears begin to form in Urushihara's eyes.

"And even if you never worked a day of your life, what are you planning to *do*, anyway? How can you shut yourself inside if there's no room to shut yourself into? If you try pulling some stunt like what you tried with Olba, I swear you're gonna regret it."

"It is your right to intrude upon others and refuse to aid them in any way, yes, but could you ever truly be *proud* of that? Assuming you even *have* the utter nerve to leech on the goodwill of a total stranger without singing for your supper!"

"Mommy? Suzu-Sis, don't pick on Looshifer!"

Alas Ramus, aware that Urushihara was besieged but not of much else, raised a concerned face in his defense. It was yet another blow to his pride.

"Hmph. Well, Devil's Castle can take care of its own business. Not like we're obligated to worry about you."

"Indeed. Nothing more than a wayward goblin cast away from the heavens. I am sure his work ethic and sense of shame must have flown into oblivion with his holy garments!"

"Dude, stop! I'm gonna cry, okay?! I'm seriously gonna cry if you keep going with that crap!! You're just as jobless as I am, Bell! Where do *you* get off?!"

Urushihara's face reddened as he shouted, voice in a telltale waver.

"Bell's jobless in Japan, yeah, but when she returns to Ente Isla, she'll be an ordained Church cleric. She's got goals to strive for. And most importantly, she can cook, clean, and do laundry for herself. Maybe she's unemployed like you, but you know what? The difference is like the sun and the moon!"

"You…! Ngh! Dammit! …Treating me like an idiot!"

"Looshifer, don't cry! Boys don't cry! Pain, go away! Go awaaaay!"

"Dude, that's real sweet, but… Ughhh!!"

Swatting away the hand provided by his sole ally at the moment, Urushihara turned his teary eyes upon Emi and Suzuno.

"All *right*! All right, okay?! I'm gonna work! Once I get into it, I'm gonna make Maou look like a *slug*, with how much I'm gonna work! I'll make you take back everything you said!!"

His shoulders quivered indignantly as he lashed out, but before the women could respond, he slammed the door to room 201 in their faces. Emi and Suzuno looked at each other, relieved.

"Do you think that worked?"

"…I guess. Maybe."

"Mommy? Suzu-Sis? Don't be mean to Looshifer!"

Dodging Alas Ramus's doleful lecture, Emi turned toward the Devil's Castle door, fatigue beginning to set into her eyes.

"Becoming unemployed and homeless on the same day would set

anybody off. The Devil King and Alciel are one thing, but I'm more worried about Lucifer. He's the only one out of them to actively harm anyone in Japan."

This was the reason behind Emi's oddly cooperative behavior during Maou's time of need.

If Urushihara—never known for his cool under fire—grew unstable as a result of this crisis, there was no guessing how he might erupt. But with the three demons now back to work and under a roof, Emi's heart was filled with a profound relief.

"But Choshi is rather a long distance from Sasazuka, no?"

Chiba prefecture shared a border with Tokyo, but in terms of landmass, it was even bigger. Emi had little idea where this Kimigahara was at all. But for now, at least, she wasn't particularly worried about the demons' future plans.

"You've never met the landlord here face-to-face, right, Bell?"

"Right. We simply exchanged letters."

Emi recalled the first time she met Miki Shiba, erstwhile owner of Villa Rosa Sasazuka.

"How should I put it...? As long as their landlord's involved with them somehow, I have a feeling they won't do anything bad. Or *couldn't*, maybe, even if they wanted to. I'm not gonna leave them be, but I don't think we need to be hot on their trail for the next two weeks, either."

"What do you mean?"

Once, Urushihara and Olba had challenged the Devil King to life-or-death combat, Chiho serving as his hostage.

It was just a few months ago, but somehow it felt like the distant past.

"As Ente Islans, there are so many things, so many *powers*, we have, that the people on Earth can hardly dream of. And yet..."

I would think that you, of all people, would understand the power behind people's thoughts, and wills.

"...And yet, there are people on Earth with powers that we can't even imagine."

Suzuno arched her eyebrows in confusion.

"That, and there's Chiho, too."

"Chiho?"

"Whether she likes it or not, she's pretty deeply involved in this. Even if we followed the demons over there, we need to make sure she stays safe. Otherwise, I don't know if I can leave Sasazuka."

By now, Chiho was known both to Ente Isla and the world of heaven as someone caught in the battle between the Hero and Devil King. Erasing her memories, like a celebrity erases an embarrassing tweet, wouldn't do much to hide the facts. Emi and Maou cared about her, and that was impossible to change now.

And they couldn't even describe the regret they'd feel if she wound up Sariel's or Gabriel's hostage yet again.

Emi crossed her arms, deep in thought.

"It'd be great if we had permission from her mother to come along…but that's probably gonna be tough. It'd be nice if her parents could take a trip out of the country or something for us."

"Be serious."

One couldn't just trundle a teenager around to and fro like that. Real life didn't work that way.

＊

The day after Amane Ohguro's unexpected job officer, the demons of Devil's Castle frantically prepared for the next two weeks.

Bowing their heads down deeply to the Church cleric next door, the Devil King and his inner circle of generals received a promise that she'd transport their refrigerator and other belongings into public storage with her own appliances.

"Ah, how I wish I could take a photograph of this and send it to the Church! A blessed sign of the Devil King's subservience to our cause!"

That was how thoroughly Maou had to kowtow to her.

Once that was squared away, the next item on the checklist was all the stuff they'd need starting tomorrow. The Devil's Castle resident househusband was roused to action.

"This may be a divine bit of fortune, Your Demonic Highness, but we must prepare thoroughly...lest we allow the golden ticket to fall through our hands!"

Amane didn't suggest much apart from some study beach sandals, but it wasn't as though they could set off with a T-shirt, shorts, and nothing else. They were staying there for two weeks, which entailed bringing at least enough clothes for that.

"I expect, my liege, that four days' worth of a wardrobe should be enough. We should be fine, as long as we are diligent with our laundry."

"Yeah, I don't think they got a uniform or anything, so we better bring stuff we won't be embarrassed to work in."

"Ah. Yes. In that case, my liege, we had best divide our wardrobe between business and pleasure. Knee-length shorts should suffice for the job."

"I could just roll up the legs on my jeans, but... I dunno. Like, when everyone's usually got the same uniform on the job, it's kind of weird to think about wearing other stuff."

"Yes. I can imagine. You recall the four different emblems our demonic forces wore on Ente Isla, my liege, representing the continental army they were aligned with."

"Huh. Maybe we could just buy a bag of T-shirts at UniClo. That way *we'd* match, at least."

"Ah, that reminds me of our days in short-term temp work, my liege. Remember how they'd force us to purchase uniforms from them?"

"Oh, yeah, with the company logo and stuff, right? We still got some of those, but I think they're all long-sleeved."

"Quite true. Certainly not late-summer outdoor gear."

As Maou and Ashiya organized their baggage, ransacking their way through the clothing carefully stored in the closet, Urushihara stared on without so much as a whisper.

The look on his face was strangely resolute. Some bizarre twist of divine providence was driving him to help them out.

But his performance earlier in the day—oil still stuck to the dishes after he washed them, shirts folded into oddly-shaped parallelograms, blankets falling to the ground after he hung them out to dry—went beyond incompetence and made him nothing but a nuisance. So he sat silently in a corner instead.

"Like, everyone sucks at it at first. Why're you being so mean?"

The drive to help was a thing of the past. He was back to moaning about his plight.

Maou and Ashiya were once leaders, powerful generals charged with unifying thousands of demons to a single cause.

Give a man a fish, and he'll eat for a day. Teach him how to fish, and he'll eat for the rest of his life. But if it was the fallen angel, ex–Great Demon General, and commander of the Western Island invasion force, he'd call out for pizza and go home before you could hand him the fishing rod.

The Hero Emilia's rebellion began at the Western Island. Maou was starting to wonder if it was his appointed general's lack of leadership skills that had spelled his ultimate doom.

And even if he kept himself from dwelling on the connection between failing to stop the Hero's advance and failing to wash dishes properly, the what-if thought of being blown to Earth with this talentless shut-in instead of the gifted, hardworking Ashiya made him shiver.

"Ashiya...I can't even tell you how glad I am you're here."

He placed a hand on Ashiya's shoulder as the heartfelt words came out.

Ashiya stared blankly at the hand for a moment. Then, once his brain processed what Maou meant, he kneeled before him in a panic.

"I...I, I appreciate such a kind, magnanimous compliment, my liege, but what drove you to say *that* all of a sudden?! ...Uh, I mean, I would *never* bristle at your lofty praise, but..."

Ashiya looked around the room, flustered, before his eyes settled upon something.

"U-Urushihara! Go wrap our plates in that stack of pennysavers and put them in a box. You can surely do *that*, at least."

"I'm not *that* stupid!"

Urushihara was genuinely put off by Ashiya's command—so plainly brought on by his awkward embarrassment—but he didn't have anything to retort with. Pouting, he stood up, brought the newspaper and cardboard boxes to his spot in the corner, and silently began to wrap up the kitchen breakables.

"Y'know, though…I don't wanna encourage Urushihara or anything, but do you really think he's okay?"

"You mean how I might be wanted and stuff…? I didn't notice any surveillance cameras or anything when we were on the run, but…"

The way he so freely discussed his short-lived career as a street mugger in Japan like it was the day's weather was suitably demon-like.

"Yeah, but you don't look too much different now than you did as a demon. Try to use your head a little when we're out there, okay?"

"Well, what, dude? I wasn't thinking that *this* would happen."

Urushihara sullenly turned his back to Maou, who was currently busy trying to wrangle the cape from his Devil King days. All the frills and embroidery made it devilishly difficult to fold properly.

"Oh! Your Demonic Highness? I think we had best put some insect repellent inside your cape. It's thick enough that it might get moth-ridden in this humidity."

The ex–Devil King was not interested in *Better Castles and Gardens* cleaning tips.

"…*I* wasn't exactly picturing myself mothballing this cape two years ago, either. No point dwelling on the past, y'know?"

Scowling at Urushihara as he tried to stifle a snicker, Maou meekly followed Ashiya's suggestion and stuck a packet of repellent into the box.

"I mean, did the cops even arrest Olba?"

After Maou quelled Olba and Urushihara's conspiracy to destroy the city with his newly recovered demonic force, Olba was taken in by the local police force. That much, the demons saw for themselves.

"I'm pretty sure they did. For weapons charges, at least."

"Really?"

"Yeah. It's been a while ago, but I saw it talked about on the net. Guess it wasn't exciting enough to show up on TV or in the newspapers."

"Uh, that's kind of bad news, isn't it?"

"I would doubt that, my liege."

Ashiya interjected.

"I read the same coverage myself. It described him as a foreign national who entered Japan illegally and was destroying property with a gun. They speculated that he was some kind of secret agent or mafia operative. He was already suspected of armed robbery before that point, as well…"

"Yeah. Not like we took *that* much from people, though. The big sites probably wouldn't pick it up unless we actually killed someone."

"Pfft. Good thing we got the criminal *right here* to set the record straight. Where'd you see that, Ashiya?"

"Oh, on our computer. Or Urushihara's, I should say."

Ashiya turned to the laptop PC that was now exclusively Urushihara's net-browsing device.

The fallen angel insisted, of course, that the computer was coming with them. Along with their wireless hotspot. Of course.

"He may just be an idle layabout these days, but back when that happened, I was quite ready to turn him over to the authorities."

"Whoa! Dude! You really didn't trust me *that* much? That's kind of a mean way to put it."

"From that day to this one, have I ever said or done anything that indicated I *ever* trusted you?"

Ashiya's icy sneer silenced Urushihara.

"But regardless. Ever since then, my liege, there's been nothing related to the events surrounding Olba."

"Nothing reported, anyway."

Maou's hands stopped as a thought came to him.

"Hey, Urushihara. Olba didn't use up all his holy energy, right?"

"I don't think so. He definitely went all-out fighting you and Emilia, so I dunno if he has enough force left to open a Gate or anything. But…what? You worried he'll do something nasty in Japan with it?"

"Well…pretty much, yeah."

"Hmm… 'Cause I wouldn't believe it."

Urushihara shrugged.

"Olba doesn't know what happened to me, and besides, he's got Emilia to worry about too, right? There's no way he could break out of jail and try to get revenge on her. Not without some more holy energy. His only choices are either to finger me as his accomplice or use some of his magic to bust out. And it's not like going back to Ente Isla would help. Bell's trying to expose the corruption in the Church. No way he can get back to a position where he has any power over the archbishops. Not any longer."

"Yeah, it's that 'fingering you' thing I'm scared of the most. If people find out I'm harboring a criminal, that'd make me seriously unhireable."

"If the long arm of the law ever makes its way to Devil's Castle, I will refuse to admit any knowledge of you, you realize. My liege must be protected!"

"Great, thanks! But the cops have already *been* here, remember? And they didn't do anything."

"Oh… Yeah. When Suzuno crushed my bike."

Maou was chewed out by an officer at Devil's Castle for leaving the twisted remains of the first Dullahan in front of the Tokyo Metropolitan City Hall. At first, Maou feared the cop had burst in to seize Urushihara.

"So it'll be fine, dude! We're just going to Chiba for a little bit. It's not like they got my poster up in the train stations. You guys are way overthinking this."

"You're kind of underthinking it, man… Maybe we should poke around a little when we have some free time, though."

In some ways, the presence of Olba Meiyer was like a tiny fish bone stuck in the throat of the demons' peaceful coexistence in Japan. Like a sesame seed between the teeth or a piece of lettuce in some unreachable corner of the mouth, it was something that could make them anxious at the drop of a hat.

"Are you done wrapping those dishes yet, Urushihara?"

"Yeah. I mean, they're mostly plastic, dude. They're not gonna break on you that easy."

Even when demonstrating a desire to help, Urushihara couldn't help but whine. Ashiya took the bait.

"If the coating comes off of them, they might become infected by all kinds of horrid bacteria!"

"Ugh. Sorrrrr-eeeeee. Neverrrr miiiiiind!"

Urushihara put his hands to his ears.

"Damn youuu…! Oh, have you contacted Ms. Kisaki yet, Your Demonic Highness?"

"No, I'm about to. I figured I'd say good-bye in person. The construction guys are gonna start showing up today, but she said she'd be around 'til the evening."

"Very well. In that case, perhaps the sooner, the better, yes? I think our belongings are squared away, by and large. Now we just need to shop for supplies."

"I could buy the stuff for you on the way back."

"No need. We have to buy some manner of luggage, after all, and I think I know how large a one we'll need. Unless you have a preference, I can purchase sandals and such while I'm out as well. That, and I have someone I need to say farewell to myself."

"Oh, *do* you?"

Maou never heard anything from Ashiya about his acquaintances, or where, if anywhere, he worked. As he asked the question, he began to realize how little he really knew about his aide's private life.

Although he never asked for details, he knew Ashiya still engaged in the occasional temp work to beef up the Devil's Castle coffers, aiding the budget for their search for demonic power (a quest Maou mostly put out of his mind these days).

It was best to grant this request to his closest confidant. Besides, he knew Ashiya had their shoe sizes memorized. That's just how he was.

"Well, cool. Thanks a lot."

"Yes, my liege. I hope things go well with you and Ms. Kisaki…for the sake of all of our tomorrows."

"Yeah, and our food budget after that, too."

As he saw the two of them off, each walking down the streets of Sasazuka for their own respective purposes, Urushihara had an uncharacteristic bout of worry.

"Are they, like, really plotting to take over the world, or what? Isn't that what they're working for? If not that, *what*?"

Suzuno, Chiho, even Emi asked the same question at one point or another. But at this point in their acquaintance, there was no way Urushihara could guess where Maou's true intentions lay.

Scaffolding was already set up in front of the MgRonald, an anti-dust tarp covering most of the exterior. Maou heard a voice calling for him as he approached.

"Maou! Are you feeling okay?!"

Chiho claimed she was there to schedule shifts for the second half of August, once the remodel was complete. But she demonstrated far more concern for Maou, whose googly-eyed swoon in her living room last night would no doubt be a family story shared around the holiday table for years to come.

"Yeah. Thanks again for last night. It was just kinda...well. Yeah. It's fine. Fine like wine."

His landlord began to belly-dance across his brain. He felt dizzy for a moment.

Chiho stared up at him, brooding, but refrained from speaking further. Starting tomorrow, after all, he'd be off to some faraway workplace, someplace she would never see.

"Wh-What's up, Chi?"

Maou sensed this sudden change in atmosphere. Chiho weakly shook her head.

The awkwardness continued as they accompanied each other inside, hoping Kisaki would help them cast it away.

"Oh, you found somewhere good, huh?"

Kisaki nodded her firm approval as Maou explained that he'd be working at a beachside cabana in Chiba that his landlord had pointed him to.

"So you're coming back, right?"

"Huh?"

The unexpected question made Maou hesitate.

"Well, you aren't gonna commute from Sasazuka to Choshi every day, are you? I didn't know if you had a place up there, or you were planning to move or something."

Kisaki studied the handwritten shift request form Chiho gave her, eyes turned away from Maou.

"You're free to work wherever you want to, of course. But I've raised you to the point where you're practically my right-hand man around here. It'd be a shame to let you go."

She was smiling, albeit flatly. But she never told a joke unless she wanted people to laugh, and she never lied to her staff. What she said just now was Kisaki's honest appraisal of him.

"I'll be staying up there for just a little bit. I'm definitely gonna be back."

Maou knew it, too. That was evident in the sudden strength behind his voice.

The self-assured conviction to his words even lightened Chiho's heart slightly.

Kisaki betrayed a satisfied grin and finally looked Maou in the eye.

"Perfect. I haven't forgotten how you talked about being a successful permanent employee here someday. Your performance up to now tells me you definitely weren't lying. That much I can see."

"I kinda messed *this* up, though..."

"Aw, come on. You've been a model employee here from the start. Seeing you make these kinds of mistakes sometimes reminds me that you're human, you know? It's cute. Make as many as you want, I say, as long as you can make up for them. Because that experience will help you down the line. Trust me."

Being called "human" to his face gave Maou mixed emotions. Kisaki, blissfully unaware of this, flashed another grin.

"Besides, this is what you get for ignoring an important notice and possibly affecting our business. You better work harder than ever once we're back open, okay?"

Maou, feeling Kisaki pat him on the shoulder, felt something warm bubbling up from beneath his eyes.

"And I know you're off for two weeks, Chi, but try not to kill yourself once you're back, okay? I know you like working with Marko, but you should spend your summer on something besides work a little. While you're still young, if you follow me."

"Ms. Kisaki!!"

Kisaki's light reproach gave Chiho the impression her boss knew she hadn't given up on eloping with Maou.

It was enough to put Maou out of sorts as well. His eyes wandered off somewhere as Kisaki smiled warmly at the two hormone-laden young adults in front of her.

Then she changed the subject.

"By the way, Chi, I saw that you didn't ask to be transferred or anything. Don't tell me you're gonna run off to Choshi on me, huh? 'Cause Marko's going there, if you didn't know."

Chiho's eyes rolled into her sockets.

"Uh, you, I, um, that."

Her response was understandable enough as it was. The frenzied side glance at Maou midway made it all the more clear.

"Well…I've always wanted to go there…not just because of Maou or anything…"

"Oh?"

"Have either of you heard of the Choshi Electric Railway line?"

Maou had, of course, given he was the one who brought it up first last night. Kisaki's eyes turned upward for a moment as she scanned her memory.

"Choshi Electric… Oh, isn't it that local line that was about to go out of business, but one of the workers sold a bunch of sesame crackers or whatever to keep it running?"

"That one, that one. I read a news article about how a high-school girl in Choshi, the same age as me, was involved with developing the sweets they sold. It was like, wow, here's this girl my age trying to help out the rail company and her hometown, so I thought I'd like to see what it's like sometime."

Kisaki and Maou exchanged glances as Chiho launched into her inspired speech.

"You always were serious-minded like that, weren't you?"

Her boss sighed a sigh that could easily be interpreted as a chuckle in the right conditions.

"Huh?"

"Oh, nothing. I'm just impressed at that intellectual curiosity of yours, is all. Just make sure you get your parents' permission first, all right? It's a pretty long field trip."

A common-sense response in Kisaki's mind, but it was enough to take Chiho's slightly eased heart and encase it in darkness once more.

"Right. Certainly."

Chiho tried to sound as cheerful as she could in response. But she wasn't sure Kisaki heard it that way.

Then, after a few more pleasantries, Maou and Chiho walked out of the MgRonald together.

"…"

They stood there, demonstrating exactly what it meant to be lobotomized to passersby on the street, until Sariel ran right into them on his way to delivering the day's rose bouquet.

"Oh, Sariel…"

Chiho had only just recently begun to shed herself of her physiological hatred of Sariel. He stopped at her voice and lunged toward the pair, his heaven-gifted Evil Eye of the Fallen wide open and sparkling.

"Maaaaaaaaaaaaaaaaaaaaaaaaaaaooooooooooooooooooooooooooouuuuuuuuuuuuuuuuuuuhhhhhhhhhhhhhhhhhhhhh!!!!!"

"Gahh!!"

The small-statured Sariel grabbed Maou forcefully by the collar, almost sending him toppling to the ground.

"What is the meaning of this what sort of evil scheme do you have afoot why is the restaurant of my eternal goddess shutting down *spit it out* you conniving monster and tell me where you hid my goddess or else I will *incinerate* you with the sheer pathos streaming out every pore of my body!!"

Sariel, in his own way, was proving just as unobservant as Maou was. He must have missed the notice on the window Kisaki claimed she posted up.

"Ow-ow-ow! Get those roses off! The thorns…!"

The rose bouquet raked across the bridge of Maou's nose.

"Have you forgotten the noble act of selflessness I committed when I refused to cooperate with Gabriel you putrid demon and if you were shutting this down then why didn't anyone *say* anything to me if only I *knew* then I could have pooled my courage and my finances together to make the most momentous confession of my entire liiiiiiiiiiiiiiiiiiiiiiife!!!"

Maou was ready to poke Sariel about what his finances would accomplish, or how effective he thought any kind of confession would be, but the thorns were going to penetrate skin shortly. Chiho was kind enough to react first.

"S-Sariel, wait a second! What do you mean, cooperate with Gabriel?!"

"Oh?"

Chiho put a hand around one of the arms Sariel had on Maou's collar. Instantly:

"Pfft! I never refuse the invitation of a beautiful woman. How would you like to join me inside Sentucky to enjoy our brand-new Tandoori Chicken Twister over some iced tea?"

Now it was Chiho's hand in his grasp, as Sariel knelt down to kiss it. It was not quite the reaction she intended. But she had been through hell with him before. Her very life was threatened. And precious little of it made any sense to her. This relatively benign level of sexual harassment wasn't going to faze her anymore.

"I'll tell on you to Ms. Kisaki."

It came out even colder than intended, the disappointment of not being able to join Maou in Chiba squeaking out with it.

Sariel, in response, flashed an expression that deftly combined hope and despair on one face.

"Mhh... I, I hope you wouldn't do anything so drastic... But is my goddess still inside?!"

You didn't need a knife to kill Sariel. All you needed was the word *Kisaki*.

"If you want to know, then tell me. What did you mean when you said you refused to cooperate with Gabriel?"

"Ermm, that was, I..."

Sariel couldn't formulate a response. The words had apparently slipped out of him, and he clearly regretted it.

Maou watched on with more than a bit of awe as Chiho expertly wrapped him around her finger.

"You've gotten a lot stronger, Chi..."

It was a deeply moving sight. Maou had profoundly altered the life of somebody close to him, in assorted ways.

"Tell me that, and I'll tell you about MgRonald. But if you don't, I'm gonna call Ms. Kisaki and tell her that Mr. Sarue tried to assault me."

"Well, Gabriel paid a visit to Sentucky the other day. He wanted me to help him retrieve Emilia's holy sword and the Yesod fragment, so we spoke for a while."

A word or two from Chiho was all it took for Sariel to spill everything he was so hesitant about a moment ago. Not a moment of hesitation.

"And you're *good* with that?"

Maou changed this angel's life, too, now that he thought about it. Not that he cared two seconds later.

Up to now, Sariel was still on one knee, Chiho's hand in his. The stares of passing customers bothered him not a bit. He was likely fated to this sort of life, no matter where he wound up.

"The reason I came down in the first place to fetch Emilia's sword is because Gabriel failed at the job. But I didn't know Yesod was broken into that many tiny fragments, or that one of them took the shape of that young child. And I didn't care, either. My goddess is all that occupies my mind these days. What does some sword have to do with me? He hasn't been back since."

The term *goddess* was starting to grate on Maou's mind, but to sum up, Sariel was so smitten with Kisaki by this point that he no longer cared about his heavenly duties. It brought his qualifications as an archangel into serious question.

He expected nothing else from Sariel, in a way, but Maou still found the story a tad strange.

"Hang on a sec. 'That many tiny fragments'? So you knew Yesod was broken up, at least?"

"...enhh."

Sariel growled. Another slip of the tongue. He dared a glance at Chiho.

"You knew that, didn't you?"

"...Yes, I did."

Chiho offered him no room for negotiations. Sariel hung his head in disappointment.

"I was given the duty of retrieving Emilia's holy sword because it was one of the fragments we absolutely knew the location of."

Despite having met her at least once, Sariel did not initially notice that Alas Ramus was herself a Yesod fragment.

He had a suspicion that her armor, the Cloth of the Dispeller—freshly evolved after its fusion with Alas Ramus—had something to do with the Yesod, but apparently not even the heavens had a full grasp of how the fragments were evolving, and transforming.

"I guess Gabriel didn't get his hands on the sword either, did he? That's why he approached me and asked for my help with the Yesod fragment. I told him, 'No, I'm busy.' You guys owe me one now, don't you? I saved you from having another heavenly menace in your way."

Sariel managed to patronize Maou even as he spilled the beans.

But he revealed a lot. Not only did Gabriel not cry all the way back home to heaven—he wasn't giving up on Alas Ramus.

Defeating Sariel and Gabriel in succession, as far as Heaven was concerned, changed nothing. It just meant they didn't have as much muscle to enforce their will with.

And that meant Maou still remained on the defensive. There was no telling when, where, or how his opponent would strike, and that worried him.

"...?"

"Wh-Why are you looking at me like that, Chiho Sasaki? I've given you the full and honest truth."

"Oh. Well, great, then."

Chiho returned Sariel's glance. Like Maou, something on her face suggested that something didn't quite sit with her, either.

"Sariel, how are you so sure you 'absolutely knew' the location of—"

Chiho was stopped by a voice from behind her.

"Jeez, guys, you're still out here talking to each...other...?"

In an instant, Sariel's face shone like a thousand-watt bulb.

But Maou and Chiho, frozen in place by the ominous way the voice trailed off, turned around in abject horror.

There they saw Kisaki—not in her normal uniform, but in a bright gray pantsuit, hair undone and a large business bag draped over her shoulder.

And she wasn't looking at Maou, or Chiho, but Sariel, still kneeling, hand still clasped around hers. Her eyes were filled with enough rage to even stop a Devil King in mid-hoofbeat.

"...What are you doing to my crewmember, Mitsuki Sarue?"

Sariel somehow kept up a timid smile in the face of this withering gaze.

There's an old Scandinavian fairy tale about an evil mirror, shattered into splinters that penetrated the hearts and eyes of people, making them susceptible to the sweet words of the Snow Queen.

The main difference between little Sariel and the boy in that tale was whether his Snow Queen of choice had even a shred of love for him.

"N-No, I, this was a kind of *negotiation*, you see. I was forced into this in a feeble attempt to determine my goddess's location..."

"I've been willing to put up with you as long as you're a paying customer. But someone rotten enough to lay his hands willy-nilly on an underage coworker is no customer of mine! From now on, you're banned from the property until further notice!"

"Rrgghh?!?!"

The archangel Sariel, powerful enough to annul the almighty force of Emilia's holy sword, was frozen by a single word from a single woman. He shattered to pieces and helplessly clinked to the ground.

"Get on going, you two. Marko, you were with Chi the whole time! Why didn't you do something about him?"

"Oh, um, sorry."

Maou apologized as Chiho flailed her hands around, staring at the shiny chunks of ice that used to be Sariel as they melted in the summer heat and flowed toward the curbside gutter.

"L-Let's go, Chi."

"Go? Oh. Sure, um... Okay. Thanks again, Ms. Kisaki."

Maou and Chiho hurriedly trotted away, down the Koshu-Kaido road, still looking terribly confused about it all.

"I, I think maybe we were meaner to Sariel than we should've been..."

"Hey, think of it as payback for having Suzuno kidnap you, huh? He kinda had it coming. I'm amazed Ms. Kisaki would even deal with that hard sell until now."

Their appraisal was as cruel as it was justified.

"But you know, Maou…"

"Yeah. I know."

There was no point trying to extract anything else from Sariel. But Chiho didn't have to say it. It stuck out in Maou's mind, too.

He said that Emilia's Yesod piece "was one of the fragments we absolutely knew the location of."

The heavens let Emi run around unfettered in Japan with her holy sword for over a year. How did they ever get a bead on the sword's location, and hers?

"…Well, it doesn't really matter. If they weren't after me, then it's Emi's problem, not mine."

In terms of cold logic, this was a dispute between Emi and heaven. Outside of that first attack from Urushihara, Maou had almost zero stake in it. So there was nothing left to think about—

"Don't you care about what happens to Alas Ramus?"

Chiho squinted as she asked it, expertly cutting off his thought before it could advance any further.

"I mean, Yusa's sword is pretty much Alas Ramus herself now, isn't it?"

"It… But I can't fight at all in Japan anymore. Emi's a ton stronger than me, so why do I even have to do anything…?"

"That's not the problem. What kind of dad doesn't try to protect his little girl? You're gonna make her cry, you know."

"Jeez, Chiho, whose side are you on?"

The question wasn't sarcastic. Maou was inexorably conflicted.

"I just want everyone I like to play nice with each other. I kinda want us to be together. For the long term."

There was a twinge of sadness to the reply.

"…What? Is there something up?"

This was the Chiho who once burned in flaming jealousy after mistaking Emi for Maou's evil ex-girlfriend. Lately, though, she was acting…mature beyond her years, perhaps. Or maybe preoccupied about where Maou, Emi, and Alas Ramus were going with their lives.

"Mmm, I guess I can talk about it if you want…but are you ready to listen? 'Cause it's kind of heavy."

"Huh? Uh, sure."

"Well, you told me a bit ago that you believed in me, right? That you relied on me and stuff. But…I can't keep this going as it is right now."

"K-Keep what going?"

"I mean, I can't fight the way Yusa and Suzuno can, and it's not like I've known you forever the way Ashiya has. I just happened to be near you, and then I found out the truth. And even if I get all worried about Urushihara being all lazy and screwing it up for you, it's not like we could go to Chiba together."

Even under the whining cicadas overrunning the trees lining the sidewalk, Chiho's voice had the strange power of ringing loud and clear in Maou's head.

"So I want to study more, and learn about the world around me. And when I'm all grown up, I want to be able to help you when you need it. You said you relied on me, so I want to answer that, you know?"

"…Yeah."

"And I haven't gotten an answer from you yet, either. But if I'm going to get one, I want it to be a *good* one. So I really want to try harder from here on in. That way, someday…"

Without warning, Chiho fell silent and crossed her arms, chin and chest held high in the air as she let out as low and foreboding a laugh as her voice could manage.

"I can become a Great Demon General in your reformed army and duel against Yusa for the right to have you!"

"Bfft!"

Maou performed an unrehearsed spit-take.

"Wh-What part of our conversation made you my Great Demon General?!"

"Ashiya promised that he'd recommend me a while ago. I said no at the time, but if *that's* how it is, maybe I should apply after all, huh?"

Chiho was acting like she'd just volunteered to run for student council.

"Which, maybe that's just a joke and everything, but if I'm going to win against Yusa, I need to be more grown up. I need some weapons to fight her that she can't use against me. I want to go to college, broaden my horizons, and become the sort of woman you can rely on. Here, *and* on Ente Isla."

The sheer passion behind her wish surprised Maou. The August heat must have been making her feverish.

"College, huh...? But...Chi, you've been a huge help to all of us already, you know?"

Chiho frowned in dissatisfaction as her eyes met Maou's.

"Maybe 'Maou' relies on me. But 'Devil King Satan'? All I do with *him* is sit around and wait for him to save my life."

Maou stared at her agape.

"I want to be someone you can put your trust in with anything. Anytime. Whenever."

Maou hadn't noticed it at the time, but what he told Chiho after being lectured by Kisaki the other day must have emboldened her like a bolt of magic.

"I..."

Seeing such dedicated feelings from a human being made it hard for Maou to figure out a response. He trolled around for an answer, but hemmed and hawed in awkwardness instead.

"Oh, it's Ashiya!"

Chiho, ever thoughtful, turned her attention somewhere else.

Ashiya had just stepped away from the Sasazuka rail station building, trundling a wheeled suitcase along with him. Maou knew they'd be using that on the trip, although he couldn't guess why he'd taken it on the train with him to...wherever he'd gone.

Attracted by Chiho's voice, he approached them with a breezy wave.

"Good afternoon to you, my liege. I see Ms. Sasaki is joining you?"

"...Yeah."

Chiho's eyes were on the suitcase Ashiya pulled behind him.

"We ran into each other at MgRonald. Are you taking that to Choshi? That's a pretty nice-looking bag."

"Yes. We'll need to bring along what we need over there, so I had some trouble deciding on which to choose…"

Ashiya still looked hesitant as he placed a hand on the oversized, caster-equipped travel suitcase, offering more than enough space for the clothes, underwear, towels, and any other essentials three demons would need on the beach.

"We aren't allowed to leave anything in the apartment, so we need space to bring our bank records and other valuable documents. And there is no telling what the security situation might be like, so I thought something sturdy and lockable would work best for us."

"Oh. Yeah, that might be a good idea."

"Did you take the train someplace to buy it?"

"Yes, Your Demonic Highness. There was more of a selection downtown, and considering our long journey tomorrow, I decided to take the train instead of walk to conserve my energy. That, and I wanted to use the public phone in the station."

Ashiya was so cheap that he'd cheerfully walk the half hour or so to Shinjuku, Tokyo's central hub, on a regular basis instead of paying the 120-yen train fare. But under this muggy summer sun, wheeling a heavy suitcase halfway across Tokyo would wipe the smile off anyone's face.

Plus, with all the sandals and extra clothing Ashiya had to buy for the trip, Maou wasn't about to criticize him for hopping on a train for a quick round-trip jaunt.

Maou was still curious about who Ashiya wanted to reach out to along the way, but not even the Devil King felt he had the right to invade his subordinate's privacy.

Ashiya was generally not the sort of demon to hide things from people. He must have had a good reason to do so this time, but the phone call couldn't have been anything with major repercussions for anyone else.

After neatly wrapping up that question in his mind, Maou examined his suitcase. It was brand-new, tag still attached, explaining how the bag allowed airport security to unlock and inspect it without damaging anything.

"That really *is* a fancy bag you got, huh?"

"The time may come, my liege, when we must travel overseas in order to restore your demonic powers. I considered it a smart investment for that day."

"Ooooh! So you can conquer the world, right?"

There were few people on Earth who could so freely toss around terms like "conquer the world" in front of an arch-demon who really *did* conquer the world. That is, another world. Nearly.

"Precisely, Ms. Sasaki. Oh, and by the way, we will be sure to buy a souvenir or two for you over there. The least we can do, after all, to repay you. Choshi, I hear, is one of the most well-known fishing harbors in Japan."

Judging by Ashiya's unfazed response to the high schooler's observation, the concept of "conquering the world" held about as much weight with them as a helium balloon.

"Oh...well, thank you."

But Chiho's heart grew heavy for other reasons. It was to be expected, but within Ashiya's mind, Chiho wasn't part of the Choshi caravan. But something else then occurred to her: If Maou was going to Choshi, what kind of people were absolutely *certain* to be on the train behind them?

"...Speaking of conquering the world, though, have Yusa or Suzuno discussed anything about traveling to Choshi with you?"

Maou and Ashiya flashed each other a glance, as if to confirm that yes, they really *were* going to conquer the world someday. Not now, but, you know, whenever.

"Come to think of it, they haven't, really. I figured she thought you were trying to run away from her, too. I was expecting this epic rant about how she'll chase you to the ends of the Earth and so on, but nothing."

"Yeah, she probably thinks we'll mind our Ps and Qs as long as we're with someone who knows our landlord. She's met her before, so. But Urushihara told me the two girls pushed him to the corner and made him cry about what a lazy bum he is last night, too. It's weird, how cooperative they've been with us finding work. It's like they *want* it."

"You're…right, huh? I was just thinking that Yusa's been really kind to you lately, too…"

It was impossible to think that Emi would let the demons simply waltz out of Tokyo without batting an eye. But if she had a plan in mind, she was sure taking her time executing it.

And Sariel's unsettling piece of news made Chiho worry as well. If Maou didn't know what Emi was doing, or vice versa, that could put Alas Ramus in danger.

Not that it meant, of course, that Emi would work together with Maou if she knew about this new development. That was simply impossible to imagine.

"Just make sure you get your parents' permission first, all right? It's a pretty long field trip."

"Take the road you have to. As long as you don't do anything to embarrass yourself or your family, I'm not going to say anything."

The voices of two top authority figures in Chiho's life rang in her head.

Filled with a new sense of determination, Chiho took out her cell phone.

This was probably the first time in her life that she did something so completely self-serving. It would involve taking the bad-faith move of deceiving her parents without actually lying to them.

But it was worth it.

Having the people she held dear that far away was dangerous. She wanted to curtail that danger, as much as she could.

Nodding at Maou and Ashiya, Chiho took a few steps away and called home.

"Hi, Chiho. What's up?"

The landline in their house had a caller ID display. Her mother immediately knew who was on the line.

Chiho took a deep breath, soothing her quickening heartbeat.

"Mom…?"

"Hmm?"

"I wanna go see the Choshi Electric Railway. Is it okay if I take a day trip out there with Yusa and Suzuno?"

THE
HERO
HELPS
THE
DEVIL
REMODEL
HIS
WORKPLACE

"Wow! Look at that train! It's so cute!"

At Choshi rail station, the endpoint of the JR Sobu line, Chiho squealed in pure glee at the sight before her.

It came at the end of a long journey, one laden with unfamiliar transfers—Sasazuka to Shinjuku, to Kinshichou, and then to the Chiba central station, where they boarded the Sobu Main local line. Their journey, taking them due east of Tokyo, took just over three hours.

The train that arrived at the Choshi Electric Railway platform, modestly located on the edge of the much larger JR platform in Chiba station, was like nothing Maou, Ashiya, or Urushihara had seen before.

It had been not quite two years since the demons first set foot on Earth. As such, the idea of a "train" being a four-door car made of stainless steel with long, bench-style seating on the inside was firmly instilled in their minds.

But the "train" trundling up to them now blew away their urban-oriented assumptions in the blink of an eye.

Aerodynamics was not the top priority for its boxy, rectangular body, the lower half a drab shade of red and the top half a sooty sort of black. Lighting was limited to a single round lamp smack-dab in the top of the train's front. Despite being a single car in length, it made an enormous clatter as it bumped its way across the line.

The polished-steel Sobu Main rail car they had lounged on for the past while was something from the far-flung future by comparison. To be as frank as possible, this was old.

When it finally reached the platform, the noise when the conductor applied the brakes was shrill, almost painful—the grind of metal against metal.

"Dude, is that really a train?"

The first words out of Urushihara's mouth were characteristically unappreciative. Chiho rolled her eyes at him.

Maou's brain shut off for a moment upon sight of this strange, alien rail line. Suddenly, though, he noticed that the scene around him was starting to fill with an odd air of excitement.

Even Maou could tell that the other passengers offered nothing but smiles to this preposterously old-fashioned train.

It was "cool." It "really brings me back." It "is totally retro." The people around it were "soooo glad [they] came." The sense of wonderment was palpable.

Then the crowd whipped out their phones—the somewhat more dedicated rail nerds had their digital cameras and tripods at the ready—and started snapping.

"Well! I suppose people like *you* wouldn't sense the elegant nostalgia exuded by this car, hmm?"

"...You've been here for as long as we have, you prick."

Maou sneered at the mocking words pelting him from behind.

There, he saw Emi, Alas Ramus in her hands, and Suzuno, her hands gripping a sun parasol.

"Hmm. This is the Choshi Electric Railway De-Ha 1001 series. A native to this rail line since 1950. Although, according to the literature I read first, these types of trains ran all over Japan back then."

Suzuno studied the free pamphlet she picked up at the station.

The question of where she picked up her research materials, how she consumed them, and why that led her to the "ditzy postwar housewife" look she so expertly pulled off was still a mystery.

"But where do we purchase tickets?"

The Choshi Electric platform began where the JR one ended.

There was no turnstile or anything between the two; all they saw was a small computerized card reader.

But all this gang of pleasure-seekers had on them were the tickets they purchased at the Shinjuku service counter.

"Hmm. I suppose we buy them on the train, or perhaps from someone on the platform. That gentleman, perhaps? He has a hole-punch in his hand."

"Whoa. They do it all by hand?"

"What are you so agog about? Just a few decades ago, every turn-stile from Shinjuku to Ikebukuro and Shinagawa was manned by ticket-takers."

Something about discussing the Japan of the past—the early-to-mid-twentieth century in particular—always added a tinge of excitement to Suzuno's tone.

In the era she had studied for her cultural orientation prior to traveling to Japan, the JR staff still punched every ticket in the nation by hand. But it may as well have been centuries ago; even Chiho, the only native Japanese in the group, was born well after the whole system was computerized.

All Suzuno knew about *that* era was what she learned from books and TV. And that applied equally as much to Maou and Emi.

"But why do they go through all that trouble? Like, there's a commuter card reader right there."

"Don't you see? That's the whole point. People *like* this whole process."

"Seriously?"

Ignoring the dubious Maou, Emi took Alas Ramus to a nearby station agent.

"One adult and one child for Inuboh. Oh, but I think she wants a physical ticket, too..."

She had learned somewhere that children rode for free, Maou supposed. But Alas Ramus's eyes twinkled with anticipation, transfixed on the well-used hole-punch holstered on the agent's belt.

Once her ticket was stamped and handed back to her, Alas Ramus beamed in joy, carefully clutching it in her hands.

"Well, thank you very much, little lady!"

Her sheer bliss was enough to even make the agent smile a bit.

"You see how it works?"

Suzuno looked on in triumph.

"One would never expect that level of service with those cold, impersonal automatic turnstiles!"

"...No, I guess not."

Maou accepted that much, not that he cared.

Ashiya copied Emi's procedure to purchase his own ticket, although Chiho was too busy shooting pictures of the train to pay attention.

Urushihara, meanwhile, was slumped over a platform bench, the heat proving too much for him.

"You know, though... I really didn't think *you'd* join us."

Maou shrugged as he regarded Suzuno. Her face peered out below her parasol, revealing a breezy smile.

"How many times must I say it? We are hardly in pursuit of you. We merely happened to choose the same destination for our summer sabbatical."

This was beyond bald-faced.

It all began several hours ago.

As Maou arrived at Sasazuka station at eight in the morning, he found Chiho there, attempting to catch her breath.

He thought she was just wishing him good-bye at first. But Chiho was carrying a pretty hefty sports bag, making him wonder if she was off on a trip of her own someplace.

From a common-sense viewpoint, no matter how much Chiho's parents trusted her, there was no way they'd permit her to join a small gaggle of men in their stayover summer job on the beach. At the time, the idea that Chiho was joining him to Choshi hadn't even registered in Maou's mind.

"You going somewhere too, Chi? Guess we're sharing a train to Shinjuku, huh?"

"Well," Chiho cheerily replied as they went through the turnstile, "a little longer than that, actually."

Not even thirty seconds later, Maou realized what was going on.

"Oh, good morning, Chiho. Hey, who're those three guys behind you?"

"Goodness, Chiho, I thought we would be waiting until the end of time! You ran into the Devil King and his minions, I see. Quite the coincidence, hmm?"

"Daddy! Chi-Sis!"

There, on a bench at the Shinjuku side of the platform, he saw Emi, Suzuno, and Alas Ramus seated next to one another.

The unpleasant shock was difficult for Maou, Ashiya, or Urushihara to express in words at first.

Thanks to their early-morning departure, they hadn't thought to say hello to Suzuno on their way out.

Emi and Suzuno must have arranged it so they'd ambush them at the station. Their faces—as they made it a point to greet just Chiho and express innocent surprise at the suspicious individuals behind her—betrayed how much they enjoyed the harassment.

Perched in front of them was a medium-sized carrying bag. No doubt about it: They were hell-bent on following him.

"So anyway, we won't be on the same train just until Shinjuku. It's actually gonna be Choshi. It's okay, though. I've got my mom's permission and everything."

Chiho certainly picked a grandiose way to answer Maou's previous question.

The three demons' jaws dropped. What kind of world was this, where a pair of well-meaning parents would agree to *that*?

"You guys aren't getting the wrong idea or anything, right?"

As Maou struggled for an answer, Emi sneered at them from her seat.

"She might be going to Choshi, but not because she's following you guys. She's just coming along with us, is all."

"...Oh, joy."

That was too much of a whopper for any of them to believe.

"Like, what're you freaks doing for work, anyway? You're planning to stay in Choshi for two whole weeks?"

Emi smiled breezily.

"I took some time off. I needed some to help Suzuno move, anyway. But what do you mean 'two weeks'? We're just three free-roaming girls, checking out some of Japan's quaintest and most historic rail lines. What makes you think we're gonna stick around for *that* long? You aren't keeping anything *secret* from us, are you?"

Maou stared daggers into Emi's eyes. Her sheer malice was clear between the rhetorical questions. But:

"Hey, Daddy, guess what! Guess what!"

Then the excited Alas Ramus blocked his view, preventing him from firing back.

"We're gonna go to the *beach*!"

And thus, everything fell into place. Maou hung his head, dejected. Time passed.

Upon reaching Shinjuku, Maou and his unexpected traveling companions hopped on the Sobu line, marveling at the looming sight of Tokyo Skytree as the express train arrived at Kinshichou station. That took them all the way to Chiba, where they nibbled on *ekiben* box lunches sold right on the platform as they waited for the local train to Choshi. After another short while, they passed by the city of Asahi, near the line's final stop in Choshi.

"Chi-Sis! Windmill! Windmill!"

Alas Ramus was perched on Chiho's knee.

Emi and Suzuno were with them, occupying the entirety of a four-person booth inside the train car as they innocently shared snacks with one another. The three demons sat in the booth across the aisle, ignoring the overweight businessman already occupying one spot, and soon found themselves both physically and mentally cramped.

Gazing out the window, Alas Ramus was beside herself with excitement. Just before reaching Choshi, she spotted one of the gigantic wind turbines generating power outside of the city.

"Wow, Alas Ramus. You learned the word *windmill* and everything, huh?"

"Hee-hee! Uh-huh!"

By the time the turbines fell out of view, the intercom announced

that the final stop of Choshi was near and advised passengers to prepare for arrival.

Now, on the Choshi Electric Railway platform, Maou attempted to
plead his case as Suzuno stared upward at him.

"I mean, I *guess* Chiho really does have an interest in this rail
line, so that's fine and all, but why do *you* stalkers have to hound me
every day of my life? You're just here to tail us under the pretext of
joining Chiho!"

Suzuno's response was almost a little too well-rehearsed.

"Think of it what you may. There is no telling what dastardly deed
you may try while away from us. I hope, for your sake, you will
exercise sound judgment in your destination, just as in Sasazuka.
Remember—our eyes hang from every wall, our ears from every
ceiling!"

"Look, you've known me in Japan long enough, right? I'm like a
walking, talking personification of kindness and sincerity here."

"A Devil King is a Devil King."

There was little he could do to deny that.

"You don't feel stupid at all? Asking the Devil King to exercise
'sound judgment' out on the beach? What, do you think I'll push
you in or something?"

"Hmph. Well. As I believe I have mentioned before, we simply
happen to share a destination today. So go ahead. Run off to your
new workplace. Pay us no mind!"

"All right, *seriously...*"

They intended to follow him all the way to the beach house. That
much was bleedingly obvious.

"Your Demonic Highness, I've purchased a ticket for you."

Ashiya stepped in, paper slips in hand. Urushihara, for his part,
lurched his way into the train and threw himself limply on a seat.
The heat must have done a serious number on him.

He and Ashiya didn't bother prodding them any further, already
resigned to these distasteful riding partners. It was something they
half-expected anyway. Besides, Emi, the woman they had the most

to fear from, would no doubt be forced back to her own job before too long.

Although it brought to question whether there was any hope at all for the demonic races, given that their former supreme leaders were so willing to be watched and observed by the Hero on a daily basis, where and when she felt like it.

"...Doesn't look much like a ticket to me."

The paper Ashiya handed to him was a thin piece of paper, torn off on one edge, with every station along the Choshi Electric line listed on it.

"Hello there, young man. This your first time in Choshi?"

"Eep!"

Maou's body twitched involuntarily at the sudden voice from behind.

Somewhere along the line, an elderly woman in a broad sun hat had sidled up next to them, shopping bag in hand.

"Quite the old little train, isn't it? I bet *that* was a surprise to you. Certainly not the sort of thing you young folks probably wanna be seen in, hmmmmm?"

"Oh, no, I, um..."

Maou had trouble replying to a total stranger sizing up his personality in such frank terms.

"But, you know, *this* paint job is the most popular one around here. This line's picked up all kinds of rail cars from this place and that, so you'd be amazed at how many different cars you'll see. Ohhh, yes! But this black-and-red little bugger's the most popular of all. Like going down memory *lane*, they all say!"

"Memory...lane?"

"Of course, *we* ride it every day so it's nothing special to *us*, but you don't see train cars this old being driven around much anymore, hmmimm? Why, this De-Ha 1001 car here's been running to and fro ever since they built it in 1950!"

There was a sense of pride to the woman's voice, like she was praising a member of her family.

"The entire line was in danger of closing, you know. Several times, in fact! But more and more young folk like you showed up, and the children that live here worked so hard on everything, that a lot of people really like our little train line nowadays. So thank you!"

It wasn't like Maou had done anything in particular. The woman must have been several times his (human) age. But Maou smiled and nodded on cue, not seeing the need to rain on this old lady's nostalgia-tinged parade.

"So are you here to see the sights? You going to Inuboh?"

"Um, yes, ma'am. Kind of sightseeing...ish."

"Oooh! Well, good. Wait'll you see the sun rise above the horizon for the first time. Why, I bet you'll flip your lid, son! Been watching it every day for years, I have. But even now, it just cleanses my heart. Get as old as I am, and *you'll* start waking up that early, too. Oh, yes!"

"Y...es?"

Amane Ohguro mentioned that, didn't she? Kimigahama, their ultimate destination after reaching Inuboh, saw the sunrise before anywhere else in Kanto.

"Oh! And if you're going to Inuboh, I *assume* you'll want to try some of our *nure-senbei*. The *nure-senbei*, I said. Try those. They're scrumptious!"

The conversation continued anon until the train was due to depart, allowing Maou to escape Suzuno's ever-vigilant eye for at least a little while.

It was a tad uncomfortable for Maou at first, but soon, the woman was giving a rundown of every station along the Choshi Electric Railway, in detail that would make a tour guide feel wholly unqualified. Chiho and Emi joined the fray as she went on, and despite nobody knowing one another's names, the chat took on an endearingly affectionate tone.

When the appointed time arrived, the demons and humans helped themselves onto the De-Ha 1001 train car before it languidly departed the station.

The car was fuller than the trip on the Sobu Main line, but from Maou's spot, he enjoyed an excellent view of the conductor's seat and the tracks ahead of them.

"Wowww! The tree tunnel!"

Chiho let out another now-familiar squeal as she took in the view.

"This is turning into…quite the adventure."

"Whoa…"

Ashiya and Urushihara found themselves similarly stirred into words.

The train ran through a tunnel of sheer green, the sun trickling in through the tall trees that loomed over it on both sides.

Summer flowers bloomed just clear of the tracks, the old "iron horse" under the train roaring into action as it thundered its way uphill.

They passed by a crossing, a simple affair composed of a few lines on the ground and a wooden electric pole.

It felt like an era from the past, one that only ever existed on paper from Maou, Ashiya, and Urushihara's perspective.

"It's…quite nice. Quaint."

The old woman nodded sagely at Ashiya's blurted-out impressions.

"Ooh, it is, it is!"

The woman eventually excused herself at Nishi-Ashikajima, an unstaffed station—little more than a platform and a vending machine.

"We didn't think to ask her name."

The thought occurred to Ashiya after they departed from the station.

"Ah, well. Maybe it's better that way. To her, we're just another echo from the modern era. Someone she can touch, but never really embrace herself."

"…What're you talking about? Did you finally get heat stroke?"

The rude rejoinder came from Emi, eyes transfixed on the view out the conductor's window as she held Alas Ramus. It didn't faze Maou much.

"Yeah, well, I was just thinking a little about… You know. World conquest, and so on."

"Oh, *really*? Ready to give it up and live out your life in Japan yet?"

Emi, like Maou, put little heat into replying. Maou fell silent after that, and she pursued it no further.

The train shuffled its way on from Nishi-Ashikajima, through the Ashikajima and Kimigahama stations before finally reaching Inuboh, the easternmost point in the Kanto region of Japan.

Ashiya, leading the crew as he wheeled their bag along, wiped the sweat from his brow.

"Certainly a fancy-looking station, isn't it?"

The station was done up in white tile, evocative more of Mediterranean Europe than Japan. Several station agents manned it, ready to handle the regular trainloads of summer tourists.

Maou stepped off the train, dodging the onlookers photographing the car before it moved on to its final stop in Toyama, and followed the group to the station building. The scene was drenched in summer sunlight outside, but the brown tile–lined interior was refreshingly cool, calm, and refined.

As they followed the other passengers into the building, Maou noticed a woman in the shop on the right-hand side grilling up *senbei* rice crackers by hand.

"Oh, hey, are those the *nure-senbei* that lady told us about?"

Chiho descended into the shop.

"That's it! The savior of the Choshi Electric Railway!"

"Mommy, what's that?"

Emi, wiping Alas Ramus's sweat away with a handkerchief after sitting her on a nearby bench, turned toward Chiho as she scurried inside the shop.

"They're called *senbei. Sen-bei.* You like them, don't you, Alas Ramus?"

"Oh! *Senbeeeiii!!*"

The mention of the word was enough to make Alas Ramus bat away Emi's hand and toddle toward Maou and Chiho.

"Hey! Wait! You're going to trip and fall!"

"Daddy! Chi-Sis! *Senbei!* I want *senbei!*"

"Hmm? Oh, you having Mommy buy some *senbei* for you, Alas Ramus? Kind of young for *that*, isn't she, dumbass?"

Maou directed the final sentence at Emi.

"They have soft vegetable *senbei* for babies. She can chew on her own, so she'll be fine with that."

"Well, the *nure-senbei* are moist enough, she could probably handle those, too. Oh, but I wouldn't want to ruin your lunch. Would you like to go halfsies with your big sis, maybe?"

Chiho crouched down as she asked. Alas Ramus raised both arms to the air.

"Halfsies!"

The instinctual drive to eat, writ large.

"Well, you heard her. ...Oh, don't worry, Chi. Emi'll pay for it."

"Aren't you supposed to say 'I'll pay for it'?"

"Yeah. You."

Emi made a face at Maou as he took the extraordinarily chintzy approach of currying Alas Ramus's favor with other people's money. Ashiya looked on, his face far more morose. His liege was in full-on, fanny pack–sporting tourist mode.

"...Your Demonic Highness! We need to contact our ride."

"Oh, right. Sorry, sorry."

Maou awkwardly nodded an apology as he took out his cell phone and walked outside, into the forecourt.

Out of the corner of her eye, Emi spotted Maou exiting while she stood in front of the shop's cash register.

"All right. Can we talk a second, Chiho?" Emi's voice was hushed as she called Chiho over, pulling her to one side of the building.

"I was really surprised yesterday, you know. You *did* get your mom's permission, right? Because if so, wow."

"...Sorry I called you out of the blue like that."

Her mother had all-too-readily agreed to her blatant cover story of touring the Choshi rail line—as long as she was allowed to speak with her traveling companions Emi and Suzuno first, that is. Emi had been shocked, but agreed to the idea nonetheless.

"I was figuring I'd make sure you were totally safe first before I staked out the Devil King. So *this* is kind of a godsend for me. And *also*..."

Emi grinned as she turned back toward Suzuno.

"Chiho. I have a message for you from your mother."

"Um?"

Suzuno removed a sheet of paper from the carrying bag.

"According to this, as long as we report to the inn your mother specified and one of us telephones her on regular occasions, you have been granted permission for a two-night stay."

"Huh? Um? *Huh?*"

Chiho almost dropped the *nure-senbei* she went halfsies on with Alas Ramus.

"Now we all get a chance to see whether they're actually doing any work or not. No repercussions!"

"Wh-Why...?"

Chiho was more than content with a simple day trip—so she convinced herself, anyway. That was her full intention, too. And why would Emi and Suzuno have a message from her mom in the first place?

"Well, if I'm traveling with you, your mom needed someone to contact in an emergency, you know? So I gave her my phone number, and then she called me up later on."

"I may perhaps be a tad biased, but Chiho is such a bright young lady. She never lies to me, either. She's worried about what will happen to Mr. Maou, of course, but I think she's also concerned that if something goes wrong with his job, that'll make all of you drift away from her, too."

Riho, on the other end of the line, was serious, almost somber in tone.

"And if Chiho is willing to relate that much to me, I'm sure there must be something inspiring all that concern. To me, it seems like you and Ms. Kamazuki are very important people to her. Someone she relies upon on a daily basis. So I apologize in advance for such a selfish request, but I just thought, if there's something you could to do to help wipe away Chiho's fears..."

Emi gladly accepted Riho's request—she was far more apologetic for involving Chiho in the affairs of Ente Isla than anything her mother could have guessed. The two then engaged in a drawn-out period of friendly bickering over who would pay the hotel costs.

Chiho never discussed anything about Ente Isla with her mother.

But if she felt "something inspiring all that concern," Riho was apparently willing to place her full trust behind it.

To Emi, who had met Riho personally, it didn't seem like a case of excessively free-range parenting. Chiho's mother's words were backed, no doubt, by the harmonious mother-and-child relationship they'd built over the years.

She couldn't deny that it made her jealous. She'd only learned who her mother was a little while ago. Then she went missing again. Plus, she wasn't even human.

"So basically, to sum up, Chiho, I think your mother's given you her full support. And in exchange for leaving your father all by himself, she wants you to pick up some of the simmered *tsukudani* fish they make out of Pacific saury around here. We'll go find some of that together, all right?"

"...Boy, this... My mom is just..."

Chiho's eyes clouded just a bit as she hung her head downward.

"But what's this all for, anyway? I mean, why'd you make such a bold move in the first place? It's not just because you're worried Lucifer's gonna get them all fired, is it? 'Cause if so, you would've volunteered to go the moment they played that video."

Chiho sniffled, just once, then placed Alas Ramus on the ground.

"...Sariel told me something the other day. He said Gabriel hasn't given up on Alas Ramus."

The sudden mention of Gabriel's name made Emi and Suzuno both betray a slight panic.

"And I know we beat him away once, but...Maou and you and Alas Ramus keep running into all of these dire situations, but you managed to work your way out of them...because you weren't alone. Right? I'm not asking you to forgive Maou for everything he did in Ente Isla. Nothing like that. But if things get really dangerous again, I just thought having both of you nearby would be a lot safer. But...I dunno, it just kind of seemed like you were really happy to see Maou run off, Yusa, so..."

"Ohh..."

Emi unconsciously nodded.

Their previous handful of team-ups were all the result of desperation. It just kind of turned out that way. Never by design.

Emi had indeed avoided the worst, thanks to Maou or Ashiya or Urushihara being around. But she never actively pleaded for their help, either.

She demonstrated no special interest in pursuing Maou to Choshi, given that he'd be under the watchful eye of the niece of that enigmatic landlord, Miki Shiba. But it must have aroused the suspicion of Chiho, not knowing what kind of woman this landlord really was.

"I mean, the fact that Maou, and you, and Suzuno, and Ashiya, and Urushihara... The fact that you're all in Sasazuka, right nearby me... It's all just a bunch of little coincidences. It's a delicate balance. And if we ever tipped it, you'd all go away, and that really scared me once I realized it. I know that's really selfish, but that's how I feel. So I thought I could try to keep things balanced on my side..."

Chiho kept an eye on Ashiya and Urushihara, seated on a faraway bench and sharing what looked like a half pint of ice cream with each other.

"I know you might all have to return to Ente Isla and settle things for good someday. But if you want to do that, then... I don't know. I want you to work together for it. Just, when you need to. That'd be just fine."

Chiho, to her credit, wasn't driven this far simply out of pure affection for Maou.

"I don't know if Maou himself's realized all of this. But Sariel said something else, too. He said that he knew all along where your holy sword was, Yusa. All your attackers must have known exactly where you were before they came over here. So I thought that...that if Gabriel struck again while Maou was off in Choshi..."

Emi beat Gabriel once in a one-on-one battle. But the archangel might not risk another brazen solo attack next time.

Everything Chiho said, everything Chiho saw, was the honest truth.

Even as Emi and Maou went around calling themselves the Hero and Devil King, neither of them solved any of the threats that followed them into Japan by themselves, strictly speaking.

If anything, they were being too proud of their powers, far more often involving Chiho, Emi's coworker Rika Suzuki, and all manner of other Japanese people in their battles—even if nobody besides Chiho ever realized it.

"...You are a wise young woman, Chiho."

Suzuno's whisper betrayed her admiration.

"The road may have proven twisty and convoluted indeed, but Emilia's ultimate goal is to settle things, as you say, with the Devil King. And in this world, if either Emilia or the Devil King is missing, nothing will ever be settled. We must never allow ourselves to mischoose the foe we must truly face up to, if we want to achieve our supreme objectives. ...Is that what you are telling us, Chiho?"

Chiho lightly nodded.

Thanks to her "mischoosing" the foe she needed to face up to, Suzuno had once been in a position where she ruthlessly eliminated those that blocked the path to peace. She hated that "elimination" was the only method allowed to her. It pained her. Internally she screamed to herself, begging to know who her true enemy was.

Now, the foe that Suzuno and Emi needed to slay was both the Devil King and *not* the Devil King.

It was this...someone. Someone wearing the mask of righteousness, while attempting to empty the world of all that remained good within it.

This someone, or someones, could prove far more powerful than either the Hero or Devil King. And, until now, they had never acted to throw this delicately balanced world of humankind into crisis.

"We've all gotten along so far because I was so selfish. Because I didn't know anything about Ente Isla. ...But now we have Alas Ramus. Alas Ramus, who loves all of us so, so much. I don't want anything to happen that would make her sad."

"This *senbei*'s yummy!"

Chiho nodded slightly again at Alas Ramus's meek reply.

"Chiho?"

"Yes... Agh!"

Emi cut off Chiho with a gentle hug.

"No wonder your mother trusts you so much. You were born into such a peaceful country, too. Where'd all that resolve in you ever come from?"

Emi patted her on the back to calm her.

"All right. I'll sign on to your idea. This child's just as important to me, too."

She released Chiho, then placed a hand on Alas Ramus at her feet.

"But one thing I want to make clear: I have *zero* intention of making friends with the Devil King, or being together with him, or getting—*pah!*—*close* with him."

She spat visibly to drive the point home as she watched a sweaty Maou talk on the phone outdoors.

"If things get *really* bad—like, if there's just *nooooooooooooooooooooothing* I can do alone and I'm absolutely positive I need some help—I promise I'll ask for it. No, I *swear* I'll take up all the help I can. *Consume* it, right down to the core. And once I'm done with it, I'll toss it into the compost pile."

The somewhat overaffected declaration was greeted by a beaming Chiho, bowing her head in appreciation.

"I apologize for the trouble. Thanks a lot."

"Anyway, let's just keep an eye on 'em while we kick back in Choshi, all right?"

"Indeed. We have just completed a long journey. Traveling this far only to surveil the demons as they live their impoverished, pointless lives would be a wasted opportunity."

Suzuno's wry whisper was just the wedge the girls needed to clear the lingering urgency from the air.

Just then, Maou came back inside, sighing contentedly at the temperature difference, blissfully unaware of the portent of the girls' previous conversation.

"Oh! Hey, what's that you're eating there?"

Maou protested at the cup of ice cream Ashiya and Urushihara were tucking into.

"*Nure-senbei* ice cream. It's pretty good."

"I apologize, my liege. I was so taken by curiosity over what it could possibly taste like, I couldn't help myself... Would you care for some?"

That explained why Maou seemed so oblivious of Emi and Chiho. He was too distracted by his demon cohorts resorting to frozen treats to keep themselves from dying of thirst before even reaching their new job.

"Well *yeah*, of course I'd care for some!"

Maou fished some coins out of his pocket as he sauntered toward the shop. Emi twisted her face in disgust as she watched him.

"So I can't protect myself unless I accept the help of a demon who can't resist that tacky souvenir ice cream? That's...kind of hard to swallow."

"Oh, but that *nure-senbei* ice cream is supposed to be really good! It's a new local treat for the summer, I read."

"Chiho, Chiho, Chiho. The taste is not the issue."

Maou, meanwhile, licked his lips as he savored the indescribably unique flavor texture inside his ice cream cup.

"So...what's that chick like, anyway? Ohguro, right?"

Maou and Ashiya stiffened at Urushihara's casual tossing around of the name.

"Could you try not to bring that up? I'm trying to keep that out of my mind for as long as possible."

"What, dude? I'm scared! She's the niece of the lady from That Photo!"

"B-But she sounded kind of young over the phone!"

"There is no need to fret over it. We are committed for the long term. We must do everything possible to face our fates...no matter what they may be."

"Yeah, but how? We haven't even seen her place yet! ...Oh, hey."

Maou's phone began to ring.

The three demons stared at each other for a moment. A beat, and then Maou answered the call.

"Hello?"

"Oh, hey, Maou. I'm in front of the station now. The white van!"

The moment of truth was here.

The three demon nobles took a deep breath, composing themselves in anticipation for whatever might come next, then warily strode into the sun-drenched forecourt in front of Inuboh station.

Chiho and the ladies followed behind, walking up to the tiled front area.

There they saw a long-bodied commercial van idling, its color less white and more a well-worn shade of cream.

Maou swallowed nervously just as the person in the driver's seat noticed them. She removed her seat belt and exited the vehicle.

When the figure stepped out into the bright sunlight, Maou's, Ashiya's, Urushihara's, and Emi's eyes shot open.

"You Maou?"

"Um, yes. Yes, I am. You're Ms. Ohguro?"

"Sure am! Thanks for making it all the way out here. Welcome to Inuboh!"

In a word, she was beautiful.

Her long black hair was tied up carelessly in the back, framing her black T-shirt, a well-worn green apron, some heavily-chafed jeans, and a pair of sandals. A rough exterior, to be sure, but Maou could still tell that her proportions could easily give Kisaki a run for her money.

She had no makeup on, but her eyes, and the brows that arched over them, told the story of a woman with boundless willpower. They were a perfect match for her healthily bronzed skin, almost evoking the chiseled looks of some long-ago warrior princess.

This girl was really Amane Ohguro? The niece of *that* landlord?

Apart from the fact they were both vertebrates and females from their respective species, she had absolutely nothing in common with Miki Shiba.

"Bet you're thinkin' we don't look too much alike, huh?"

Maou must've stared in silence at her a little too long to be tasteful. Amane Ohguro looked at him, a tactful smile on her face. Maou snapped out of it and...

"Um..."

...had trouble figuring out whether to nod or shake his head.

A woman of her sensitive age, would it be prudent to say she resembled *that* landlord? The question required serious debate.

"Ha-ha-hah! Sorry, sorry. I guess you'd never really know anyway!"

"Um...yeah..."

"Aunt Mikitty and I look pretty alike once she takes off her makeup. If you saw some of her photos when she was more my age, she's practically a dead ringer."

If that was true, time was *such* a cruel mistress.

As rude as Maou knew it was, imagining his landlord without any makeup on reminded him of the skin of a 65-million-year-old dinosaur.

"But anyhow, I'm Amane Ohguro, more or less the girl who runs Ohguro-ya. Nice to meet you."

"Oh, sure, um, my name's Sadao Maou."

Ashiya stood straight up, following close after Maou. Urushihara, despite the signs of excitement he betrayed a moment earlier, played it far cooler.

"And I am Shirou Ashiya. Thank you again for your generous offer."

"...Hanzou Urushihara."

"Ashiya and Urushihara...and..."

Amane Ohguro's eyes focused on the women behind Maou and his cohorts.

"Sure are a lot more of you than what I heard!"

"No, that, um, it's just us three guys..."

Maou hurriedly tried to come up with an excuse. After a day of being pushed around and bothered on the train by this posse of unwell-wishers, Maou wasn't about to let them screw up his job offer.

"The rest of them...uh, they're just kind of following along by themselves. Yo! How long you girls planning to shadow us, anyway?!"

"My name's Chiho Sasaki! I work together with Maou back home, so I thought we'd tour around and check out the place he's staying at over here."

Chiho bowed politely, saving Maou from having to explain things himself.

"Uh, Chiho? Did you hear my question or anything?"

The other two girls approached, paying Maou no mind.

"I am called Suzuno Kamazuki. He is my...neighbor, one could say."

"Emi Yusa. And this little girl is Alas Ramus."

He was hoping they would step up to dispel Chiho's claims, but they did nothing of the sort.

The six of them had collectively decided a while ago not to make up a more authentically Japanese-sounding name for Alas Ramus when introducing her to others. The girl was far too young to understand what the ruse was for, and besides, she didn't look particularly Asian anyway. So far, at least, nobody called them out on it. Amane didn't, either, nor did she seem offended at the women butting in on Maou.

"Wow! You sure brought a variety pack along with you, huh? Who're the lucky parents?"

Urushihara pointed straight at Maou. Chiho and Suzuno drew a finger toward Emi. Ashiya stared into space, pretending he was somewhere else.

"Hey!!"

The lucky parents' response came in perfect harmony.

"Well, I can't blame you for having all these hangers-on. It's what you get for working in paradise, huh? Tell you what, how would you all like to check out my place before we open it up? You can go swim out on the beach if you like, long as you stay within eyeshot of me. I could tell you what to check out around Choshi, too."

Amane's eyes turned toward Emi.

"...*And*, I'm sure you'd like to see where your husband's working, right? Boy, Maou, you could've told me over the phone that you had a pretty little thing like that! I thought you were coming alone!"

"N-No! No, it's not...like that...!"

It was their mission, and Chiho's curiosity, that made them want to examine Maou's workplace. But neither of the "parents" were at all interested in being treated like family.

Emi protested from the bottom of her heart, but Amane paid it little notice.

Everyone except Urushihara found their eyes attracted to Emi and Chiho. Emi had an annoyed scowl on her face, but Chiho, oddly enough, had her normal smile out for the world to see.

"All right, well, how 'bout you guys hop in the van? No point baking out here. And you too, ladies. Oh, lemme go set up the child seat first, okay?"

Amane took the child seat out of the rear storage space, as if she'd known all along to expect an infant, and strapped it into the front passenger seat.

The six of them exchanged distinct glances with one another as they piled into the van.

With Alas Ramus up front, the women took up the entire second row, the three demons crammed in behind them.

After tossing all their baggage into the back, Amane made one final announcement before climbing in.

"Great! I'll try to be careful with the kid ridin' shotgun, okay?"

Then she cranked the starter motor, which belied its age as it creakily powered up the engine. Soon, they were away from Inuboh station, the suspension already rattling everyone's rear ends.

The first sight along the road was a gaggle of signs advertising the nearby hotels and resorts. None of them had seen any sign of water since departing Chiba, but—just as Amane promised—the view opened up significantly after just five minutes' driving.

The moment they turned onto a road running along the coastline, the Pacific Ocean suddenly loomed to their right.

"Wowww!"

Chiho all but cheered.

"I've never seen the sea over here... It's so blue."

Emi sighed, her voice soft. Even after her end-to-end journey across Ente Isla, she'd never witnessed a shade of blue as beautiful as the one the Pacific sported.

"Such a graceful blue, is it not? We never saw anything of the sort in our homeland."

Suzuno was just as profoundly moved. Both of them took care not to have Amane overhear them.

"Mommy! Blue! All blue! All Kehsed!"

Alas Ramus, meanwhile, shouted out in glee, blurting out the name of the Sephira who ruled over the color blue in the process.

"This is Kimigahama Coast. If you look back to the right a little, you'll see a cape, right? That's the Inuboh-saki Lighthouse."

Craning their necks back as instructed, they saw an impressive chalk-colored lighthouse standing atop a craggy bluff, surveying the ocean like some giant creature as it was framed by the deep blue of the sky behind it.

"What's that in front of the cape...?"

"Oh, you spotted it? That's Ohguro-ya, right there."

There was a building smack-dab in the middle of the wide beach that formed Kimigahama Coast.

At first glance, it looked like just another old one-story house.

The moment they realized what they were looking at, Amane turned off the road and entered an open clearing that apparently served as the beach parking lot.

Ashiya peered ahead from his seat.

"Hmm. There aren't as many people as I pictured."

Amane had promised them a busy two weeks, but only a few cars dotted the lot she just pulled into.

Given that their only experience with the beach was opening up travel guides and marveling at how every square inch of sand was filled with people, beach towels, or both, this was something of a disappointment.

Amane shut off the engine, removing her seat belt as she did.

"Yeah, that's because the beach doesn't open 'til tomorrow. Right now, there ain't gonna be much besides a few surfers."

Maou accepted this, otherwise unaware of how beach access rules worked around here. Chiho, however, put a hand against her forehead as she surveyed the empty beach from out the car window.

"Tomorrow...?"

She sounded dubious before spotting something bobbing in and out of sight between the waves.

"Oh, I see them. Offshore a little ways..."

"Ms. Sasaki? What's up?"

The way Chiho kept trailing off caught Ashiya's attention. There was something awkward about it.

"...Oh, nothing."

She declined to explain. He dispelled the question to the nether regions of his mind.

"This beach is pretty popular with joggers and people coming over to see the lighthouse or the sunrise. We still get a pretty decent stream of folks even before the beach opens up."

They began to notice a few more people on the beach. Some dog-walkers, along with a handful of men and women tanning themselves on top of wide beach blankets.

"Anyway, we better get your bags inside. Lemme show you the guest quarters first."

The group headed downhill, toward the beach and the house they had spotted earlier.

Amane led them as they left the car, each one exhibiting different levels of excitement, and arrived at a semi-eroded wooden door at the rear of the shop.

"There's pretty much nothin' in here except some futons, but hopefully that'll be enough for you after you're done workin'."

Amane opened the door as she spoke, revealing a sight that made Maou's, Ashiya's, Urushihara's, and Suzuno's eyes bug out.

"...This is nicer'n our place, isn't it?"

Urushihara's hushed whisper summed up everyone's impression.

The room was maybe around 150 square feet, counting the closet and a kitchen space similar to the one in Devil's Castle. The sun pouring in through the large window lit things up brightly, but the space was still invigoratingly cool.

"Dude, I wanna hole up in here forever."

Urushihara's eyes were fixated on a point near the ceiling.

An air conditioner.

It had an air conditioner.

It was an old one, yes, but the small box whirring above their heads was unmistakably a running AC unit.

"The humidity on the beach tends to make the tatami mats on the floor go all warped and uneven, but hopefully you won't mind that too much."

Compared to the glory of the AC, this was the minutest of details to the three arch-demons.

She might have said there was nothing in here except futons, but that was still more than the Devil's Castle was equipped with.

For a moment, the lure of this new living space made Maou forget all about MgRonald.

"It's probably freezing in here come wintertime, though."

Ashiya's pointed rebuff of Urushihara's reverie was enough to make Maou snap out of it, too.

Beachfront restaurants like these were, after all, seasonal affairs. Once summer was over, so was their employment here.

"Well, I'm glad you all like it! I usually head back to my own place once we close, so don't forget to lock up at night, okay?"

Leaving the entire building in the hands of these raw hirees indicated the level of trust their boss had in them. That must be how much Amane valued a recommendation from Shiba, Maou figured.

"Right. Well, I wish I could let you relax, but once you get your stuff all set up, you all mind coming out front for me? I got a job for you."

Urushihara was the only one to wince in protest at the mention of the word *job*. One of his companions was keen to pick up on this.

"I'd be more than happy to put your stuff away, guys. You can go ahead and start work!"

Chiho, beaming like the sun above her as she all but wrested the traveling bag from Ashiya's hand, turned around just long enough to make eye contact with Maou.

He nodded his thanks and, without any further discussion, he and Ashiya each grabbed one of Urushihara's arms.

"Wh-Whoa! Dude! I didn't even *say* anything yet!"

The Devil King and his right-hand man showed off their practiced teamwork as they dragged Urushihara up, ignoring his objections.

Amane, to her credit, declined to comment on the display as she walked out the door and toward the coastline just outside.

Emi, Alas Ramus, and Suzuno meekly followed behind.

The so-called guest quarters was connected to the restaurant by a simple connecting corridor, allowing Maou and crew to enter the shop from the back if they wanted.

There was something about a brand-new workplace that summoned a whirlpool of emotion, just by setting foot inside it for the first time.

Maou and Ashiya were feeling it now, that mixture of nerves and anticipation, as they stood in front of their new job site.

All that raw emotion went limp once they set eyes on the exterior. "...Huh?"

It literally took the words out of their mouths.

Ohguro-ya, a one-story wooden house on the beach, had a fairly decent-sized restaurant and store space. If you took Mr. Hirose's bike shop, wheeled all the bikes out, and roughly doubled the indoor space, it would be about this large.

But the place was...less than spotless. Dust ruled this kingdom, from corner to corner.

A patio-like space jutted out toward the beach, containing a weather-beaten table and set of benches whose splinters made them a less-than-exciting beachfront hangout.

A set of narrow doors lined one wall—shower stalls, probably, judging by the spigots they could see inside. A sign, half-rusted by the salt breeze so it was impossible to tell when it was made, read 10 MINUTES 100 YEN.

The bathroom featured a full-on flush toilet, at least—about the most modern appliance in the whole place—but it was a toss-up whether the creaking coin-operated lockers worked at all any longer.

The sign out front—the beach house's public face—was thoroughly rusted out by years of wind and rain. The cushioning on the backless stools was torn and eroded, revealing the top panel of the chair below. The brass pipes that Maou surmised were a set of beer taps were all equally green with rust.

A vertical ice chest for holding drinks sat next to the cash register, almost empty except for a few achingly lonely cans of Kola-Cola.

The fact that the iron griddle used for frying up *yakisoba* and such wasn't just as rusty was one of the place's few saving graces.

The several-generations-old anime characters printed on the inner tubes and beach balls hanging down from the walls only added to the forlorn scene.

There was old, and then there was *old*. No matter how inexperienced Amane was with running a beach house, why did she abandon it *this* thoroughly?

The place has *to be shutting down next year.* That was Maou's first impression.

And it was Amane's father's place, even. The sight made Maou wonder if the family had any real passion for business at all.

An indescribable storm of apprehension raged across the hearts of everyone on hand.

"Grooooossss!"

Alas Ramus, always eager to say exactly what was on her mind, innocently lobbed a fastball right down the middle, eloquently expressing what everyone was thinking in one word.

"Um... Ms. Ohguro?"

Amane flashed a thumbs-up sign at Ashiya's probing question.

"Jeez, Ashiya, I'm not running a funeral home! Call me Amanecchi! That's what everyone else does!"

They would gladly call her any dumb nickname she demanded. That wasn't the issue. The issue was that *now*, at least, they were sure she was linked by blood to Shiba.

Ashiya soldiered on, wearily:

"...Amane. When did you say the beach opens to the public?"

That was all he ventured to ask. His tone indicated to Maou that he had a similar impression of the space.

"Tomorrow!!"

The breezy response thundered in loud and clear.

"So, uh, you know, I'm kinda in panic mode here!!"

"Yeah, uh, I don't think we can make this into a sunny family fun zone that quick..."

For once, Urushihara was exasperated. The layer of grime covering every inch of the building offended even his tastes.

"Well, I told you guys that I'm 'more or less' running the joint, right? I kinda didn't really know what I was getting into, and besides, I had my day job too, soooo…"

She didn't say what her day job was, but it was clear to Maou that it absolutely did not involve customer service.

"Okay, Maou, I put all of your and Ashiya's stuff away—whoa."

Chiho, dashing in from behind, lost her voice midsentence. It only made the situation starker, and more urgent, to everyone.

"'P…pan'… Mommy, what's 'panty-mode'?"

"…You don't need to know yet, Alas Ramus."

The uniquely toddler-esque attempt at Amane's "panic mode" almost made Emi burst into laughter. She stifled it, moving on to her main point.

"I…probably wouldn't wanna go shopping in here, I don't think."

The final blow. Amane looked up at the ceiling, not bothering to defend the obvious.

Suzuno's impressions were similar to Emi's, but now something else caught her eye.

"Dev—Sadao, what is it?"

Maou, who had yet to say a word, was muttering something to himself that she could just barely make out.

"The place is a heap, but it's still gonna be a busy summer… We're gonna have customers… We got a monopoly. A thousand yen times three ain't cheap… Which means… Say, Amane?"

"Yah?"

Amane took her eyes off the ceiling long enough to acknowledge her name.

"I was just wondering… If we can fill this joint up with people, do you think we could get some bonus pay?"

"Uhh?"

The entire room gasped at the completely unexpected words.

"Fill it up…? Well, if you could, then absolutely, but…I mean…"

I mean, what about this sordid scene indicated to him that the thought was at all possible? As Emi said, it was not at all clear whether anyone would even dare to step inside.

"Ashiya. Urushihara."

"Uhm?"

"Uh, what?"

The two of them looked up.

"We're gonna pack this place full."

Maou had a flair for the dramatic when he felt like it.

"Is that okay by you, Amane?"

"Well, sure, I mean... Go ahead. But that's kinda crazy talk, isn't it?"

Amane did not have a flair for managerial charisma.

"'Cause I gotta admit it, you know... Just like your wife said, I probably wouldn't shop in here, either."

"I *told* you, I'm *not his wife*!!"

Emi's objection was lost to the crashing waves.

"Well, it's good to have a lofty goal to strive for, I'm just saying. If you put your goal up high first, then even when you start faltering, you'll still accomplish a lot more than if you kept the bar low. That..."

Now there was a twinge of tingling excitement to his voice.

"And a store's appearance and selection is like a businessman's suit. You aren't going to earn much more than pocket change if you approach your customers wearing a wrinkled shirt and a stain-covered suit. It won't be enough money to connect you to the next thing. You need to provide service that lives up to that level."

There was something a tad halting to his speech, but his point was clear enough. If you wanted customers to come in, you had to be as prepared as possible for them.

"...And you call yourself Devil King."

Emi sighed, as if resigning herself to what undoubtedly came next.

"...So, what are you saying you're gonna do?"

Maou furrowed his brows at Emi's question.

"Why are *you* asking me?"

It was a fair question. Ashiya or Urushihara were one thing, but why would the biggest threat to his continued non-dismembered state care at all?

Emi scrunched her face up, a little crestfallen, and looked to her side toward Chiho.

"Don't give me that. I'm helping you out here, all right? You could at least *notice* that!"

Something about the smile that erupted on Chiho's face, off to her side, annoyed Emi to the extreme.

The totally unexpected offer was enough to leave all three demons dumbfounded.

"Wh-what's with you, Yusa? You drink some sour milk, or what?"

It was hard to criticize Urushihara for making sure.

"I'm just doing you enough of a favor *now* that it'll be worth collecting on later."

Only Suzuno and Chiho understood what she meant.

"In that case, I'd like to help out, too. Are you okay with that, Amane?"

Chiho lined up next to Emi to volunteer her own efforts.

"Y-You too, Ms. Sasaki...? Are you sure about that?"

"Oh, of course. I was hoping I'd be able to pitch in a little anyway. And if Yusa's joining in, I don't wanna lose out to her."

Chiho raised a defiant fist in front of her as she answered Ashiya.

"I apologize, but I did not bring with me the necessary garments to join in this work. Instead, I would be glad to care for Alas Ramus in your stead. I hardly expect she will be asked to scrub the floors as well."

"Suzu-Sis go home?"

Suzuno shook her head as she accepted Alas Ramus from Emi's arms.

"Your father and mother are going to be working. We need to leave them alone. Let's go play in the sand instead."

"In the sand?"

The concept didn't seem to ring any bells in the girl's mind.

"Perhaps we could start with a sand castle."

"Okeh!!"

"Very well. I will take responsibility for Alas Ramus for the time being. In the meantime, I wish you the best of luck. Try to keep the demons from losing their jobs."

With those final words aimed at Emi and Chiho, Suzuno took Alas Ramus's hand and walked off toward the shore.

Emi frowned as she watched her go, then lightly slapped her cheeks with both hands, mentally prepping herself for the job ahead.

"So! What now?"

She glared at Maou, like a swordsman about to unsheathe her weapon.

"...Are you serious? You seriously want to help me out?"

"That's what I said, didn't I? Stop asking me again and again. You're gonna make me say no."

"Behold, Urushihara...! Today is the glorious day when the Hero has finally fallen to her knees at the might of His Demonic Highness!"

"...That's really not how I want you to describe this, Ashiya."

Chiho simply looked on, a content smile on her face.

"Chi and Ashiya know this already, but I can be a real slave driver sometimes, you know."

"Would you mind not treating me like a wimp for a change? You need to build one *damn* thick shell if you want to survive in a call center!"

"*Ooooooh.* Yeah, we'll see about that. Right. From here on in, I want all of you to follow my instructions. And no whining or running off on me, got it? Good. I'm assuming you guys didn't bring any extra clothes, so I won't give you any of the heavy lifting."

Despite the high-and-mighty tone, Maou demonstrated at least a tad of sensitivity for the crew he'd just press-ganged into action. Next he turned his eyes toward Amane.

"You still good with this, Amane?"

Despite it all, Amane was still the (more-or-less) boss here. Maou wanted her final say before going forward. As ready as Emi and Chiho apparently were to begin, he didn't have the authority to start hiring whomever he wanted.

"Well...I can't say I know what's gotten into you, but sure. I don't mind. If you can actually get this sty into presentable shape in time for tomorrow, you guys all get a bonus from me for today! This is my screwup, anyway."

The reply couldn't have been more carefree and easygoing.

Confirming his boss's assent, Maou sized up Ashiya, Urushihara, Emi, and Chiho in order.

"Awesome. Let me just get this straight before anything else: We ain't gonna pack the place from the very first day or anything. We've got more people now, but this space is pretty big, so we're only gonna get to so much today. Given that..."

Given Amane's lack of enthusiasm, it was totally up to Maou to build a positive work environment for his staff and build the shop up to the point where customers would gladly give them money for their goods.

Sadao Maou, de facto assistant manager, set foot on the golden sands of Kimigahama, the fate of his future salary resting squarely on his shoulders.

"It all comes down to this. From here on in, we're gonna have to fake it as much as we can!"

✳

Maou kicked things off by running a full check of the beach house's equipment.

The electricity and kitchen equipment worked fine, at least. The high-humidity refrigerator in the back was a brand-new Tsukizaki model, much better than the old, chugging fridge at the MgRonald in Hatagaya.

The drink cooler was showing a lot of age, between the yellowed top panel and the rusted-out feet, but they could hide it well enough if they positioned it in the right spot.

The brass drink server, featuring two taps fed by a single pipe, probably saw a lot of beer run through it in its time.

Deeper inside the building, the group found a dust-caked, hand-operated, shaved-ice machine.

It cranked, albeit haltingly. It wasn't critically broken, anyway.

After checking the rest of the outlets and lighting, Maou nod-ded sagely to himself and called out to Amane, lurking somewhere behind the counter.

"Amane! How much petty cash do we have on hand?!"

"Petty cash" was the term for cash kept by a business or depart-ment apart from their regular bank account, meant to pay for small daily expenses or unexpected situations.

It wasn't an accounting item Maou saw much of at MgRonald, given how location finances were mostly handled by the regional HQ. But they would sometimes dip into petty funds to cover trans-port costs for supplementary crew, or the paper and pens they used throughout the shifts.

In the case of Ohguro-ya, a family operation without much in the way of fiscal regulations or real company procedure, they'd use petty cash for things like running off to the supermarket to buy some *yakisoba* sauce if they ran out.

"Uhmm, I think about twenty thousand yen or so! I could prob-ably spot you a little more if you need it, though."

The response came from the back room. Since Chiho was a minor, Amane was preparing a contract that she wanted parental permis-sion to enact. Maou had to hand it to her: When it came to legal paperwork, at least, Amane had a decent head on her shoulders.

"Twenty thousand oughta be more than enough. Yo, Emi!"

Maou grabbed a pen and notebook from next to the register, jot-ting down a note and passing it over to Emi.

"I want you to find out from Amane where the nearest big store is and purchase all this stuff for under five thousand. That, and take some of the ten-thousand-yen bills out of the register—not the petty cash, the regular bills—and break it all down into hundred-yen coins at the bank."

"Um…I know what the coins are for, but…one new inner tube, an air pump, construction paper, and some sandpaper? What's all of that for?"

Emi was clearly dubious. Maou didn't skip a beat.

"Just get it all for me, okay? And make sure you bring back a receipt."

"A receipt?"

"Yeah. As long as all the items are printed out on it, the receipt from the store's register oughta be fine. If it doesn't itemize everything, though, have 'em write it out by hand so we can account for the petty cash."

"Okay. I've done some expense-account stuff at work; I know that much, at least. Should I write it out to 'Ohguro-ya' and expense it as 'goods and services'...?"

Emi meekly walked over to Amane for the details she needed.

"Ashiya, I want you to get the floors spic and span before Emi comes back. Don't leave a single grain of sand on it."

"Y...Yes, my liege...!"

Ashiya stumbled over his reply as he sprang into action, asking Amane to direct him to the cleaning equipment. Chiho jumped out onto the store floor just as he began sweeping.

"Ms. Sasaki, could I ask you something...?"

"Sure, Ashi— Ashiya?! Why are you crying?!"

Tears welled in Ashiya's eyes, his nose turning red and sniffly, as he began to sweep, broom firmly in hand. It, to say the least, unnerved Chiho.

"Emilia... Emilia, the Hero of Ente Isla! The sworn enemy of every demon that lives and breathes! She has been touched by the glorious aura that seeps out of my liege's every pore! She has prostrated herself to him, putting herself at his every beck and call! Watching this dazzling sight unfold before me...I...I don't know how to express my emotions...! This is one small step for a demon, but one giant leap for the demon realms...!!"

Tears began to stream down Ashiya's cheeks, nothing left in his heart to restrain them any longer. Chiho smiled uncomfortably as she watched.

"I...guess I can see why that makes you happy, but you're probably getting the wrong idea here. And I think you kind of owe Neil Armstrong an apology, too."

"Ohhh...how glad I am to be alive, to overcome those days and nights of hopeless desperation..."

Faking a smile to placate Ashiya—although she still wasn't quite sure what caused this emotional breakdown—Chiho edged back toward Maou.

"Oh, hey, Chi. How'd it go with your mom?"

Chiho had readily agreed to help out, but Maou knew he was placing a fairly major burden on her during her supposed vacation. Judging by her face, though, things turned out well with the family.

"Ms. Ohguro came on the line, too, so Mom said it was okay. I think Amane's in the back room now, writing up contracts for all of us…"

Chiho halted toward the end, choosing her words carefully.

"She really said yes? Seriously?"

Riho must have assumed that whatever Chiho was doing in Choshi, it had to involve Maou in some nontrivial manner.

He didn't have any awareness of Emi and Riho's conversation, but even without knowing that, the idea of Chiho's mom allowing her to work during her vacation struck him as pretty ballsy.

The permission she gave for her daughter's flights of fancy was no doubt backed by the trust they had. The trust a mother had not just for her daughter, but for all the people that she, in turn, trusted.

Under no condition could Maou afford to do anything that damaged those bonds.

"…Guess I'll have to bring Mom a gift from Devil's Castle once we get back, huh?"

"Huh? Oh, no, you don't have to go that far. I'm doing this 'cause it's fun, basically."

Of course Chiho would say that. Maou shook his head.

"But I have to do *something*. You and your mom being really nice to me… Man, maybe I really *will* ask you to shack up with my army someday, Chi."

Maou intended it as an offhand remark.

"…Wow. That's a little exciting to hear."

But even he could hear Chiho's muffled gasp.

Only then did Maou realize the remark went a lot deeper than intended.

"Uh? …Oh! No, um, I, I didn't mean anything major with that, but…you know, it was just a turn of phrase. It, it wasn't the 'response' you were talking about or anything. Oh, but don't take that to mean 'no' or… Huh? Wait."

"If…if you left out the 'with my army' part…that… I'd definitely… the…ughhh…"

"Huh? What was that?"

Chiho fumbled around for words in her mouth, making it impossible for Maou to hear her.

"N-Nothing… I, I just…you know, really…someday…"

"…Uh, dudes, TMI? If you don't have any work, I'm going out back and sittin' in the AC."

"Whoa!"

"U-Urushihara?!"

Maou and Chiho jumped into the air. At their feet, Urushihara's voice emerged from under the beer counter.

"Uh, no…I mean, yes, I got work for you. Just wait a sec!"

"I-If you were there the whole time, why didn't you *say* any-thiiiiing?!" Chiho protested loudly, face red as a ripe tomato. Urushihara looked up quizzically.

"What, like you wouldn't have bitched at me no matter when I spoke up?"

Urushihara, for once, was completely right.

It was proving to be an embarrassing confrontation for both of them. Luckily, Maou returned just in time, bravely attempting to save face as both a Devil King and an awkward young man.

"Ah-hem! Right! Come over here, Chi. This ain't anything too exciting, but…"

Beckoning Chiho into the kitchen with a loud cough, Maou took some salt and vinegar from the spice shelf and picked up a scrub brush from the sink.

As Chiho looked on in confused curiosity, Maou took out a small bowl, added a tablespoon of salt, and poured in enough vinegar to cover it up before stirring it with the brush.

Bringing the mixture to the tarnished beer taps, he began scrubbing the brass surface with the brush.

"Ooh! Wow! It's coming off!"

The golden sheen of the brass emerged from the spot Maou polished up.

"The salt granules act as an abrasive that helps the acetic acid in the vinegar penetrate and remove the rust. Now, it's gonna take some time, Chi, but I'd like you to polish these taps until they're sparkling."

"Sure thing! I'll give it a try!"

Her face still showing a twinge of pink, Chiho eagerly took the scrub brush in hand.

"If you run out of salt and vinegar, just add a little bit to the bowl. Lemme know when you're finished."

Chiho nodded and went to work, just in time for Urushihara to pipe up again.

"Where'd you learn *that* household hint? You didn't have any TV or Internet 'til I showed up."

"I studied up a little after I got to Japan. All the joints I worked at as a temp... There were some pretty ugly-looking workplaces."

"Oh? You mean like the place that made you buy that long-sleeved logo shirt?"

"Right. Most of the time we'd just be moving heavy things around, but sometimes we'd be installing stage props, or standing on street corners with sandwich boards, or keeping track of how many cars passed by... All kinds of crap. I learned that rust trick when I was helping clean up a retro-themed *izakaya* before they opened. A lot of bare-bones stuff like that that doesn't require any special tools."

"Huh. Never know what's gonna help you in life, huh?" Urushihara chuckled to himself, in rare agreement.

"Yeah. And since *you* don't know what kind of help *you're* gonna be in life yet, I'm gonna have a few jobs for you, too."

"Nothing that's a pain in the ass, thanks."

He didn't shoot it into Amane's ear or anything, but it was still one step too far for Maou's tastes.

Pulling Urushihara out from his cubbyhole, he pointed him toward the customer seating.

"See the padding on those chairs? Pull it off for me."

"Huh?"

"You can use scissors or whatever else you want. Just rip it all off, down to the wooden surface. Got it?"

"Rip it all off...? Well, sure, but, like, what for?"

"Customers from the beach sit on those chairs with their wet bathing suits."

Maou pointed out a particularly water-stained piece of padding.

"Nobody wants to park their ass on something like that, right? These seats used to have vinyl-leather covers that made them waterproof, but now that they're like this, they'll just sop up water like a sponge."

"Huh? But, dude, if you rip all that foam off, you're just gonna be sitting on bare wood."

"That's fine. The important thing is that customers have some-place to sit right off the beach that isn't all soggy and gross, okay? That, and there's no point making them more comfortable than nec-essary. That'll just torpedo our turnover rate, and I'm not expecting a ton of customers at first anyway. With the amount of time we have to work with, I wanna focus more on getting people in and out of here instead of the individual customer experience. So once you get that foam off, you'll take the sandpaper Emi's getting for us..."

"Oooh, I get it. Sand down the edges of the wood so it's all smooth, right?"

Amane peered in from the side. The sheaf of papers in her hand must have been the part-time work contracts Chiho mentioned.

"You sure are coming up with a lotta ideas, huh? You ever run a shop before?"

"Oh, not really. I mean...I can explain why I'm doing everything I'm doing here, but as for what inspired me to try it, it's mostly just guesswork."

There was nothing Maou instructed his work crew to do that was purely his own idea. He were merely building what he thought were the "best practices" the place needed—anything from his past expe-rience, and what he had learned at MgRonald, that could connect to customers wanting to purchase that little bit more from them.

"I'm sorry, though. It probably looks like I'm busting everything up in here."

"Oh, it's fine, it's fine! The place needs it anyway. Besides, after that little speech of yours, you've sure convinced me. Most of the beach houses nearby have a bunch of patio chairs lined up, but we didn't really have the money to invest in that stuff, so... If we can patch up this place without breakin' the bank along the way, then bring it on, I'd say."

It was hard to tell whether Amane was being serious or just trying to keep Maou at ease, but either way, she ended her appraisal with a hearty laugh and a slap on his shoulder.

"All right, Urushihara. We got our boss's permission. Skin that chair down to the wood. And clean up, too. I don't want to see any foam or leather bits on the floor afterward."

"...I *knew* this was gonna be a pain in the ass," Urushihara whined, though he was at least kind enough to keep it to a low murmur in front of Amane as he went to work.

"I'm gonna go check in with Suzuno for a sec, so if you have any order forms for the local liquor store or farmer's market or whatnot, I'd love to see them."

"Sure thing. I printed out some contracts, too, so take a look once your wife comes back, 'kay?"

"She's not my wife, Ms. Ohguro..."

Maou frowned and jogged outside, not waiting for her response.

A bit in front of the shoreline, Suzuno was building a sand castle with Alas Ramus.

Or, to be more exact, Suzuno was tending to the job by herself.

"Daddy! Suzu-Sis is awesome!!"

Alas Ramus had reason to be excited. Suzuno, sand stuck against the hemline of her kimono, had completed a castle. A real one. "Sand castle" didn't do this work of fine architecture justice.

It wasn't a Western-style medieval castle, but a full Japanese-style *donjon*, golden whales adorning both sides of the sloped main roof.

She attended to every detail in an amazingly short amount of time, right down to the seawater-filled moat surrounding the edifice.

Most very young children, when greeted with this sight, would immediately go all movie-monster on it with their hands and feet. Not Alas Ramus. Her budding sense of appreciation for the arts must have been stimulated to overload by Suzuno's masterpiece.

"...I had no idea you could do that."

"Mmh. Devil King. The child was begging me to carry on, and I became a little...wrapped up in the work."

The smile on her face belied her obvious pride. It really was an impressive effort, one you wanted to take a picture of and label it "Greetings from Himeji Castle, Japan" just to see how many people you could fool with it.

"It is nothing that impressive. Some of the ascetic monks of our faith devote a lifetime to the study of church architecture or religious sculpture. Working with sand is far simpler by comparison. One can always start over if things turn out poorly. Though, sadly, the wind is already causing the structure to deteriorate."

A Church cleric versed in architecture and religious sculpture, making a model of Japan's world-famous Himeji Castle out of sand, was news to Maou. But, given that he was expecting little more from her than an hour or two's worth of distracting Alas Ramus with sea-shells or whatever, the sight made him rethink matters a little.

"Listen, Suzuno, I gotta ask you a favor. Could you, like, build that next to the beach house later on? 'Cause Amane'll probably pay you for it."

"This? The sand castle? Very well...but what would be the purpose of that?"

"You seriously don't know? 'Cause if you don't, that's just scary."

Maou scrutinized the miniature Himeji Castle intently.

Emi and Chiho were working with a restricted schedule. But Suzuno, by and large, was a free woman.

If he procured lodging for her, produced a daily salary, and begged her on hands and knees long enough, he could convince Suzuno to build sand sculptures for him on a daily basis. There couldn't possibly be a better way to attract customers.

"...But anyway. Thanks for taking care of Alas Ramus for the time being."

"By all means. What would you like to build next, Alas Ramus?"

"Ummmm… Mommy!"

"Emilia, then? Very well. Off we go!"

Given her Himeji Castle masterpiece, human sculpture was no doubt a piece of cake for her. Suzuno might even build a sand golem to attack Maou if he wasn't careful. Leaving them behind, he walked back to the store.

"Here's all of our main supplies. And here's the menu list we had for most of last year."

Amane had spread a litany of documents out on the counter, next to where Urushihara beavered away at the seats.

"All right. We should probably keep the menu small the first day. It probably won't be until tomorrow morning when we get all the ingredients in here, and we'll run out of time if we try doing up everything right then. We'll just have to do what we can on the griddle at first, and… Hey, uh, what kind of work do you do anyway, Amane?"

When it came to Emi, Chiho, and Suzuno, Maou couldn't count on much work from them beyond today. Which meant that starting tomorrow, he and Ashiya would have to cover as much as possible for Amane, who had let the house fall into de facto ruin, and Urushihara, who could barely even finish a sentence when talking to a stranger.

Still, if Amane had any experience working with customers or cooking, maybe, he might be able to count on her for food prep or something, to some extent…

"Me? Um…soldier of fortune, kind of?"

"Sol…what?" Maou replied, before he had the words fully parsed.

"Welllll, as far as food goes, anyway, I'm pretty much a home-ec dropout. I can't even cut up lettuce or anything."

And she was running a shop and snack bar? This was starting to make Maou anxious.

"Otherwise…yeah. I guess you could call it job security work."

Not the kind of "home security work" Urushihara provided by shutting himself inside Devil's Castle 24/7, hopefully. She mentioned over the phone that this used to be her parents' business. A mental picture was forming in Maou's mind of a lazy, shiftless father foisting his dingy, underperforming beach shop on a daughter who couldn't care less about making an honest living.

He couldn't take a gamble on letting Amane run the kitchen.

But she understood what "petty cash" was, at least. She knew the basics of business operation. Maou felt safe enough leaving all the store's financial needs in her hands.

As a matter of course, then, it'd have to be Ashiya manning the griddle.

"For drinks... I guess we'll focus on mineral water and 5-Honest Energy, plus Kola-Cola, orange soda, sports drinks, tea... Maybe too much?"

They only had a single four-tier cooler to work with. Unless they limited the number of brands, running out of a single item would make the rest of the cooler look like slim pickings.

"Why 5-Honest Energy? Doesn't that come in those little tiny bottles?"

Maou nodded.

"Yeah, so we can stick a boatload in the cooler, sell 'em cheap, and make money out of the volume. If everything in the cooler's a hundred and twenty yen except for one item that's a hundred, whether you buy it or not, you notice it, right? Plus, I don't think people are carrying around a bunch of bills if they're going in the water. The lockers and showers are a hundred yen a pop in here, so once they ask us for change, our customers are gonna have a bunch more coins in their pocket. Having something they can buy real quick with what they've got on them helps boost the average sale per customer."

That was something he learned from MgRonald's "100-Yen Mag" value menu.

"Also, I'd like to get some of this."

Maou pointed at an entry on the order sheet touting "5-Honest Energy Campaign Pack – Buy 2 Cases for 1 Set of Movie-Size Promotional Posters!" As long as they ordered two cases, the advertising came free with it.

"Oh? You looking for one of those bikini-girl posters, Maou?"

Amane grinned as she spotted the smoking-hot young girl—no doubt blissfully refreshed after being dosed with as much caffeine as the leading cup of premium coffee—in the poster illustration. Maou stoically shook his head.

"Retro-style posters like that can help cover up some of the stains on the walls. And if we put the pin-up-girl posters near the cooler to attract people's attention, I figure that'll keep them from noticing how beat-up the cooler is. That, and cute girls never hurt, I suppose."

"Aww, you're no fun. Or... What, you got other tastes, know what I mean?"

This wasn't the kind of feedback Maou was hoping for.

"That's why I'm having Chi...er, Ms. Sasaki polish up those taps, too. If those are all sparkly inside of here, that'll draw people's eyes to it. And when someone's ordering a soft drink, if we can get some kind of beer poster in addition to the energy drink one, that can lure people into checking out both the beer and the other menu items. It'll be perfect."

"Huh... Neat."

"Same deal with the inner tubes, too. If we take the spanking-new one Emi's buying and put it up front, the older ones we have in stock will look less 'old' and more like funky variations. The point is that, as long as we're providing the bare minimum as a beachfront bar and rental place, we win. Then we can *really* go on the offensive after that."

"Yeahhh..."

As Amane looked on in admiration, Maou suddenly received a phone call.

"Hey. What's up? I guess the world's gonna end tomorrow if you're actually calling me, huh?"

"I'm hanging up."

By the tone of her voice, that wasn't all Emi wanted to do.

"I'm at this supermarket right near Choshi station, but what kind of inner tube should I be looking for? With all the other stuff I gotta get, I doubt I could buy more than one for five thousand yen."

"Maybe a child-sized one. Something gender-neutral. Are there any *Pokétures* ones?"

Pokétures, short for "Pocket Creatures," was a game and merchandising franchise now large enough that it spawned a new anime film like clockwork every year.

A lot of the toys MgRonald sold as part of their "Happiness Set" kid-oriented menu were based on *Pokétures*, too.

"Sorry. I think they're out. It's all *Pretty & Pure* or superhero stuff... Oooh, here's a Relax-a-Bear one..."

"You're not shopping for yourself, all right? Chill."

"It's *fine*! I mean, boys would be okay with Relax-a-Bear, right? Barely?"

"No."

The denial was flat and low-pitched.

"Oh, come on! I mean, you'd pretty much *have* to be a demonic monster not to think this is cute... Oh, *Pokétures*! Oh—wait. Never mind. That's a kiddie pool..."

Listening to Emi fumble her way around the summer-goods section struck Maou with a sudden revelation.

"Emi! How big is that pool?!"

"Um? Not that big. Maybe six or seven feet in diameter. It's a kiddie pool, so it's not too deep, either..."

"Six or seven feet... Perfect! Buy that for me, now!"

"Huhh?! Buy *this*? It's gonna put you way over budget..."

"I'll pay you back, okay? And go ahead and take that Relax-a-Bear inner tube, too!"

"...All riiiiight. Fine. I'll be back in a little while."

Maou hung up before allowing Emi any more time to complain.

Then he flung himself to the cash register and hurriedly thumbed through the phone book.

"Choshi's a harbor town... There's gotta be something to keep the...fish fresh and stuff... Here we go!"

Seemingly spotting an ad on a random page, he immediately whipped out his phone.

Amane stared on in wonder as, after finishing the call, Maou threw a fist into the air in a classic "yes!!" pose.

"Who'd you call?"

"The icehouse. It's called Nanchou Ice Manufacturing."

"Icehouse?"

"I figured in a port town like this, there had to be a company out there providing ice to the local fisheries. So I called 'em up, and they said they could give me a deal on a pretty small order if I wanted. I'm sorry to bother you, Amane, but would you mind picking it up in your van tomorrow? I reserved some edible ice to make shaved-ice treats out of, and some colder pure ice for freezing purposes."

"Freezing?"

Maou turned around, facing the store space, and gestured at it with his hand.

"We can't move the cooler very far. There's no place else to plug it into. So I figured we'd fill the kiddie pool Emi's buying with ice water and toss in cans of soda and stuff for sale. That'll help attract customers, and even if they don't want to go inside, they'll have something to buy from us. Then we can devote the cooler space to things that people who wanna sit down and enjoy a meal would prefer. That way, we can offer more variety."

"Hohhh... Boy, you're just full of ideas, aren't you? But...were you plannin' to use *that* thing to make the shaved ice?"

Amane looked at the hand-cranked shaved-ice machine Maou had plucked out of storage earlier.

"I mean, it looks easy, but you're gonna need some real muscle to crank that thing. You think we'll have the time for it tomorrow?"

"Sure. We can have Urushihara handle the drinks and shaved ice."

"Wh-Whoa! Dude! You're crazy!"

Urushihara, still pecking away at the seat-cushion foam, bugged his eyes at Maou.

"Um, I really... I don't think Urushihara might be up to it..."

"I agree, Maou. There's no way at all."

"Uh, dudes, I already said I can't. You don't have to rub in like that, do you?"

Urushihara puffed up his cheeks as Ashiya and Chiho, both still busy with their own work, chimed in with their own appraisals.

But Maou stood tall, brimming with confidence.

"Don't worry about it. I'm gonna be inside here taking care of whatever comes up, so if it gets too hairy, I can come over to help out. Otherwise, Urushihara can totally run this by himself. He's guaranteed not to screw it up. And even if that machine doesn't work too well, the customers are never gonna complain about it. It's the ideal system."

"Huhh?"

"Wh-What are you *talking* about?!"

"Urushihara can...do that by himself?"

Maou had a satisfied look on his face as he surveyed his disbelieving crowd. What was this wonder system that would make a shut-in fallen angel handle several work posts at once? He began to explain.

And when he was finished:

"Huh. Now I get it. ...You'd need a place like Ohguro-ya to pull that off, for sure. It definitely wouldn't fly in MgRonald."

Chiho barely croaked it out, such was her surprise.

"Indeed... As long as he can open and close a refrigerator door and read prices, it is certainly possible. Absolutely *cunning*. You've thought of *everything*!"

"It's nothing *that* amazing, Ashiya. You're really starting to make me pity you, you know."

Urushihara, for his part, looked supremely relieved.

"I dunno, but...I think I can do that, you know?"

It was rare to see him exude such positive vibes.

✳

Amid the calm sea breeze, a whirl of colorful flame danced a rondo of light in the darkness.

"That... That's got a lot of kick to it, huh?"

At the far end of the stick Ashiya gingerly held in one hand, sparks shot off in a seemingly neverending cavalcade of color, eerily lighting up his pained-looking face.

"Mommy! Sparkly sparkly sparkly!"

"We can just watch together, okay, Alas Ramus? You're still too young for that."

That was doubtful, considering her daughter could turn into a sword powerful enough to make archangels cry to their own mommies. But like any small child, bright lights and loud noises could often make Alas Ramus break into tears.

Their vantage point on the beach gave them a good view of the whizzing streams of light, but placing even a plain old sparkler in her hand would probably be too much for her.

"So, like, what's so fun about these things, anyway?"

Urushihara, crouched down on the beach nearby, was never going to be particularly engrossed by the small black-snake pellets and their undulating lines of ash in front of him. Emi didn't bother commenting, preferring to focus on her motherly duties.

The Ohguro-ya beach house now at least looked the part of a welcoming snack shop and beach retreat—enough so that Amane had the time to host a beachside fireworks party to welcome Maou and his pals.

"Hey! Ashiya! Gimme a light! I'm gonna try four of these at once!"

Now he was attempting to light four heavy-duty sparklers at the same time off the one Ashiya was carrying.

The almighty King of All Demons had his arms thrust into the sky, four different varieties of color sparklers in his hands.

"…I am gladdened to see you in good spirits, my liege."

Ashiya stuck his sparkler toward Maou's smorgasbord of fire sticks…but not in time.

"Ah, too slow…"

His sparkler sputtered out halfway down the stick, leaving him time to light only three of Maou's.

"…Aw, man! The sticks were all different colors, but the light's all the same."

The Lord of Demons was a little disappointed.

When Emi returned to the beach house that afternoon, she was just in time to catch Suzuno and Alas Ramus, both a little bored of playing in the sand. They took a quick break as Ashiya experimented with making the kind of huge *yakisoba* batches they'd need with only the ingredients on hand. That wound up being everyone's lunch.

"Ohh, if only we had this kind of firepower in Devil's Castle..."

The temperature of the liquid propane gas-powered griddle was enough to astonish him, to the point where he kept muttering that plaintively to himself.

After the lunch break, Maou enlisted Suzuno to pick a spot shielded by the wind and build a full-on version of her previous Japanese-style sand castle. Emi left the work crew temporarily to keep Alas Ramus distracted.

Urushihara was busily sanding away at the tops of the chairs he had just ripped the foam away from.

Ashiya, studying the core recipes for Ohguro-ya's food menu, attempted to prepare them with what he could find on the shelves. Chiho, looking on, took up the construction paper Emi purchased and started writing out the menu items in large lettering, making her characters as cute and girly as possible as she did.

Meanwhile, Maou, under the direction of Amane, staged a full-frontal attack on the shower rooms, the yardstick by which any beach cabana was measured. From corner to corner, not a single speck of mildew could escape his murderous rampage of soap and scrubbing.

The sun began to duck below nearby Byoubugaura, a famous beachside cliff popular with sunset photographers, as the sky descended into a dark-blue dusk.

Ohguro-ya, a dump that Emi declared she'd never set foot in a few hours ago, a place nobody expected to see in any kind of presentable shape in time for tomorrow, was now restored to the point where an impartial (or, at least, very charitable) observer could identify it as an old, beat-up, but still-operating rural shop.

There was nothing they could do immediately for the cracks and stains in the walls, not to mention the rusted-out sign—so many years' worth of wear wouldn't come off that easily. All they had left to focus on was tomorrow's food deliveries and the final touches.

By this time, Suzuno's masterpiece of sand—"Sarou-Sotengai," she called it, or "Blue-Heaven-Covered Sand Building"—was complete.

"Dang, Kamazuki! We should just move the shop in there, huh?"

Amane had a point. It was a huge, elaborate edifice.

There was no telling what kind of magic she pulled with the sand. You could even poke at the walls and they wouldn't crumble at all.

As Suzuno put it, the sands of Kimigahama were perfect for making sculptures. If you mixed water and sand in just the right proportions and sculpted the results after it hardened, it would easily remain intact for one or two days.

Emi and the ladies took this opportunity to walk over to their inn—a Japanese-style *ryokan*—ten or so minutes away from Kimigahama. After wrapping up dinner over there, they returned to the coast, eager to have their first up-close fireworks experience.

"Oh, what, so you *are* staying here?!"

It was at this point when Maou finally learned the extent of their plans. He protested loudly, but once Chiho explained she had her parents' permission, he fell silent, still not very convinced.

Outside of Amane and Chiho, nobody in the group had any experience with fireworks.

They knew what they were, of course—a year or so spent in Japan taught them that much—but actually getting to grips with them made them realize just how much care went into these cheap little playthings.

There was no type of magic, demonic or holy, they knew of that could generate such mesmerizing colors and sounds.

"Hey, Alas Ramus! Look at this!"

Chiho took a particularly long and ominous-looking sparkler, showing it to the child.

"Wow, what's that? That's a pretty big one."

Emi was similarly enthralled. It was a long stick with a hexagonal folded paper thing on the end serving as the fuse, even bigger than the fountain-type fireworks you stuck to the ground.

Making sure the coast was clear around her, Chiho brought the tip up to a candle they had placed inside a hastily-dug hole to keep it safe against the wind.

"Ooooohhhh!"

Alas Ramus exclaimed her rapt surprise.

The hexagonal paper tube at the tip spun around and around, spitting out a rainbow of colorful sparks every which way.

It only lasted ten or so seconds despite its size, but what happened next made Alas Ramus's eyes shine with wonder.

"Birdie!!"

Out of nowhere, the spinning paper tube split in half, turning into a sort of papercraft birdcage. Inside was a cartoony yellow bird.

"Birrrdiee! Tweety-tweet-tweet!!"

She tried her hardest to touch it.

Chiho handed the stick over to Emi.

"It's still kind of hot, so maybe wait a little bit before letting her at it, okay?"

"That's pretty impressive… A lot more than you'd expect from a toy."

"There're some others that fire parachutes, or those strings of little plastic flags from all over the world. Too bad we can't have anything that shoots out stuff on this beach."

Rocket-type fireworks were banned on most of Japan's beaches. The tidal winds were strong enough that there was no telling which way they would go.

"Tweety-tweet!"

After checking the heat level, Emi handed the stick to Alas Ramus, her eyes gleaming as she looked at the bird inside the cage.

"Hang on, Alas Ramus. What do you say to Chiho?"

"T'ank you!!"

From far away, Amane and Suzuno smiled as they watched Alas Ramus express her gratitude.

"Hmph. That would be three in a row for me."

On the other end of the beach, Maou—finally tiring of his fire-stick

sword moves—sat in a circle with Ashiya, Amane, and Suzuno in her night kimono. They were busy playing "Sparkler Sudden Death," where they competed to see how long they could make a basic sparkler last against the sea breeze.

"Dammiiiiit! Well, who cares, is what I say! She looks so cuuuute in that kimono, with the sparkler and everything! Right, Maou?"

Amane nudged Maou's shoulder as she appraised Suzuno's slightly coquettish look.

"No, I wouldn't really…"

"You must not lose! Victory shall be ours next time!"

On his other side, Ashiya, playing referee, took out three fresh sparklers from the box.

"Mommy, Mommy?"

"Hmm? What's up?"

"Izzat tweety, too?"

Alas Ramus, birdcage still delicately held under her arm, was pointing at something besides Maou and his fireworks game.

It was a series of lights from a group of fishing boats, plying their trade offshore during the night. It seemed like a fairly large group, and when you looked at it, the lights were almost the same color as that birdcage job they had lit earlier.

"I don't know. But, you know, Alas Ramus, I bet you wouldn't be scared of those little sparklers. Why don't you go to Suzuno and join the fun?"

"Suzu-Sis!"

Gently shifting her attention back to the fireworks, Emi dropped Alas Ramus down on the sand and pushed her forward.

Alas Ramus ran toward Suzuno as fast as she could, although the sand almost tripped her up once or twice.

Seeing her off, Emi's eyes turned toward the sea.

Faraway lights, floating atop a distant horizon out at sea, were never a good omen.

On Ente Isla's Southern Island, the spirit fires that flitted atop the sea were considered the very personification of evil.

Anyone who laid eyes on these balls of light—supposedly released by the spirits of the dead—would be cursed by some kind of disaster from the gates of the underworld. That old tradition still held strong on the Southern Island.

The armies of Malacoda, one of the Great Demon Generals, were gifted in the ways of necromancy, the magic of death. It was the perfect weapon to wage war with in the Southern Island, a land where superstition still rang true to most people.

This, of course, was Japan, and Emi knew they were just lights on fishing boats. She knew the natural phenomenon they called St. Elmo's fire on Earth was perfectly explainable by modern science.

But, on Ente Isla, they were nothing short of grotesque harbingers of doom.

"What's up? You believe in that St. Elmo's fire stuff or something?"

Emi raised her head at the sudden question. It came from Amane, standing as she watched the horizon Alas Ramus pointed toward.

She dodged the question with one of her own.

"Are you done with the sparklers?"

"Oh, man, no way could I beat those guys! Kamazuki ain't wearing that kimono just for show, y'know. I had Chiho tag in for me."

Emi never heard of any relationship between sporting a kimono and being blessed with godlike sparkler skills. Amane continued, undeterred.

"You know, I'm not trying to spook you or anything when I say this, but here in Choshi, there's an old story about these guys called the *moren-yassa*."

"Moren-yassa?"

"Yeah. The moren-yassa, you know, they're these seafaring ghosts that appear on really foggy or stormy days out on the sea. They go up to fishermen and try to make them drown to join their ranks. They say 'Lend me your *inaga*'—inaga is an old word for a water ladle—and anyone that lends 'em one, their ship sinks, right on the spot. They say that when you see lights out on the ocean like that, a moren-yassa's got to be near. There's a story like that down in Kyushu, too, I think. Common theme, I guess, spirits that can't find their way to heaven playin' tricks on the living instead."

Amane's eyes remained transfixed on the fishing boats.

"You see that a lot, I guess. Ghosts going back to our world and messing around with the living. But it really makes no sense to me."

"No?"

"Well, I mean, that's the whole point of the Obon ceremonies in Japan, right? To help the dead make a quick return trip to Earth to hang with their families or whatnot. It's a lot more benign than all that 'ooh, I'm coming to take your soul' stuff. I think anyone who started gettin' scared about vengeful spirits and stuff...I bet they lived pretty evil lives. Enough so that they got all worried about what happens to them in the afterlife."

"Yeah, but everybody's afraid of dying. Is there more to it than that?"

Urushihara butted in from the side. In front of him were ten or so snakes, their ashes starting to crumble and blow off into the sands. He must have liked them after all.

"Well, being afraid of death's one thing, but being afraid of the dead reaching out and touching you is totally different, no?"

It was a very sudden opening to Amane's debate about their views of life or death. Suzuno probably would have been better qualified to participate.

"I'm just saying, why all the hate for spirits just because they maybe had some regrets in life they didn't get around to atoning for? I mean, what's *really* scary..."

Amane's eyes darted over to the edge of Cape Inuboh-saki, and the tower throwing its light upon the dark waters.

"What's really scary, are people who live on forever. Immortality's always gonna be a lot worse, in the long run. Plus which, most of the things we see as bad omens, there are scientific explanations for. It's all just a bunch of coincidences. So...I guess what I'm trying to say is..."

She returned her eyes to the beach.

Ahead of her were Maou, Ashiya, Suzuno, Chiho, and Alas Ramus, happily grasping at the sparkler Chiho was guiding into her hand.

"Try not to raise your child so she starts discriminating against spirits, okay?"

"...Amane?"

"What'd you mean by that?"

Emi and Urushihara, not following Amane's point, both interjected. Then, they were interrupted.

Buoooooooooooooooonnnnnnnnnnnn...
Buooooooooooooooooooooonnnnnnnnnnnn...
Buoooooooooooooooooooooooooonnnnnnnnnnnnnnnnnnnn...

A low-pitched, siren-like blare echoed across Kimigahama.

It was sudden enough to make everyone except Amane twitch in shock.

"Uhm?"

Alas Ramus, still busy with her sparkler, stopped and swiveled her head, a dissatisfied look on her face, dropping her still-sparking stick as she did.

"It, it's okay. Nothing's wrong."

Chiho nimbly gave her a reassuring hug, caressing her cheek to assuage her. But the incessant blare made Alas Ramus's face morph closer and closer into crying mode.

"It's all right! There's nothing wrong!"

She tried her level best to calm her down, but by now, Alas Ramus was a millisecond away from exploding. This supernatural being, who once stood (more like floated) proud in the face of Gabriel, was just as weak against the ominous and unfamiliar as any other baby.

Then another salvo of this unfamiliar rumble stormed across the beach. That was the trigger. The tears began to flow.

"Nnn-*waaaaaaaggghhhh!!!*"

"Oh, dear, dear... That always does unnerve the young'uns a bit."

Amane, perfectly composed, turned her eyes back toward the lighthouse again.

"Um, *we* were kind of startled too, but..."

Another blare sounded off as Emi replied.

"Well, that's the sound of the lighthouse's foghorn. It doesn't mean we're in danger or anything, so you don't have to worry about it."

"Foghorn?"

Emi parroted back the unfamiliar term.

"Yeah. It's a horn in the lighthouse that makes that droning blare whenever the fog's real thick to warn the boats. To keep 'em from running aground, you know. I guess there's some fog out there, huh?"

If the conditions allowed it, fog could appear just as easily in the summer months as it did in the dead of winter.

"Yeah, but wasn't it totally clear just a second ago?"

Everyone on the beach gasped a bit as they looked up at Maou. There, on the faraway ocean, a white mist appeared, as if from thin air. It had already enveloped the fishing boats, their lights now hazily shimmering in the distance.

"It...is certainly fast."

Ashiya darted his eyes to and fro around the area, as Chiho hugged Alas Ramus tight to keep her from panicking any further.

"Yeah, it's sure coming in."

There seemed to be a hint of nervousness to Amane's voice.

"Kimigahama used to be called 'Kirigahama,' or 'Fog Beach,' back in the day. That's how notorious it is for the stuff. We might see it here on land before too long. Sorry, guys, but the firework show's over for now."

Amane nodded to herself as she pointed the burnt firework casings out to Maou.

"Would you mind cleaning that up for me? I'll take the girls over to the inn. Once that fog rolls in, it can get so thick that even the locals don't leave their homes."

The snappy, order-giving Amane was a far cry from the laid-back stoner act she stuck to earlier.

"A-all right."

Maou and Ashiya teamed up to collect the spent casings. Alas Ramus refused to stop crying.

"*Feehhhhhhhraaaayaaaiaiaaaaa!!*"

"...She doesn't pitch a fit like *this* very often..."

Maou's eyebrows bunched downward. Even he could tell how quickly the fog was threatening to consume the shore.

"Can you take care of Chi and Alas Ramus for me, Amane?"

"Whoa, what about Kamazuki and your little lady?" Amane

wisecracked back at him, though she still nodded her approval. There wasn't much time to play around any longer.

"Sure thing. But you guys try not to linger outside too long either, okay? We'll all be up early tomorrow, so try to get some sleep while you can. Ladies, you ready to go?"

The women, guided by Amane, hurried their way off the beach. Maou and his cohorts watched them go, their minds not entirely free of concern.

By the time they made it to the inn, the town was already swallowed up by fog thick enough to cut visibility down to just a couple hundred feet.

And yet Amane, after dropping them off, was oddly eager to dive right back into the soup.

"Right. Good night, folks. Stop by tomorrow to pick up your wages, okay?"

"Amane, the fog is still terribly thick. Would it be wiser to wait in the lobby, perhaps?"

Suzuno's suggestion seemed like common sense to anyone. Anyone except Amane.

"Nah, I got a couple small things I gotta take care of. Kind of related to my day job, you know? Sometimes I get called to work if the fog comes out, so... Don't worry, though. I'm pretty used to this. See you tomorrow."

With that hurried reply, Amane plunged into the night fog and disappeared before they could stop her.

Emi, Chiho, and Suzuno watched the fog anxiously, the now-silent Alas Ramus finally giving them a moment of peace.

Amid the dense mist that so filled them with disquiet, a single beam of light—probably from the lighthouse—plowed its way through the murk.

✳

Maou and Ashiya stared out their guest-room window.

"Man, this fog is nuts."

"If we stepped outside right now, we would quite literally be in a fog, wouldn't we?"

"Hey, your phone's ringing."

Stirred to action by Urushihara behind him, Maou reached for his cell phone.

"Ooh, Chi sent a text… Guess they made it to the inn."

Maou opened the message, reading through it before his eyes stopped on the final few words. He tilted his head in confusion.

"…Uh. What?"

"What is it, my liege?"

Maou turned toward Ashiya.

"She said Amane walked away. Right into the fog."

"So? She lives here. She probably just went back home."

"Well, yeah, maybe, but Chi didn't say she 'went home.' She said she 'went off somewhere.'"

Maou turned off the screen and put the phone in his pocket before turning toward the fog one more time.

He never had found out what Amane's day job was. Did it have her running outside on a night like this? Because you really couldn't see more than a few dozen feet ahead right now. *Hopefully she doesn't get in a car accident or—*

Buoooooooooooooooonnnnnnnnnnnnn…
Buoooooooooooooooooooooonnnnnnnnnnnnnn…
Buoooooooooooooooooooooooonnnnnnnnnnnnnnnnnnnnn…

The window glass vibrated as the blare echoed again.

Perhaps this is what the roar of some ancient, massive dragon sounds like.

It was enough to tear right through the fog, making the entire beach seem to shake. It caught Maou right when he was deep in thought, startling him so badly he thought his heart exploded.

"Jeeeez, that scared me!"

The fog grew even thicker as the horn continued to peal.

The view out the window was now a uniform white. The Cape Inuboh-saki bluff was now the mere suggestion of a shadow.

"Y-Your Demonic Highness!"

"Gahh!"

Just then, Ashiya shouted for his master's attention right next to Maou, startling him into a muffled scream yet again.

"D-Do-Don't freak me out like that, man! Eesh!"

"I, I apologize, my liege, but…did you see something in the fog just now?"

"Huh? In the fog?"

The only thing piercing through the layers upon layers of fog was the strobing lighthouse beam, the nearby beach, and the demons themselves, reflected against the window. That, and:

"…A person?"

They saw the figure of somebody in the fog. It looked like it was walking toward them, but it was staggering, eerily lumbering, like a broken pendulum. And even worse:

"Uh, pretty huge, isn't it?"

"It is, my liege."

The approaching figure was impossibly enormous. Not just tall, or rotund, but gigantic.

Big enough to dwarf the entirety of the one-story Ohguro-ya beach house.

"Hey, what's up?"

Taking note of Maou and Ashiya's increasing sense of panic, Urushihara took his own place by the window. Then he saw what Maou and Ashiya saw.

"Well, look at this fog. It's probably one of those Brocken specter things, right? Just our shadows being cast back at us?"

"B-But that'd mean one of us was casting that shadow. We couldn't be."

"Uh, dude, are you saying that story Amane told Emilia just a sec ago…"

The moren-yassa. The legend of the seafaring ghosts of Choshi.

"No way. They show up on boats, right? That…that guy's gotta be on land…"

"Ssshh! I... Those are footsteps..."

It might have seemed comedic, the sight of these former rulers of the demon realms quaking in their boots as they desperately tried to gain a view of the giant stomping around outside. But even demons could be afraid of the unknown.

"It, it's coming..."

As Ashiya gurgled it out, the fog parted...and it appeared.

"Nhh..."

It was hard to say who uttered that groan out of the three.

It really was a giant, tearing his way through the fog. One all of them knew well.

And as they watched, the figure, just a bit away from them, fell to its knees with a mighty crash and a ballooning puff of sand.

"Is that..."

"My liege! Lucifer! We must go at once!"

"S-Seriously?!"

Watching as the figure collapsed a hairbreadth in front of Ohguro-ya, Maou regained enough of his senses to storm out of the guest house.

It was virtually right on top of the door to their quarters.

And as they looked down at the fallen figure, amid the fog and the swirling sand, Maou, Ashiya, and Urushihara found themselves at a loss for words.

<"Gr...rr...rhh...">

It emitted a guttural, nonhuman grunt, but it had the shape of a human being.

Its size, though, was nearly twice that of a normal man. Its armor-like skin was the color of rust, and a single horn extended from its forehead.

Most unique of all, however, was the intricate tattoo covering its entire face, completely surrounding both of its eyes.

The effect of the ink made it appear that just one large eye occupied the top half of its head. It rang a bell with all three of them.

"Is, is that...a demon?"

Ashiya whispered it, seeking confirmation from Maou. Maou swallowed, then shouted out loud.

"A...A cyclopean?! What the hell is a cyclopean doing over *here*?!"

<"I...I couldn't see... How could...a human have such power...">

The words this beast they called a cyclopean spoke had meaning: They were from one of the languages of the demon realms. The sound of them suddenly made the scene much less of a dream and far more of a reality to them. Ashiya found himself striding forward, exuding confidence and authority.

"You! Cyclopean! What is the meaning of—"

"Ashiya! Get away!!"

Suddenly, the fog began to swirl atop its enormous frame.

Maou grabbed Ashiya by the scruff of his neck, dragging him off his feet and away. Just above them, multiple streams of fog zoomed past like snakes slithering in the air, converging toward the creature.

Unable to react in time, the three demons watched as the fog imploded within itself, illuminated by a powerful flash that made them avert their eyes. Then, enveloped in the fog, the cyclopean that never should have existed in Japan vanished.

The dragon's roar returned to their ears.

"It's gone..."

Once the swirling fog disappeared, all that remained was a depression in the sand. That, and:

"Must've been a younger cyclopean... But he was definitely there. Wounded, too."

Right there, where the hulking mass once lay a moment ago, they could see something red seeping into the sand.

Ashiya gaped at Maou's quick analytical skill.

"But this...this is Kimigahama! In Chiba! What's a demon doing here?!"

"Uh, what's the Devil King and that archangel doing in Sasazuka, huh? We can probably expect Sapporo to elect a Church archbishop mayor soon. Maybe the Eight-Forked Serpent from Japanese mythology will show up in Isla Centurum before long."

"This is no time for jokes, Your Demonic Highness! It was right here! Where we stand right now! This is a crisis, my liege!"

"I'd like to think it was a coincidence...but no luck, huh?"

"Kinda *sudden* for that, don't you think?!"

Urushihara looked around warily. This was enough to unnerve even him.

"Perhaps someone in the demon realms has tracked down our location..."

Ashiya blurted out the assertion, as if it only just came to mind. But even that sounded too optimistic.

"Doubt it. Why was that cyclopean in such bad shape, then?"

"That..."

Ashiya fell silent. Urushihara was right: There was no way to be sure, but those had looked like battle wounds.

Where did the Gate open up? Who opened it? Was it injured before entering the Gate, or afterward? Depending on the wheres and whens, the story could branch into all kinds of possibilities.

And considering the demon was a cyclopean, a demon race Maou and his generals knew well, an even larger question loomed before them:

Why, even after falling into Japan, did the cyclopean retain its demonic form?

The situation didn't give Maou any time to ponder over matters.

"...!! Whoa! Ashiya! Behind you!!"

Behind Ashiya, deep in thought, stood another demon.

It was a beast demonoid, its bottom half that of a carnivorous beast, its top a twisted, demonic monster. Many were those in the demon realms that praised the heroic exploits of this race.

<*"Grrnnnnngghhhh..."*>

But this demon, like the one before it, was gravely wounded, groaning and writhing in pain.

It looked like a midlevel demon, the sort Maou and Ashiya would have assigned an army unit to in the past. The armor it wore was in tatters, the swords in both hands so dented and nicked that it was a wonder the blade remained in one piece.

"A beast demonoid?! From Satanas Arc?!"

There were many half-demon, half-beast races in the demon realms, many of whom lived in Satanas Arc, the de facto capital.

<"Humans...of this world... Do you seek battle with me, too?">

The demonic tongue was invitingly familiar. It screeched across the air like a buzzard's cry, but even with their human ears, Maou and Ashiya understood it perfectly without the need for an Idea Link.

"H-Humans? Us?!"

All three of them understood the demon's speech. But, as he still failed to fully comprehend the situation, Ashiya found Japanese coming out of his mouth, a language that seemed much more natural to him by now.

"You insolent fool! I am Alciel, Great Demon General of the—"

<"Enough with your nonsensical warbling. Let us fight, so I may show you how my sword tastes!">

"Phwaaahhh?!"

To the wounded beast demonoid, the rantings of the thoroughly offended Ashiya sounded like little more than an alien from another world prattling on about nothing.

Its twin swords had long lost their sharpness, but now it swung them high, thrusting them down upon Ashiya.

"Ashiya!!"

With a pointed shriek, Maou barreled into Ashiya, sending both of them rolling in the sand. They felt a sword whiz above their heads.

<"Sheathe your swords! I am not your enemy!"> Maou, still sprawled out on the ground, shouted at the beast demonoid. He could see the hesitation in its ghoulish face.

<"Ashiya, calm down! He's not gonna understand Japanese, dude!">

<"Oh. Er. Right.">

It took Urushihara's scolding for Ashiya to finally figure it out. Flustered, he switched his brain from Japanese to demon-language mode.

<"Ngh... The demon tongue... That demonic power... Who are—">

"!!"

"Huh?!"

The end of the beast demonoid's sentence never reached their ears. Just like the cyclopean before, the demon's body was enveloped by snakelike whorls of fog. An instantaneous flash ran across this miniature tornado of mist, and then there was nothing.

Then, that dragon's roar again.

"What the hell's going *on* here?! Is the Church attacking us?!"

"I, I've never *seen* that manner of holy force before!"

Right before their eyes, two wounded denizens of the demon world had appeared...then disappeared.

They left not a trace of demonic force. Nor did any hint of the power that whisked these demons away reveal itself.

No... *Now*, they felt another force.

"Above us! Here comes another one!!"

This time, Maou and Ashiya and Urushihara could feel the demonic power before it approached them.

"?!"

With a boom like someone blew off an artillery-grade firecracker, the fog above them began to shimmer.

As it did, something began to fall, aimed squarely at the beach Maou stood upon.

"Get away!!"

The three demons nimbly dove for cover.

Another few moments, and then the demon that hurtled downward at such speed that Maou thought it was blown in by an explosion unfurled its wings, touching down for a soft landing.

In terms of size, it was much smaller than either the cyclopean or the beast demonoid. About as tall as Ashiya, the birdlike demon was covered in an array of jet-black armor.

He, too, sported several open gashes. Although he landed on his feet, he soon fell to his knees.

"D-Damn it all...! How could anyone wield such force in this realm...!"

Unlike the previous two demons, while this demon fighter's armor and helmet were all but destroyed by the ravages of battle, the sword hilt and scabbard by his side were in sparkling condition, the colorful jewels that festooned them shining in the dim light.

It was a sword of some notoriety. That much was clear. But Maou and Ashiya paid it little heed. Their eyes were focused on the avian demon's face.

They knew it.

"C-Camio?!"

"Sir Camio?!"

The avian warrior, his round, evocative eyes a rarity for a demon, raised his heavy head at the call of these strange humans.

"You... Humans. Why do you know my name...? Rgh!"

Blood poured from the demon's beak, his sharp eyes glaring at Maou and Ashiya.

"It doesn't matter! Camio, what happened to you?! Your wounds...!"

"My liege! The fog!!"

Maou attempted to run up to the warrior, but for a third time, the snakes of fog were too fast for him.

He had no idea what was driving this living, breathing fog, but there was no telling what would happen if it chose to smother him. He stopped.

"Ugh! Shit! This is all or nothing!!"

Urushihara's voice rang out, and then a strong wind began to blow.

The next moment, the fog around the three demons fell back.

"Urushihara?!"

Behind Urushihara, they didn't see the black wings of a fallen angel. These were white, bathed in holy energy as they hung in the air.

With a single flap, they summoned a more powerful gust, bringing the entire space between the demons and Ohguro-ya back into clear focus.

"Uh, why're your wings white—"

"Couldn't you tell that something's *up* with this fog?! Hurry up and get Camio inside!"

"Oh! Right! Jeez, this is nuts... Ashiya, you take that side!"

"Y-Yes, my liege!"

The two of them held the avian warrior by the shoulders, bringing him back into Ohguro-ya. It wasn't far. All of this had happened practically on their doorstep.

Urushihara continued flapping his wings to keep the fog at bay as he took rear guard, shutting the door behind him once everyone was inside.

Buooooooooooooooooonnnnnnnnnnnn...
Buoooooooooooooooooooooooonnnnnnnnnnnnnn...
Buoooooooooooooooooooooooooooonnnnnnnnnnnnnnnnnnnnnnn...

The haunting scream, like that of a carnivore whose prey had slipped through its talons, boomed across Kimigahama.

"Your Demonic Highness! The fog!!"

After setting the warrior down, Ashiya looked out the window, only to find the fog receding just as rapidly as it came, as if the guttural scream just then had scared it away.

Several more moments, and Kimigahama was back to its normal nightscape—the moon, the stars, the lights out on the sea, the town overlooking the beach, and the lighthouse.

There was no sound, apart from the ebb and flow of the sea. The events of the past few minutes seemed like a passing daydream.

"Camio! Camio, hang in there!"

The three demons looked on, concerned, down at the wounded warrior.

"I know not who you are...but meddle with me, and it will cost you your lives... Know your place, hu..."

Strangely, the words coming from the warrior's beak didn't match the cyclopean's or beast demonoid's speech. It was fluid Japanese from the start, a bit of a mismatch for the creature's visage.

"Can't blame you. Satan and Alciel look pretty much totally different now."

The warrior fell silent at Urushihara's voice.

"But you can still tell who I am, I bet. Right, Devil Regent?"

The avian warrior's face shot up.

Urushihara was dressed in a baggy T-shirt, shorts, and hoodie, but his pure white wings were still there as he stood before the warrior.

The sight was enough to make him gasp.

"Lucifer... Is that you, Lucifer?!"

"Sure is, Camio. You never *did* call me by my full title, did you?"

Ignoring the pouting Urushihara, Camio refocused his eyes on the other two men watching on.

"Alciel? ...Satan? ...It couldn't be. It couldn't be..."

The words fell shakily out of his beak.

"General...of the Eastern Island..."

"...I look like this now, it is true...but yes, Camio, I am Alciel."

Ashiya kneeled down to gain a closer vantage point to the demon's eyes.

"And, and you... Could it truly be...?"

"Camio, what happened to you? Tell us."

Maou's and Camio's eyes made contact.

"Lord Satan... My Devil King... You're alive...! What a glorious stroke of luck..."

"Yeah, sorry we've been neglecting the demon realms for so long. But I kind of wasn't expecting to see you in Ja—in this world. What's going on?"

"My...my apologies, Your Demonic Highness."

The avian warrior Camio attempted to rise, in order to prostrate himself before his rightful king. Maou tried to stop him, but he shook his head in refusal.

"I...I was unable to keep your realm protected during your long... departure. I can hardly bear to face my Great Demon Generals... nor your dearly departed comrades from the north and south..."

"What do you mean?"

"My liege... The demon realms...and Ente Isla. They both face chaotic times once more. I was powerless to quell the waves... I...I am..."

"Whoa! Camio! Camio! Speak to me! Hey!"

The flame of life rapidly flickered from Camio's pupils.

As it did, a dim light enveloped his entire form, his body growing smaller and smaller.

"My liege! What is this…?!"

Perhaps it was the start of his transformation into human form, following the loss of its demonic power. Or perhaps, with his energy gone, this was the end for him.

The three swallowed nervously as they looked on. However, the transformation was complete in but a few seconds.

"The hell…?"

Urushihara's eyes were as wide as saucers.

Even Maou himself was rendered speechless.

As the light faded, all that remained on the futon was a shattered black battle helm, a stained and torn black cape, a glittering sword still in its scabbard, and:

"Huh. Kind of cute."

A limp, but seemingly uninjured blackbird.

THE
DEVIL
MARVELS
AT
THE
WIDE
WORLD
(AND
CHOSHI)

The morning after the night of the postponed fireworks party, the demons were forced awake by a presunrise phone call from Amane.

Apparently she was aghast that they came all the way to Inuboh and didn't bother watching the sun rise from the horizon. From Maou's perspective, he honestly couldn't have cared less.

It was beautiful, no doubt, but from his personal chamber in the Devil's Castle on Isla Centurum, he was greeted daily by an unobstructed panorama of that world's sun making its debut.

Urushihara, in a zombielike state, stood around long enough for the sun to clear the horizon. Then he burrowed back into his futon.

The previous evening's events made for a difficult night's sleep. Maou and Ashiya, both still drowsy themselves, couldn't blame Urushihara for his refusal to remain conscious.

But the fog now seemed like a faraway vision. The weather in Choshi, and along Kimigahama, was gorgeous. Even this early, the temperature was high enough to make Maou break into a sweat just standing outside.

The night before, Chiho texted them that the girls were at the inn and Alas Ramus finally chilled out. The only real concern left was how many customers they'd have to deal with today.

This was the first day Maou and Ashiya were running the place. Now that they were awake, they set out to prepare for the grand opening.

It was still painfully early as the sun rose upward. But if they fell asleep again, they might wake up to find an angry delivery truck driver waiting for them.

Amane arrived at six AM, giving Maou an excuse to beat Urushihara awake as the four of them ran one final check before the big moment.

Would anyone really show up? Just as Chiho and Ashiya noted concernedly yesterday, the beach was barren of people.

It was August 1, and Maou was ready to rumble.

By the time the clock struck eight, however, the beach—wholly uninhabited until the previous day—began to fill with vacationers, wiping away the bit of anxiety still bouncing around Maou's mind.

They were coming in droves. So much so, in fact, that despite having four people on the Ohguro-ya staff, Amane, Maou, Ashiya, and Urushihara had no time at all to rest.

Right from the start, a small crowd of people began to form around the beach house, attracted by Suzuno's exquisitely detailed Sarou-Sotengai sand castle.

Then, the crowd grew.

By ten AM, they were beginning to form a line, lured in by the smell of Ashiya's *yakisoba*.

Ashiya had to focus on cooking the noodles, but his mind was almost fully occupied already with handling to-go orders from customers.

Maou and Amane, meanwhile, were busy handling customers sitting by the tables for a rest and some grub.

The chairs Urushihara and Chiho sanded and polished could hold twelve people. But once they began offering service to beachgoers seated on the nearby ground or rocks, things grew profoundly busy in the blink of an eye.

And, of course, the beach house offered more than just fried noodles on the menu.

They had cut down on the offerings so they could more quickly prepare for the onslaught ahead. The focus instead was on dishes they could make in the same cooking area without a lot of fuss.

To be exact, they got rid of the ramen—no time to bring noodles to a boil, nor to delicately place all the extra bits and bobs in the bowl—and offered both regular and seafood *yakisoba* instead.

Having every square inch of griddle space occupied by *yakisoba* meant that *okonomiyaki* pancakes were out of the question, too. Instead, Ashiya took the space meant for ramen prep and used it for curry, pairing it with some presautéed chicken and pork to customer taste.

Writing out the menu items across the dining space, one per sheet of construction paper (including drinks), successfully diverted customers' attention away from how few offerings were really on hand.

As a result:

"Thank you very much! Two pork, one chicken, one seafood to-go on number four, please!"

"Two sauce, one seafood, on number three, two on the ground with two sauce to go!"

"Five chicken on rock two! We good right now?! ...I apologize, sir, we've got some chicken cooking right now. I'll bring it out to you when it's ready, all right?"

Maou was forced to constantly shout at the general direction of the kitchen.

"Sauce to go" and "seafood to go" mostly referred to customers who were eating indoors, but wanted to take some orders back to their beach towels for the family.

The numbers referred to chairs...or the rocks lining the outside of the store, depending.

"Maou, I've got four regular at number one! Can you get that out for me? I gotta go cook up some more pork!"

"I'll be right there! Urushihara!"

"No! I can't! I can't!"

Maou reached out to Urushihara for help. But the fallen angel was about to suffer an engine blowout himself.

The system he'd devised for Urushihara, one that seemed so foolproof and revolutionary yesterday, was about to fall apart, thanks to one unanticipated reason.

Maou was picturing customers operating the manual shaved-ice machine themselves while Urushihara simply collected money—the kind of easygoing business management that only a mom-and-pop joint like this could get away with.

The machine was pretty difficult to work, but since Ohguro-ya didn't have any of the equipment needed to sell ice cream, shaved ice was the only frozen treat they could easily offer.

They put an ample supply of ice out on the counter, with Urushihara instructed to go fetch some more if they ran out. Thanks to the entertainment value of customers grinding up the ice themselves, nobody was going to complain if the results came out less than uniform.

Simply making the shaved ice would bore some customers, though. So Maou decided to sacrifice profits a bit and offer full self-service on the syrup toppings, too—your choice of strawberry, lemon, melon, or Blue Hawaii.

Thus, the customers would put in all the effort, finely crushing the ice to their own liking, then spatter their choice of syrups on as a sort of greedy reward.

All Urushihara had to do—on paper, at least—was give them change and put ice in the machine. The tourists would handle everything else.

They ordered a ton of shaved-ice cups and spoons, so they weren't going to run out of those, either. Then they could just toss a bunch of drink cans in the ice-filled kiddie pool Maou had Emi purchase for him, have Urushihara sit down in front, and just make him be a money-taking robot for the day. Easy. But...

"I got about a fifteen-minute wait! And I'm out of strawberry syrup, too, so don't ask me for that! Please!"

Urushihara's eyes darted to and fro between the ice machine and the line at the drinks counter.

"Whaaa?"

"Aw, maaan."

Murmured complaints across the length of the line.

The drinks were moving at a much more leisurely clip compared to Ashiya's griddle, but the shaved-ice gimmick was too successful for its own good, forcing customers to stand in the hot sun for a chance to turn a crank for a few seconds.

Maou could see several of them squirm uncomfortably, stamping their feet to keep from burning their heels on the sunbaked sand.

They had only one shaved-ice machine, after all.

To keep things fair for people who messed up the shaving job, Maou had set the price on the low side. That was another reason why the line grew to levels beyond Urushihara's control. Running out of syrup was also something he never considered.

"Maou! I'm out of salt! It'll be ten minutes until the next batch!"

Now Ashiya was screaming out from the kitchen.

Maou could feel the complaints seeping out from the line behind him. He ran up to the griddle and whispered in Ashiya's ear.

"Can you handle the seafood orders I just took?"

"I have three left. We're one short on the table order I have now."

This plunged him into outright depression.

He had completely misjudged the quantities for his delivery orders. Based on how slapdash Ohguro-ya's business operations were up to now, he had ordered the equivalent of 150 percent of the previous summer's sales, just in case. Now they were running short on seemingly everything.

They had plenty of food, but there there was no time to restock everything else they needed.

"Maou! Two seafoods and sodas for rock one! Ugh, I'm starting to forget who placed an order and who didn't!"

Amane's eyes ran up and down the order slips in her hand.

Most beach houses like this, unless they had a pretty hefty number of tables, usually had customers pay for orders at the cash register before picking them up. But Maou, figuring the crowds would make this impossible, instead started generating order slips for each table.

This ensured that Amane, still not used to this, wouldn't make any accounting errors or misplace someone's change while typing in orders.

But adopting this system without practicing it first led to orders frequently being delivered to customers twice.

"Ah, jeez, we're running short on order slips..."

That, and they ran through an entire pad of slips in seemingly record time. *That* was out of left field.

"Do we have any more, Amane...?"

"Guh! I don't know! If I have any, they'd be in the closet in the room you're staying in, but I haven't been in there in ages, so..."

Maou resisted the urge to ask her—more scream at her, really—why she stuck them in there.

But if he left the store space right now, Amane would have to handle transactions, odd jobs, and drink server management by herself.

He was already noticing customers scowling and whining to their companions here and there. Unless you were a six-armed Hindu god—or the Devil King in his own world, perhaps—there was no way to solve this crisis.

All the employees' faces were red and caked with sweat. They had no reserve power on hand to deal with all these irregularities.

Maou's brain was just about to spring a flat when:

"Go look for those order slips, Maou. I'll fend everyone off while you do."

The voice flowed into the employees' ears just before they exploded.

"Shirou, you complete the orders for the regular *yakisoba*. I will prepare the seafood orders in the meantime. I just cut up the vegetables and calamari and skin the shrimp, yes?"

"Hello, Nanchou Ice Manufacturing? Do you think we could rent two shaved-ice machines immediately? Sure, you can charge us for today. They don't have to be brand-new or anything, so if you could get them to Ohguro-ya in Kimigahama ASAP... Oh, really? Great, how about strawberry and Blue Hawaii, then? Thanks. ...Whew. Sorry I took the initiative there, but if you're this busy, I figure you can shell out for that, huh? They said rentals start at three thousand yen per machine, and they'll give us syrup samples, too."

Three beams of light shone upon them.

"Chi... Suzuno, Emi... Why are you...?"

Just as Ohguro-ya's juggling act was about to end in tears, three goddesses descended from the heavens.

"What's table two…? Right there. Yeah. Two beers, one orange, and one bottle of soda? Okay!"

Not even waiting for Maou's reply, Chiho asked Amane for a table number and expertly began serving out drink orders.

"Right. Here is enough shrimp to process your current orders. What about the cabbage? Should I be shredding it, or should it be coarser than that?"

Suzuno, slicing up veggies and skinning shrimp at a clip reminiscent of a Western-film gunslinger, stood next to Ashiya. After a quick glance at the recipe, she began to make a heaping batch of salt-flavored *yakisoba*.

Emi approached Maou, the irritation clear on her face.

"The people in the shaved-ice line are crying bloody murder, y'know. Do we have anything free we can give 'em?"

The customers, frustrated by the heat and the lengthy lines, were fixated on the swimsuit-wearing female crew that just walked in.

Compared to Amane, bedecked in a sweat-stained T-shirt and spending most of her time in the back anyway, this attracted a great deal more positive attention.

"Ah, youth…"

Amane whispered the observation to herself, even though she couldn't blame anyone.

Chiho had a frilly orange bikini on, framed by a light white jacket and a sun visor that already made her look like a beachside waitress.

Deftly handling a serving tray laden with drinks, she used the footwork she'd learned at the MgRonald in Tokyo to dance her way through the crowds, delivering orders perfectly and with a smile.

For her post in the kitchen, Suzuno wrapped an apron around her waist and the simple black halter-top bikini she had on. The white ribbons on the straps well-matched the apron's basic navy blue, adding a healthy, refreshing aura to her work outfit.

And once she took a knife to a head of cabbage, slicing it to ribbons like a practiced samurai swordmaster, the formerly peeved customers in line applauded.

Emi, meanwhile, had a South Seas resort–style bikini on, fitted with a large ribbon and a wrap around her waist.

All three of them sported swimsuits that accentuated their natural beauty, but Maou's attention was focused on something different entirely.

"Uh, where's Alas Ramus?"

"...That's all you got to say?"

The question put Emi off. She discreetly motioned toward Amane.

"We went out on the beach early in the morning, so she's napping now. I put her to sleep in your room. I'm outta here once she wakes up, so..."

She tapped on the back of her head twice as she spoke.

Maou got the message. The girl was fused within her right now.

He had nothing to worry about.

But right now, there was no scaling this mountain without their help.

"Thanks! We'll probably need you for just a little bit, okay?"

"You got it!"

"Leave it to us."

"Remember, you owe me for this one!"

The three of them eagerly replied in their own ways.

Maou flung himself into the crowd before reappearing with four damp-looking cardboard boxes that he immediately foisted on Emi.

"You can use all the inventory we got on these. Pass 'em around to the crowd and tell 'em it's a freebie for lunch!"

It was their spare supply of 5-Honest Energy.

Giving away four cases' worth meant a loss of nearly five thousand yen, but they had no time to quibble over the numbers.

Right now, at this moment, if they could give the customers the service they wanted, they would make up for that loss easily.

On the other hand, if they cheaped out, they might be facing even larger, unseen losses from tomorrow forward.

Emi, more accepting than he expected, walked up and down the lines of dissatisfied *yakisoba* and shaved-ice customers.

"Our apologies for making all of you wait! We've got a free lunch bonus for all of you!"

With a well-practiced smile and what natural charm she had, she began passing out 5-Honest Energy bottles.

It was a well-calculated move. The men in the crowd certainly didn't mind Emi's swimsuit, and nobody else would turn down a cold drink in this heat.

If she could smile like that more often in normal life, one could almost describe her as cute.

Though, to Maou, their bikinis weren't as much of a surprise as the way they briskly strode in and saved the demons from a fate worse than death.

"I'll be right back!"

Checking to make sure he had a moment's reprieve, Maou ducked away and into the back in search of extra order pads.

He opened the door and immediately basked in the joyous air-conditioned atmosphere for a moment. He already knew the closet inside their quarters contained several boxes, clearly abandoned for a lengthy period of time prior.

He knew because he had dragged out one of the empty ones last night.

In one corner of the room, a large box stood safely away from both the sun and the AC vent. Maou peered in and spoke.

"...You still alive, Camio?"

"L-Lord Satan...*peep*."

Inside, the blackbird drowsily hopped around.

"Bah-hah-hah! ...Oh, uh, sorry. Glad you're still with me. I'll check up on you later."

It must have worked differently for him from when Ashiya and Maou were drained of their demonic force. Camio skipped the human transformation entirely and went straight into songbird mode.

His voice was the sedate baritone of the avian warrior from yesterday, but the way he now added a high-pitched "peep" in and around his statements struck Maou as nothing short of hilarious.

"I a*peep*...apologize...for disquieting you *peep*."

"No, no, no. There's not much I can really do for you right now anyway. You sure you're okay without food or anything?"

"I thank you, my liege...*peep*... But my demonic force has not fully drained out of my body...*peep...peep*."

"Keh-heh... All right. See you later, then."

"Yes, my *peep*."

Then the ex-proud demon warrior Camio nestled down to rest into the towels Maou laid on the bottom of the box. Maou placed a cup of water in the box and set the AC on the high side, around eighty-three degrees, so it wouldn't be too cold or hot for the demon.

For a typical bird, this would be their cue to close their eyes and wait for death. But while he looked a bit like a mynah in critical condition, this was actually one of the greatest demons from Maou's old stomping grounds, high enough in the ranks to recognize Ashiya and treat him with respect.

He was Camio, the Devil Regent.

Not every demon in the underworld set off with the Devil King's forces to invade Ente Isla. In fact, most remained in their respective homelands.

The organization Maou built from scratch, really the first true state that ever existed in his realm, needed to be governed by someone under his name while he was gone. That someone was Camio, ordered by Satan to serve as his official Devil Regent.

As Maou's representative, Camio ostensibly held all the powers of the Devil King when it came to affairs in his realm. But why was he in Japan, and so severely wounded? Maou didn't know. Camio had fallen unconscious before he could say.

The demon bird's chirping went unnoticed until the following morning, by which time Urushihara was already groggily walking to Ohguro-ya after waking up a second time, so Maou had yet to find a chance to discuss matters in detail.

One thing clear from Camio's behavior, however, was that neither he, nor the cyclopean, nor the beast demonoid that preceded him, came here in search of Satan or his general Alciel.

So what were they after, then? Why did they show up in Choshi?

And how did they retain their demon-realm forms? Riddles piled upon riddles.

But, sadly—*truly* sadly—Maou had no time to pursue any of these questions.

Out in front, Chiho and the others were meekly waiting, supporting him in the current battlefield, trusting that he would return.

"I have a job to go back to!"

Returning to the store space and prepared for anything, he was surprised to find the two rented shaved-ice machines already there.

It was not even twenty minutes since Emi placed the call. The ice seller must have been a lot closer by than he thought. In his mind, Maou gave his silent, heartfelt thanks to Nanchou Ice Manufacturing.

"Urushihara! I'll handle the ice. You just keep the lines orderly and hand out the drinks!"

"Dude, don't order me around!"

Urushihara chafed at the order, of course, but realized that Emi was right. Maou would've preferred her out in front, where her attractiveness (visually, at least) would help garner more attention. But her pinch-hitting out back was sorely needed, and Urushihara wouldn't learn anything from this otherwise.

Ignoring the silent daggers of lightning Urushihara shot from his eyes, Maou gave one receipt pad each to Chiho and Amane, leaving them to handle orders and take money as he returned to his own job.

By the time he started tackling the mountain of outstanding orders, Suzuno had restored the seafood *yakisoba* plate to the menu. She was standing in front of a large pot at the moment, filling it with curry in a mad dash to keep from running out.

If they kept this up, they might just survive the lunch rush.

It was thanks to the girls that they recovered from today's mistakes. Starting tomorrow, they'd have to learn from them, figuring out how to improve their system so they didn't need Chiho and the gang's help.

Looking back, Kisaki had been right all along, in her own way. If they made mistakes, it was fine. As long as they could make up for them all, it would never hurt in the end.

Three in the afternoon.

That's how long it took before the orders died down and everyone could breathe again.

All the tables were empty, there was some extra *yakisoba* simmering on the side of the griddle, and Maou took that as his cue to plop on a chair.

"Uggghhhhh. I'm exhaaaaausted...!"

"Here you are, Maou. From Amane."

Chiho handed him a bottle of chilled 5-Honest Energy.

"Ah, thanks."

He grabbed it, opened the cap, and chugged the contents in one go.

"*Ooooooh.* That hit the spot."

The ice-cold carbonation ran down his throat, the resulting light case of brain freeze feeling like a small vacation.

"But really, though... Thanks, Chi. If you guys didn't show up, I think we would've been screwed. Sorry we wound up putting all this work on you."

Chiho bowed her head as she sat next to him. "I'm just happy we helped you out."

"I bet some customers are gonna start asking about you tomorrow, Chi. That swimsuit looks good on you."

"...Huh?"

From heartfelt thanks, straight to a backhanded compliment. It came out so naturally from Maou's mouth that it took a moment or two for Chiho's face to redden in response.

"Ah, I, um, thank you. ...Very much. Um..."

No longer able to look Maou in the eye, Chiho wriggled her legs a bit as she stared at the 5-Honest Energy in her own hands.

"It looks...good on me?"

"Yeah. That's why I said it. You didn't...bring it with you, did you?"

Chiho earnestly shook her head as she made eye contact with

Amane, currently scrubbing the frying pan she used to sauté the pork and chicken.

Maou followed her eyes over. Amane, for reasons only she knew, gave them both a thumbs-up.

Her "go" sign, he supposed.

"Y'know, I wasn't gonna ask at first, but…well, it's a cute swimsuit and all, so…um…"

I wanted you to see it. Chiho wanted to blurt it out, but saying it out loud seemed in poor taste, so she opted to blush and stare at the floor instead.

Maou easily interpreted the words she swallowed.

"You know. We're here at the beach and all, so I thought it'd be nice if you took advantage and swam a little bit."

"Oh! Oh yeah! Sure! Uh… Ha-ha-ha-ha! Ahhh…"

Chiho picked up the conversation string, face still reddened, but suddenly let out a sigh.

"It's actually something they had on sale here at the beach house…"

"Really?"

Looking back at Amane, Maou saw her back turned to them, thumb still in the air.

Besides the food and drink, Ohguro-ya offered some extent of summer merchandise—sunscreen, beach blankets, inner tubes, beach balls, and the like.

Swimsuits hung from the walls as well, but swimsuits were much harder for a shop like this to manage. They were high-priced items—beach houses usually gambled with them, selling them at marked-up tourist prices—but generally speaking, they sold slowly, if at all.

That was the problem with such things: The sort of person who went to a beach in midsummer without a swimsuit usually didn't intend to go swimming in the first place. You needed someone enthused enough to hit the beach for some wild fun in the water, forgetful enough to leave their suit back at home, lazy enough not to run back to town and purchase one from a full-on beach supply shop, and rich enough not to mind the rip-off prices here. That didn't happen often.

Maou still wondered why Amane was so ready to give out her

dead-stock inventory as presents, but given that it allowed Chiho and the girls to enjoy some summer leisure time by the sea, he didn't regret her decision much.

Besides, Maou wasn't being polite. She really *did* look good.

"Well, I like it. I bet that swimsuit's proud it's got you wearing it."

"Oh… I… Wow, thank you so—"

"Whoa there, Maou. Kind of playing favorites a little *too* much, huh?"

Just as Chiho was about to spontaneously combust, Amane sidled in closer.

"Chiho isn't the only goddess who saved our butts today, y'know."

Her eyes turned to the other side of the shop. Emi and Suzuno looked back at them.

"Ahh, well…you know."

Amane had a point, of course. Yesterday and today, there were countless challenges that would have gone unsolved without Emi and Suzuno's help. So, remaining in his seat, Maou turned toward the pair, placed his hands on his knees, and bowed his head.

"Thanks. You really helped me out."

The unexpectedly honest gratitude made Emi and Suzuno gasp and look at each other.

"…I'm just making sure you owe me one. Like yesterday. I don't need you *thanking* me."

"Emi is correct. We simply lent a hand because it would be a drag upon our heels if you blundered yourselves out of business. We do not seek your adulation or favor."

The gratitude was heartfelt; the response, less so. He left it at that, expecting little more from them in the first place. But Amane remained unconvinced.

"Whoa there. That's it? That's not all, is it? Come on, give it a bit more oomph."

"Oomph? Oomph how?"

"Oh, Maou, don't say 'oomph how' to me! Chiho here's got some gifts, that's for sure, but you've got two other young ladies baring their all, too! Gotta compliment your wife sometime, you know? She'll start running around on you if you don't! Chiho's suit was a freebie, but those two paid for theirs. A few choice compliments could earn you some mucho attaboy points right now, y'know?"

It wasn't Amane's fault, maybe, but her skills at reading the relationship between these people proved profoundly lacking.

"Huh...?"

Maou was genuinely at a loss as he stared at Emi and Suzuno, their turned backs only adding to the awkwardness.

Why do both of them have their backs to me? Pondering over this, Maou decided to bare his honest soul to them.

"Um, I appreciate everything you guys did today, but I guess I don't know if I should be complimenting you—or if there's any *point* to it—or, like, did you really give up on the whole beach vacation thing after all?"

He understood that a swimsuit was a vital fashion accessory to a woman, and that complimenting one would never offend anyone. That was common sense. He was quite generously willing to admit that Emi and Suzuno looked beautiful in their outfits.

But in terms of their personal relationships, if you asked whether Emi and Suzuno were hoping for a compliment from him, the answer was absolutely no.

And yet...it was weird. Maou thought he gauged the situation accurately enough with his words, but now he thought he saw their bodies shiver, a dark miasmic aura looming over them.

"...Wow, are you blind, or what?"

Amane was floored. From a third-party perspective, Maou was being at best petty, at worst abusive.

"My l—Maou! Sir! Over here!"

Surprisingly, it was Ashiya who threw a life preserver to Maou.

"You are being far too honest! At least bend a bit and give them a compliment!"

"Huh? Like, even if I did, you know..."

"It does not matter *who* compliments them. Whether from a worm, or a cockroach, or even a waterbug, no woman minds a compliment! And how *dare* you say there is nothing to compliment about them! I sincerely doubt Yusa will respond as amiably as Ms. Sasaki, but it would make her feel conflicted, at least!"

"Oh, come on. You're just being mean now. Like, seriously? You're putting me on a cockroach's level?"

"And while it is with my extreme reluctance, Suzuno *does* provide a service to us every day. If you would kindly practice some social etiquette and compliment her, perhaps that would remove some obstacles going—*grrk!*"

As he feverishly griped at Maou, Ashiya suddenly rolled his eyes and collapsed on the beach.

Maou and Chiho dragged him up, unable to carry his weight. At his feet was an unusually large chunk of ice; on his head, a *yakisoba* spatula.

"We would never dream! In a million years! Of *ever*! Desiring your *compliment*!!"

"Yeah. Besides, there's nothing about me to compliment at *alllll*, right? Ohh, *noooo*."

Suzuno and Emi's twin-pronged attack, more demonic than most demons, tore into Maou.

Perhaps they didn't realize it, but the way both of them crossed their arms in order to cover their chests was a bit touching, somehow.

He wasn't going to try praising them, but it wasn't like he was totally oblivious to them, either. That was what he was trying to say, but if he did, they'd be tossing ice blocks and liquid nitrogen at him next.

"Maou...Ashiya... I've lost faith in you."

With a grand wave, Amane—the woman who both set this scenario up and tore it down with her bare hands—departed to the back room.

"Ha...ha. Ha-ha-ha-ha! Suzuno, your, uh, spatula..."

The real victim here was undoubtedly Chiho, subjected to all these horrors through none of her own doing.

"Chiho."

"Y-Yes?"

Suzuno, accepting the spatula that Chiho peeled off Ashiya's head, washed it in the sink and flashed, for just a moment, a resentful look at Chiho's chest.

"I know things are as they are, but I feel you must rethink this."

There was no way Chiho could offer a response to that.

"So, uh, what? You guys want to be complimented, or what? I don't get it."

Urushihara, safely out of the line of fire at his now-empty drink booth, fired a deviously hateful salvo at Emi as she indignantly scraped bits of ice off the machines.

"You want me to kill you?"

The way she palmed the ice pick in her hand spoke louder than her words.

"Oh. Okay. Got it."

Urushihara had at least the sneaking suspicion that Ashiya was correct, but respectfully declined to mention that out loud, lest it directly affect his life expectancy.

After that wise move, Urushihara rewarded himself by removing a can of soda from the available merchandise, opening it up, and entering full break-time mode.

"...Um, if you're free, would you mind cleaning the shaved-ice machines? It's gonna rust if somebody doesn't wipe the ice crystals off. Why do I have to do it? I'd just as soon disembowel you."

Emi's reply only seemed excessive if one didn't remember that Urushihara all but abandoned his post to her earlier.

The fallen angel turned his head toward Emi as she continued stabbing away at the ice clogging up the nooks and crannies of the machine.

"By the way, Yusa, there's something I wanted to ask now that we've got the perfect opportunity here."

"What? Where'd that come from? If you're gonna compliment me or something, I'm gonna decapitate you."

"Dude, all right, okay? Just listen."

Urushihara let out an audible belch as he took a drink from his can.

"Urp... So, like, what do you think of Olba, anyway?"

Were it not for the bright, sunny interior of the shop, the area would have felt suddenly enveloped in an anxious, dark silence.

"That's pretty sudden of you. *And* rude. ...What do you mean, what do I think of him?"

"Oh, nothing that deep. Just, like, are you enough of an optimist that you think he's just out being a model prisoner somewhere?"

"Well, no, but... It's not like I could find out where he is now, and even if I did, what could I do about it?"

"What if I said *I* knew?"

The waves, the beach, and the people around Ohguro-ya were just as breezy as before, tropical and carefree.

"What're you...saying?"

"He's being indicted at the Shibuya district jail. I don't know exactly where he is, though. They brought him up on weapons possession and destruction of property, but I'm sure that's just a stopgap until they find some evidence to connect him to our little mugging spree."

"Wh-Why do *you* know all of that?"

"What? I didn't hack into government records or anything, dude. Anybody can have it looked up if they want to. You have to jump through a lot of hoops, but still. They arrested Olba as a non-Japanese resident, too, and that means human-rights groups and stuff have to get involved. You know how the news has been going on about foreigners getting freed from jail for crimes they didn't commit, right?"

Urushihara was actually learning about Japanese society, in his own way. Emi was impressed for a moment.

"So anyway, I hacked into one of those human-rights groups' databases."

Only for a moment.

"...Well, correct me if I'm wrong, but they can only hold him in jail for a few days, right? It's different from prison that way."

"Huh. You been studying?"

"Well, you know, I watch a lot of TV dramas so I can keep up with conversations at work. Boy, when the main guy's wife got killed during season six of *Quaking Mad*, that just about blew my mind!"

Between her samurai shows and TV dramas, Urushihara began to wonder if the Hero would be staying up to watch late-night anime next.

"That's really nothing to be proud of, dude. Oh, that'll be a hundred and twenty yen. Thanks."

With a sigh, Urushihara handed a cola bottle over to a passing customer. Over the past few hours, the whole process from money-taking to soda-giving had grown smoother and quicker—something neither Emi nor the ex-angel himself noticed.

"...Anyway, a lot of the times, the prisons are so full up that people stay in jail even after they've been indicted. Olba hasn't been accused of anything serious yet, so I'm sure he's pretty low on the priority list for a prison spot. But that's not the real problem."

Urushihara's face grew stern—by his standards.

"After you guys beat me on Ente Isla, I accepted his offer for two reasons. One was, basically, he said he wouldn't kill me. After I lost, I kinda had no place to go—Malacoda and I weren't really on good terms, and it's not like you guys were just gonna let me run off somewhere."

"...Even today, I regret that I didn't run you through for good. Just *one* more thrust."

"Dude, you're gonna make Alas Ramus's vocabulary all weird if you keep that up. Hey, where *is* she, anyway?"

"I told Amane that she's in your room behind the shop. But she's in here."

Emi pointed a finger to her temple.

"She's not crying or carrying on or nothin'?"

It was a surprisingly well-considered question, by his standards.

"We woke up before dawn to watch the sun rise. We played in the water a while before coming here, too, so she's sleeping right now. ...What's the other reason?"

"Huh. Cool. ...But, Maou told you that one before: Obla told me he'd serve as an intermediary between me and heaven."

Not long ago, in front of Sasazuka station, Urushihara and Emi had faced each other as mortal enemies. Neither of them could have imagined that they'd be managing a busy beachfront restaurant and sundries shop in Chiba a scant while later.

"The Devil King's armies were annihilated, but I couldn't stay in the human world. As far as refuges went, back to heaven was just about it. I remember him telling me… He said, 'I have all the material I need to negotiate with heaven.'"

"'Negotiate…with heaven'?"

"Yeah. And he said I was one of his bargaining chips, too. I mean, taking a fallen angel people sang about in legends and reforming him into an angel worthy of returning to heaven… Like, that'd make the big guys up there flip their miters, right? Hell, they'd probably make *him* an angel while they were at it."

It depends on how you look at it, Emi reflected. By that logic, Maou taking an angel who'd fallen *this* low and forging him into an at least semi-focused hourly laborer should have earned the Devil King a spot among the clouds, too.

"But the real ace he had up his sleeve, you know, was *you*, Emilia."

"Me?"

Having her name come up unexpectedly made Emi's ice-stabbing hand stop in midair.

"Just like Maou said. I mean, we thought you probably weren't much more to him than another thorn in his side. But something doesn't add up. He literally had Emeralda Etuva and Albert Ende in a cell in Ente Isla, but he let them live. Why? I mean, Emeralda's way up there in Empire politics, right? He must've known letting her go would mean trouble for him later."

"True, yeah."

The Holy Empire of Saint Aile's relationship with the Church was undeniably unwinding. Emeralda said as much over the phone. Having Olba's crimes bubble up a bit to the surface, and offering at least broad hints of Church corruption, led to questions about its influence on the Western Island. It put the Church at a slight disadvantage in the ensuing power struggles over the rebuilding of the Central Continent and, seemingly, everything else.

"So there's something I want to check on. The Holy Silver that's used in your sword, and the Cloth of the Dispeller… Who managed that stuff?"

Emi could feel the blood drain from her head as she heard the question.

"…The Church's department of diplomatic and missionary operations—where Olba was. The missionary side handles all of the holy instruments… Those are at the very center of the Archbishops' seats, after all. The main Church building."

"Huh. I figured. Well, they all probably knew the whole time that the Holy Silver was really a bunch of Yesod fragments. I couldn't guess what else he could've tried bargaining with heaven over."

It wasn't the chill from the ice machine that made Emi shiver just then.

"He had to give the sword and the Cloth to the Hero to fight off the Devil King army. But unlike Sariel and Gabriel, he knew they couldn't just fetch the Holy Silver out of your body afterward. He figured you wouldn't be too willing to just hand it back once it was all over. And if you got into politics once the rebuilding began, the Church would lose a crapload of influence. That, and they'd never get their Yesod bits back."

"…Why was Olba so eager to make contact with heaven, anyway?"

"That, I don't know. But given how many tools he has, I really doubt Olba's just gonna sit around in prison for the next few years. We haven't worried much about him lately, but now that I'm out here and kind of, y'know, seriously thinking about things… I'm startin' to get a little nervous."

"…Lucifer…"

"Plus, the new *Monster Capturer* is s'posed to come out for the GSP portable soon. If he starts something major out here, I won't be able to buy the limited-edition version. With the custom GSP and everything."

"………………………………………………………………………"

There's just no saving you, is there? In so many ways.

"Uh, I can read your lips."

"Oh? Oh."

"Besides, the holy sword and stuff is your problem anyway, right? I'm just sayin', think about it a little."

"Yeah, thanks. *Really* appreciate that advice. That's why I'm doing you all these favors right now, remember?"

"You call scraping ice off that thing a favor? Plus, you and Maou seem to think it's all over with Gabriel, but there's no way *he's* gonna pull back, either. He's pretty well-known for being a persistent bastard like that."

"...I kind of know that, too, thanks."

There were mixed emotions to Emi's voice as she shot a glance at Maou and Chiho.

Just like Chiho worried about, Emi had yet to craft any concrete plan for dealing with Gabriel, nor any of the other unknown threats swooping down from the heavens.

"But with me and Alas Ramus right now, I really don't think I'd lose a match against them."

"Yeah. One-on-one, maybe. It's not like we know what happened last night is totally unrelated, either. Maybe they're trying some weird ruse or something to attack us where we—"

"What happened last night?"

"...Uh, you didn't notice?"

"Notice what?"

Urushihara paused. He had assumed Emi and Suzuno had picked up on the the previous night's demon attack.

The demonic power Camio flew in with last night was nothing trivial in scope. And Urushihara used his holy magic, too, though not an enormous amount of it.

He didn't know where Emi and Suzuno stayed last night, but if they were inside the city of Choshi, they couldn't *not* have noticed.

"Hey! Emi! Got a sec?"

Just as Urushihara was about to confirm his suspicion, he heard Maou call for Emi as he chatted with Chiho.

Turning upward, he saw Maou and Chiho, engaged in some silly gabfest about something or other a moment ago, now approaching them with oddly stern faces.

"I heard from Chi that you stayed on Cape Inuboh-saki, right? When all that fog came in, did you seriously not notice anything?"

"Not notice *what* of anything? I'm really not sure what you're talking about, but what's up?"

Maou exchanged glances with Urushihara, then lowered his tone a notch.

"I'm saying, you didn't notice any demonic or holy force?"

"Huh?"

He shot another glance, this time to ensure Amane was still focused on her dishwashing, then continued.

"Uh, let's go out back a sec... Hey, Amane! I'm going out for a minute!"

"Sure thing!" Amane shouted back, not bothering to turn around.

Since the bar was still open, the three of them left Urushihara at the register, nodded to each other, and headed for the guest quarters out back.

They needed to awaken the still-unconscious Ashiya anyway.

Leaving the front entrance, they found Suzuno busy repairing the Sarou-Sotengai castle as the drying sand and ocean breeze began to erode the walls.

Given that she was doing this in her swimsuit, a crowd had already formed around her. Like a practiced artisan, she focused on her work, not giving her onlookers so much as a passing glance.

It was a charming little scene, but one had to question whether she wanted to be such a public figure right now. Maou idly considered building a barricade for tomorrow as he let the other two into the guest room.

"Oh, I think she's getting up."

The moment they went in, Emi's faced turned upward in recognition as she sat on the tatami floor.

She extended her hands to form a natural cradle. As she did, a mass of light osmosed out of her body, neatly settling upon her arms before taking the form of Alas Ramus.

"Well, *that's* sure useful. I bet every mother in the world's jealous of you by now."

"Yeah, as long as they don't mind being woken up at night by screaming from inside their head, I'd love to mommy-blog some tips someday. Are you up, Alas Ramus?"

"Mnngh...uuugh..."

The newly formed Alas Ramus squirmed in Emi's arms, hands reaching out to empty space. The bird-and-cage toy from last night's fireworks show was still carefully held in her hands.

Emi brought a hand to the child's free one. She gently grasped one of her more-or-less mother's fingers as she gradually opened her eyes.

"Good morning, Alas Ramus. Is your diapey okay?"

"Oogh morring... Nnh, okay."

Alas Ramus rubbed her eyes with both fists as she groggily replied.

"Well, now that she's awake, I guess I'm off the clock workwise."

Emi held Alas Ramus in her arms as she spoke. Maou nodded. He had no particular complaint.

"Sure. Thanks for the help. But anyway, I wanted you to see *that*."

Maou pointed at the cardboard box in the corner. Behind it, something long and thin was wrapped in a threadbare, somewhat dirty black towel.

Chiho and Emi took a peek inside.

"Aw, cute."

Chiho whispered it immediately.

"Tweety-tweet moooved!!"

Alas Ramus, commenting in Emi's place, leaned over for a touch.

"No, Alas Ramus. Don't touch. It looks pretty weak..."

"Peep...peep...Lord Satan? ...Have you concluded your duties? ...Peep?"

"?!"

"Tweety-tweet!"

The blackbird's sudden question made Chiho and Emi lean back in astonishment even as it filled Alas Ramus with paroxysms of glee. It was no doubt a melancholy sight for the bird from last night's fireworks, which she now carelessly tossed aside.

"Don't do that, Alas Ramus. Chiho gave that to you, remember? You need to be nice to it."

Maou, obviously enjoying the audience reaction, picked up the toy bird and returned it to Alas Ramus's hand.

"*Peep*...mnngh... I detect humans. Lord Satan, *peep*, who are these—?"

It was clearly a small bird, cute chirping and everything, but the gravelly, ponderous way it spoke made things more than a bit eerie.

"...Is that a mynah or something?"

"It's...cute? Or maybe not so cute..."

Chiho and Emi looked to Maou for an explanation.

The response he gave was a shock to them both.

"This is a demon from my realm. He fell out of the sky last night."

Camio, the Devil Regent. Emi had never heard the name, nor the title before.

She never thought she'd receive a guided tour of domestic political affairs from the gnarled lips of a demon, either.

But this little bird Camio was a military officer, one who apparently served the Devil King since back when he first began his conquest. There was no Devil King's Army back then, no mass organization of slavering monsters at their beck and call. Ashiya and Urushihara didn't even know Maou's name yet. It was an ancient time, one when chaos still ruled the demon realms.

Satan, seeking to unify this realm under his rule, invited Camio— begged, really, repeatedly—to join his cause, although his force of warriors was still too ill-equipped and ragtag to creditably be termed an "army" yet.

Although he would be an impossibly formidable foe to your average human being, Camio was not particularly high up on the demonic social ladder.

Yet, in a realm where strength and depravity was all that counted, Camio had banded together a group of his own demons—even though a human in reasonable shape could probably have KO'd some of them in three rounds of bare-knuckle action—creating a force that could survive and fend for itself.

Seeing this, Satan recruited Camio in order to learn what it took to stay alive in this game.

Camio hardly took Satan seriously at first, nor the weak clan of wannabes he led. But over time, he found himself joining them, impressed by the young warlord's innate perception and wisdom.

The wisdom, of course, that Satan was gifted at a very young age by a certain angel.

As Maou put it, "If Camio wasn't there, no way I could have formed anything like the demon force we had."

An appraisal like that would have made Camio the instant enemy of Emi and the rest of Ente Isla. But he was one of the few denizens of the demon realms gifted in the arts of persuasion and negotiation.

He had an innate gift for language, learning the tongues and customs of each demon tribe and even deciphering the calls of all nature's creatures.

That might have been the reason why he used native-level Japanese from the moment he fell to Kimigahama, as if nothing could be more natural.

Thanks to his advice, Satan and his gang avoided confrontation with the more formidable foes of the day, occasionally rescuing other tribes from disaster, occasionally using Camio's diplomatic gifts to gradually build and expand their force.

Then, in what both Satan and Camio would call their biggest turning point in their careers, they encountered Alciel.

Just like the two of them, Alciel was a local strongman, aiming to harness his intelligence to strengthen his already-expansive powers and army.

By that point, Satan's force was a fairly decent size, his name beginning to attain notoriety among the general demon public. It was a time when infighting between different demon races gathered in the same region was threatening to explode into large-scale war.

Thanks to Alciel's timely initiation into the tribe, Satan was able to leave him with the task of managing military expansion, while Camio focused on smoothing things over with his army's recruits.

Their strength as an organization grew exponentially, and before they knew it, they were a major force, one powerful enough that demons from every region were volunteering to join the hordes.

"The one thing Camio really surprised me with when we reorganized our outfit's structure was the the concept of wyvern licenses."

"Wyvern...licenses?"

"What's a wyvern?"

Emi and Chiho tilted their heads in confusion for different reasons.

Wyverns were one of several mountable creatures the Devil King's force used as transport across the battlefield. They were best described as enormous flying lizards. But who would give out licenses for those things, and how?

"Well, there weren't too many wyverns out there, for one. We needed to be more efficient with using them. So we selected the demons that had the best knack for wyvern wrangling and gave them a combat decoration that served as their right to fight on a flying mount."

This made a knowledge of wyvern husbandry a sort of status symbol in Satan's force, vastly improving cohesion and giving rank-and-file demons something to aim for in their brutish, violent careers.

"......"

For Emi, learning about such highly...*civilized* practices being conceived of by demons from another world came as a pure, unadulterated surprise.

In the end, Satan united all the demon realms and declared himself Devil King. When his ambitions turned toward Ente Isla, Camio served as Satan's regent during the conquest, assuming leadership over the remaining denizens of his native land.

He still hadn't had a chance to ask why Camio fell straight on Kimigahama, alongside several of his demon soldiers.

Emi, meanwhile, had trouble believing any of this tale.

"So you're saying that not just Camio but two other demons just popped into existence on the beach? In that fog?"

"Hug tweety-tweet!"

Alas Ramus's focus was still squarely upon the live bird in front of her, and getting her hands on it. Emi deftly kept her nubby digits away as she looked on, her face still profoundly confused.

"Cyclopeans and beast demonoids are mostly rank-and-file melee fighters...but I seriously didn't pick up on them in the distance between here and Cape Inuboh-saki. That's ridiculous."

"Yeah, you see? I mean, I thought *you* might've ripped those dudes apart at first. But you didn't even touch 'em, right?"

"No. If I did, I would've killed them. Not let 'em run off bleeding."

"So...someone besides you, Maou, and you, Yusa, dispatched these demons from another world?"

Maou nodded his approval of Chiho's summary.

"I'm thinking about checking out that lighthouse later."

"The Inuboh-saki lighthouse? We were there this morning."

"What?!"

Chiho looked to Emi for approval. Emi nodded.

"You can, too, if you pay for a ticket. You can climb the stairs all the way up if you want. I saw the signal house with that big foghorn from last night and everything. There wasn't anything else special about it."

The foghorn that had sounded multiple times. That was the only shared experience Maou and Emi had that evening.

"They had this cartoon lighthouse guy on the signs telling you how many steps you had to go. It was pretty cute!"

Emi's idea of "special" was a bit different from the travel-magazine details Chiho gushed about.

"So the fog rolled in, these guys showed up, they were wrapped in fog, the lighthouse lit it up, and they were gone. It'd be crazy if the lighthouse wasn't involved somehow, right?"

"But this is Japan. You don't have lighthouse keepers manning the tops of those towers all night like in Ente Isla. Plus, that was built years ago. It's not gonna be infused with demonic energy or..."

"*Peeeeeeeeeeeeeeep?!!*"

"Tweety-tweet!"

Camio's sudden shrill scream stopped Emi's rebuttal in its tracks.

As the grown-ups were having their extremely grown-up conversation,

Alas Ramus slipped out of Emi's hands and leaned into the box to touch Camio…only to grab and pick up the blackbird by its tail feathers.

"Whoa! Alas Ramus, no!"

"No tweety-tweet?"

"L-Let me free! Accursed human child! *PEEP!*"

Camio continued shouting as Alas Ramus held on, peeping like mad and whipping his wings around like a hummingbird. It was a less than noble display for the Devil Regent and one of the most learned demons in all the realms.

"S-Stop it, Alas Ramus! No! The bird's saying you're hurting him!"

"It, it does! Ow! She will pluck my tail feathers before she's done! *Peep!*"

One classic way to handle a child who doesn't know how to treat animals with care is to try some variant on "See? It's crying! Can't you hear it crying?" This, however, was likely the first time any bird literally pleaded for mercy at the hands of its tormentor.

"*Gahhpeep!*"

Scolded by Emi, Alas Ramus finally let go. Camio, wings still flailing with all his might, wound up flying all the way to the wall.

The force was enough to knock over the long object concealed by the towel behind the box, trapping the bird underneath as it fell.

"Uh… Camio! You all right?"

The tubelike object made a heavy clunking sound against the floor.

"*Gnh, peep…* Y-Yes, my lord! It is not a grave injury…"

Now the surprise was enough to make Maou freeze.

"Uh, whoa, you're huge…"

Camio, whom they thought had been crushed by the object in the towel, suddenly emerged bloated to the size of a chicken, like a novelty sponge growing several times its size in water.

"Cock-a-doodle-doo!!"

Alas Ramus's eyes beamed in sheer wonder.

She nimbly escaped Emi's hands, taking advantage of her guardian's shock and awe, and attempted a full-body tackle on the rooster-sized Camio.

"Ah! Alas Ramus, stop it!"

"*Nhh!* I—I will not take this indignity a second time, *peep*!!"

Camio, to his credit, was not a willing participant. Leaping over the fallen object that crashed over him, he dug the claws of his short legs into the tatami floor, trotting just out of Alas Ramus's reach.

"Cock-a-doooo!!"

"Did you think a mere human child could *peep* capture me?!"

Trot, scamper, toddle, flap.

The black chicken, wings flapping incessantly, and the silver-haired child chasing it trundled in and among Maou, Emi, and Chiho, like a certain Great Dane and his lanky pal pursuing a spooky space alien around a haunted house.

"No! Alas Ramus, stop! You're gonna fall over…"

As if on cue, Alas Ramus fell.

She tripped on the long, towel-covered object Camio had just leaped over a second time.

Obeying at least the law of momentum, she toppled forward, doing a somersault on the floor. She looked around, a bit too bewildered to know what just happened.

"Y-You all right, Alas Ramus?! Are you hurt?!"

Maou helped her up in a panic, but Alas Ramus seemed happily unfazed as she shook her head.

"H-Huff-huff-huff-*peep*…huff… V-Victory is mine… *Peeeep*?!"

Meanwhile, Camio the black chicken, catching his breath in a very non-adorable manner by one corner, found himself grabbed by the neck by Emi, her eyes almost popping out of their sockets.

"If you hurt Alas Ramus, I'll sautée you and toss you in a curry pot. We clear on that?"

"Um, I really don't think Camio's the one at fault here…"

Chiho turned to their child, her voice a bit on the unusually harsh side.

"Come on, Alas Ramus, say you're sorry to the chicken here. You scared him, don't you see?"

Alas Ramus looked like she would tear up for a moment, but gave a pouty nod instead.

"Ooo... I'm shorrie."

"Keh... Ha-ha-ha! I am not one to grow angered over the *peep*... playful eagerness of a child. A human one, at *peep* that."

He looked far more distressed than that at the time, but Camio was surprisingly eager to overlook the rambunctious Alas Ramus's all-out attack.

Emi, brought back to reality by Chiho's semi-stern reproach, grudgingly placed the chicken back in his box.

"...Getting back to the subject, if he wasn't here to see you, what did this chicken come to Japan *for*, even? And also..."

Emi looked at the long, apparently metallic object that had smashed upon Camio's body and tripped Alas Ramus over in alarming fashion.

"What *is* that? Why'd it blow up the bird so much?"

"*Gehh*... Um, before that..."

Camio, his neck still firmly ensconced in Emi's death grasp, deftly rubbed his wings together as he looked to Maou for salvation.

"Lord Satan... Do I have your *peep*mission to explain matters to these *peep*... These people?"

"Huh? Sure. Go ahead."

Maou gave the chicken a friendly nod.

"You're right, by the way. These two are humans. This is Chiho Sasaki; she knows about me and Alciel, and she's been a lot of help to us in this world."

"Ohh, is that the case, young *peep* human girl? On my master's behalf, I offer you my utmost thanks."

The black rooster stood up in his box, extended a wing out in a sort of exaggerated wave, and leaned his head deeply downward.

"Oh, um, not at all. I mean, he...um, Satan? Has been a huge help to me, too."

Chiho found herself kneeling forward in a bow herself.

It was a historical moment—a high representative from the demon realms exchanging a cross-dimensional moment of Japanese-style understanding with one of that nation's own finest citizens.

"And the baby who grabbed your tail and this girl are the holy sword and her Hero, respectively."

"Peeeep?!"

"Hey!"

"Maou?!"

The sudden confession from Maou made Camio's, Emi's, and Chiho's eyes goggle in their own respective ways. Camio stood up once more, beak wide open as he stared blankly at Emi and Alas Ramus.

He was surprised, but not as much as Emi and Chiho.

"What're you going around just *admitting* it for?!"

Even if he looked like a petting-zoo reject, he was still a high-ranking demon in good standing.

Camio was Emi's enemy, and the opposite was true as well.

"The *peep*ro of the *peep* sword...?!"

"...Hey, you mind if I make some chicken curry tonight after all?"

"Leave him. He's not doing it on purpose."

Maou had to stop Emi from reaching into the box.

"And don't get it wrong, Camio. That's not the 'Peep-ro' of the holy sword. That's the 'Peep-ro' *and* the holy sword."

"Maou, I think you need to start being serious before Yusa goes out of her mind."

Chiho's astute observation was the only thing that saved the Devil Regent's neck from being wringed to pieces by Emi's iron fist.

"Satan *peep*."

"Uh, who's Satan Peep?"

"Satan Peep!"

At least his vocal tic kept Alas Ramus entertained.

Camio skillfully leaped to the rear, saving him from Maou's frustrated swipe.

"The Hero of the Holy Sword was the cause of our invading force's destruction. Why are you sitting here, so familiar with the Hero and her sword............*peep*?"

After all that effort stringing a sentence together, it was like he couldn't resist one little spasm at the end.

Peeping or not, there was nothing in Camio's voice that suggested resentment toward Maou. It was seeking an answer. It wanted to know Maou's true intentions. Peeping or not.

But Emi stepped up to reply first.

"...It all just kind of happened. Just remember, I'm ready to slice the Devil King's head off in his sleep anytime I want. And *you* don't try anything funny, either, or it's the dinner table for you. If you wanna keep on living, don't tell any other demon that I bear the Better Half, either."

The Hero's habit of sounding like the villain of a gangster film was well familiar to Maou by now. It cowed the black chicken into bleak submission.

"...Is *kind of* what it is, but there's more to it than that. Lemme put it in a way you'd probably understand... Even Alciel was our foe once upon a time, yeah...?"

"......*peep.*"

Maou sat cross-legged on the tatami floor, making sure he came in loud and clear to the rooster in the box.

"Remember how we managed to conquer the demon realms? I got a dream... A dream of doing that all over again here, in this country, with these humans. Maybe it all 'just kind of happened,' but me and the Hero have worked pretty closely together, y'know."

This all went over Emi's and Chiho's heads.

"Your dream of conquest...!"

This was a pact Satan and Camio forged long ago, in a realm far, far away. The decisive reason why Camio agreed to serve the young Satan in the first place.

"It *peep*...pains me so that I failed to support you alongside your great General to the East."

"*If I win this, even the foes I warred with yesterday can be tomorrow's companions.*"

He was the only demon who knew that "conquering" was about more than turning battlefields into burnt wastes, filled with the bloodied corpses of the conquered.

Maou laughed.

"Yeah, I was kinda hoping you'd be more patient, back there..."

"Wait, what're you talking about?"

"Maou?"

The Devil King grinned sheepishly at the confused Emi and Chiho.

"...We're talking about how we failed to invade Ente Isla, even after I united the entire demon realm."

"Huhh?"

"You may not believe this, but if you talk to Camio, you'd be amazed how accepting he is. He doesn't look down on anybody— Hero, human, whatever. You picked up on that much, right? Once the heavens started directly meddling with things on Ente Isla, we were always gonna be a lot more than two warriors beating each other down until someone died. Even if it winds up being like that someday, we still got Alas Ramus to worry about. If we went at it right now, we might have to have Alas Ramus kill her own parents."

Maou caressed Alas Ramus's hair.

"Nee-hee!"

She raised a fumbling hand to his.

"We all eat around the same table these days, but it's not like you keep me alive just because you accept it as fate or whatever, right?"

"Of course, but what're you trying to *say*?"

There was a tone of alarm to Emi's voice.

"Like I told you—I know we'll have to settle this someday. But if we want that to happen, we're gonna have to share at least the bare minimum of information to deal with what's going on today. Otherwise, we might expose Alas Ramus to danger. Like we did with Gabriel."

"....."

She didn't like it. He was the Devil King, for cripes' sake. But there was absolutely nothing she could do to counter that.

And she knew it, too. She knew it without requiring the demon's reminder.

"You are as direct in your s-*peep*ch as always, Lord Satan. There are times, with a hated foe, when emotions do pose an obstacle to plain logic."

Camio sighed as he watched Emi.

"*Peep*-ro of the holy sword."

"What the hell's a 'Peep-ro'?!"

"If you find it difficult to accept, *peep* of it this way: If you share a common enemy, then share what must be shared, as long as you do not interfere with each other. There is no need to fight side by side in actual battle as *peep*quals."

Camio, increasingly succumbing to the one most annoying of his vocal habits, felt himself wither under Emi's glare.

"...I know that much, all right? I don't need you lecturing me about it like my grandmother. So can we get on with the topic?! I want some answers!"

All she could do was turn her back to them in dismay. Maou and Camio, after all, were absolutely correct.

Maou, Camio, and Chiho grinned to themselves as they turned their eyes toward Emi's back.

In her own, unique way, she understood.

"All right. Go ahead, Camio. What did you come to Japan for? Why were you half-slashed to death on the way? What did you mean when you said the demon realms and Ente Isla face chaotic times once more? And what's *that*?"

Maou pointed at the heavy-looking tube hidden by the towel.

It contained the jeweled sword that once graced Camio's side.

His armor was now shattered, his body reduced to Sunday-evening dinner size, but the sword still retained its keen, dazzling shine.

It was wrapped in the cape Camio once wore, in part to keep Amane from stumbling across it, but in part because Maou surmised this was a sword of far more importance than the mere value of its jewels.

The angels who appeared from Ente Isla all had very clear objectives up to now: fetch the holy sword, kill Emi/Maou, that sort of thing.

But here, there was next to nothing to go on. Demons, coming to Japan, and not at the bidding of their lord. It was all an enigma.

"That..."

Camio opened his beak to answer the question that struck at the core of Maou's concerns.

Until someone knocked on the door.

"...Yeah?"

Urushihara wouldn't have bothered knocking. If it was Ashiya or Suzuno, they would've spoken up first. Which left only one answer.

"Maou?"

It was Amane.

Strange. It was the same voice as always, but—maybe it was the AC affecting their ears—did it sound a touch colder than usual, perhaps?

"I heard something like a chicken suffocating to death a second ago, but is everything all right? And, you know, a husband and wife skipping out on work to have an argument? I never read *that* advice column before!"

Through all the sarcasm, it was understandable that the group's now-extended absence alarmed her.

Camio's pained squawk and Emi's raised voice must've been enough to raise customer eyebrows.

"Mind if I come in?"

"S-Sure."

Maou gave Camio a "no talking" glare as he spoke. The woman didn't know a thing about him, after all.

"All right... Wow, what's with that chicken?"

She opened the door, still sweating with hair tied back, oil and curry stains on her apron, her sandals off.

Her dark eyes weren't focused on Maou, or Emi, or Chiho, or Alas Ramus. They were fixated on Camio.

The odd reaction did not escape Maou's notice.

From the moment she opened the door—before then, even—her eyes were firmly upon Camio's cardboard box, and nothing else.

It was as if she knew everyone inside this room, and everything that just went on.

If she was just here to check on things, Amane would have made eye contact with at least one of the people inside. All three of them had their eyes on her.

Amane kept her eyes upon Camio, unmoving, as she approached.

"Wow, a black chicken? You guys makin' some yakitori later?"

"*Peeep?!*"

Camio sounded petrified.

"Um...I found it last night. It was hurt..."

It sounded strained even as Maou said it. How could a chicken blunder its way on to this beach? But nothing else came to mind— and besides, he wasn't lying.

Not even Maou's excuse made Amane shift her gaze.

"Well, I don't think there're any chicken coops nearby. Maybe it's somebody's pet? We should probably check with the local vet."

"Y-Yeah... Definitely."

"Also, Urushihara's whining for you all to come back, okay? I think the rush is over, but we'll have to start closing up soon."

Maou could feel his nervousness subside, little by little.

Thinking rationally for a moment, if *you* saw a chicken in your guest house, it'd probably throw you off, too. They had been talking for a while. As their boss, it wasn't strange at all that Amane was looking for them.

Maou cleared the concern from his mind as he bowed his head.

"I'm sorry. I'll be right there."

"Great!"

With that, Amane finally removed her eyes from Camio.

"...Oo?"

Then, for whatever reason, she flashed a perplexing smile at Alas Ramus.

"Aw, look at you, little girl! Wonder what she's gonna be like when she grows up, huh?"

"Waph!"

With a few pats to the girl's head, she left.

"...Well, that's all we can discuss for now."

As long as Maou was employed, there was no defying his boss.

Beachfront businesses like these usually closed well before sunset. They would have another chance later.

But there, in a murmur:

"You can go back to work. I'll ask him about the rest."

"Huh?"

"...I *said*, I'll get the rest of the story from him! So just go to work already! If we need to take action immediately, I'll let you know!"

Emi glared at Maou, as if trying to sniper him using just her eyes.

"W-Well, sure, but...are you sure?"

"Am I *sure*? What did you guys just waste all that time *lecturing* me about?!"

Maou and Camio had no way of telling, but Emi's "you guys" included Chiho, too.

It was clear Emi didn't want to face the truth. Her face was red, her eyes liable to tear up at any moment, but she was still a seasoned warrior. She wasn't someone who didn't know what was urgent, and what needed to take priority.

"...Great. Well, go ahead. I'm counting on you."

"Don't *count* on me! I'm doing this out of my own volition!"

"All right, all right. That's fine, too. Camio, if you wouldn't mind telling—"

"That woman."

"—her about... Huh? What about her?"

"That woman... I was powerless to stop her. She had the strength of a demonic goddess."

"You're...talking about Amane?"

Maou, Chiho, even Emi doubted their ears.

The Devil Regent nodded his small beak sagely, beady eyes wide open.

"She was the one...who plunged my soldiers into the roaring of that enormous dragon..."

✳

By the time Ohguro-ya officially closed, the sky was already beginning to stain a dark red.

Once five PM rolled around, demand dwindled for nearly everything except the lockers and the shower room.

Briskly, Maou and the rest polished up the griddle, washed the drink cooler's waste-water tray, placed the covers on the shaved-ice machines, and inspected the remaining food, drinks, and other merchandise.

Amane printed a sales journal out from the register, showing off the approximate calculations for the day's proceeds to everyone nearby.

Once they emptied the lockers and coin-op shower locks, they would have a full grasp of how much they had made that day.

"Just from the register alone...we made it past three hundred and fifty thousand yen."

The smile was genuine as she held up the receipt paper.

"I still have to punch in Urushihara's drink and shaved-ice proceeds, the to-go orders from Ashiya, and the coins from the shower and the lockers...but I think we may just break five hundred thousand when it's all said and done. That's probably the first time since we opened up."

"Yeah...but if Chi and the gang didn't show up, it all would've fallen apart halfway through. We had to use a lot of petty cash to get going, too. We'll need to rein that in if we wanna keep it going."

Maou compared the day's sales record with the previous year's accounting ledger.

He'd underestimated the number of customers to expect, leading to a near breakdown in the afternoon—a point he still regretted. But simply comparing the numbers, they'd almost doubled their sales from the same day last year, an astronomical improvement.

That was thanks to Maou's sales strategy, to some extent, but the root cause likely boiled down to the happy-go-lucky, yeah-whatever approach Amane and her family took to the shop before now.

"No doubt about it. We're gonna get a *ton* of traffic. Lordy, if this is what we get every day, I don't know what I'm gonna do! Oh! Yusa, Chiho, Kamazuki, I've got something for you!"

The three women, back in their street clothes, were preparing to return to their inn when Amane called for them.

"Here's your wages for these past two days. You *really* helped out, you know? Thanks. I gave you a little bonus for that sand castle, Kamazuki. Almost wish I could ask you for one of those every day!"

Suzuno's Sarou-Sotengai masterpiece attracted some serious attention. The resulting word of mouth was undoubtedly the unsung hero behind today's sales.

Maou was already pondering over ways to harness that talent going forward.

That odd, out-of-place aura Amane emanated in the guest room was a thing of the past by the time he returned to work.

Even Chiho, returning to her own duties, was back to her usual bubbly self.

But still, somewhere inside of Maou, the anxiety was still there. Camio all but wailing "no más" in Amane's presence was troubling. That, and Emi's awkward act.

But after about an hour's work, Emi came back to the shop space, Alas Ramus in hand. The look of sheer depression on her face was obvious to anyone with eyes.

She played around a bit along the shore with Alas Ramus, along with Chiho and Suzuno now that they were off work. But a passing remark was all it took to cloud her expression once more.

"Boy, it's a shame you're all leaving tomorrow, though!"

Amane put some light pressure on them to stay, but Chiho had made a promise to her parents, and Emi didn't have any more vacation days to spare. The Ohguro-ya proprietor didn't seem genuinely interested in keeping them, but the sadness in her voice was still evident.

"...Oop?"

A vibration in Maou's shorts indicated an incoming text.

"......"

Maou wasn't foolish enough to look toward the sender.

"What's up, Maou? Your face's lookin' all dark."

It was. Thanks to a day spent working beachside, all the demons were sporting a light tan.

The tan was inconsequential, though. Taking care not to let Amane hear him as she shot a photo of herself with Chiho in front of Suzuno's sand castle, he beckoned Urushihara and Ashiya to come closer.

"I'm going out tonight. You guys're coming, too."

❋

Inuboh-saki Lighthouse was designed and built in 1874 by Richard Henry Brunton, a British architect invited to Japan to help shore up their coastline infrastructure.

After several remodels and reconfigurations to adapt it for war and peacetime, the tower was now one of only six "Type One" lighthouses remaining in Japan, its first-order Fresnel lens offering a sweep range of almost 22.5 miles.

At the base of this tower, the beam of light lazily revolving above them in the dark, Maou, Ashiya, and Urushihara faced down Emi, a cardboard box in their hands.

"By yourself, huh? What about Chi and Suzuno?"

"I told Bell. She's safe with Chiho now, just in case."

The chances of Emi choosing this moment for a final battle with the Devil King seemed slim. But was she still anticipating a "just in case" at the end of it all?

Maybe that would become clear once he knew where his beloved daughter was.

"And Alas Ramus?"

"Right here."

This time, Emi pointed not at her head, but her right hand.

"All right, so…what? You didn't call us here to fight right now, did you?"

The text that arrived as Maou closed down the store came from Emi.

He didn't recall giving her a working number. They were cyber-besties on exactly zero social networks. She must have harangued Chiho or someone for it.

The text was simple enough.

FRONT OF LIGHTHOUSE, 11 TONIGHT. BRING CUMIO. DON'T LET AMANE SEE YOU.

He didn't reply—he was too busy snickering at her rendering of "Camio"—but Emi must have known they would show up.

"That'd be kind of fun, but sadly, no. Tell 'em, Camio: Why'd I call the Devil King over here?"

"...So be it. *Peep.*"

Camio's voice was clearer, more intelligible than before. The day he'd spent recovering must have done wonders.

The three demons peered into the box. What kind of understanding did the Hero have with Maou's Devil Regent?

The ocean view from Cape Inuboh-saki was dark, murky, and foreboding.

A cold wind, strangely cold for a summer night, played with the otherworldly demons' hair.

"Lord Satan... General of the Eastern Island... Lucifer. I fear that danger is rapidly a*peep*...approaching this land."

"Uh, dude, *I* got a title, too?"

Camio ignored Urushihara's whining.

"When I heard that the Hero Emilia was here, a child serving as her holy sword... I thought I would faint on the *cheep*...spot. As we speak, there are forces—not the Devil King's demons, nor of our realm at all, but another force—in a frenzied search for the Hero's *peep*...sword."

"Not from my realm? The hell?"

Maou curiously regarded the chicken in the box.

"*Peep.* It was several fortnights ago. A human...a mere human... visited me in our capital, Satanas Arc. This figure claimed that anyone who pro-*peep*-cured the 'holy sword' would gain enough power to rule our realm, the heavens, and Ente Isla in one fell *peep*. This declaration, it pains me to say, stoked the bloodlust of many among our remaining forces, seeking revenge against Lord Satan's victor."

Ashiya and Urushihara both let out a surprised gasp behind Maou.

A human had visited the demon realms. There was not a single previous example of this in all the realm's long history.

When faced with the demonic power that coursed through the

very air in that land, a regular human would find it difficult to so much as remain conscious.

Chiho, when faced with Maou in his Satan form at close range, could barely breathe in the face of his almighty force.

"The way Camio put it, after your invasion army collapsed, the surviving troops split into two factions. One wanted to stage another invasion to avenge your death; the other took a more moderate approach, calling on the masses to believe in their lord's survival and preserve the nation's strength. Camio ran himself ragged trying to make the two sides come to terms. But this human visitor made the delicate balance he built collapse to pieces."

It was a strange picture, Emi explaining current demon-realm events to Maou. She continued, paying little heed to his suspicious sneer.

"This person said that there were *two* holy swords. And one of them…"

Without even pausing to ensure there were no average Japanese citizens milling around nearby, Emi made her sword materialize out of thin air.

The Better Half.

"There aren't that many humans who know that the Better Half is here in Japan with me."

The hint was enough to finally make Maou understand.

Why did Sariel know from the start where Emi's sword was? Where did he discover that nugget of information?

She was right. There weren't many on Ente Isla who knew the holy sword's location. Not many *humans*.

There were the Hero's traveling companions, Emeralda and Albert. Suzuno, better known elsewhere as Crestia Bell, became friendly enough with Emi to discover the truth. There were the six Archbishops who met regularly at All Bishops' Sanctuary to deliberate over Church affairs, the ones who learned of Emilia's survival from Suzuno before she left. Beyond that…

"The human arrived with the 'revenge' faction in tow before disappearing. He *peep* called himself Olba Meiyer."

"Wh-What the hell's he thinking? What's he even *doing*?! And, dude, like, *when*?!"

The name shocked Urushihara the most, given how much thought the fallen angel had devoted to him in recent days.

Olba was the only person in Japan who knew Emi was there. He engaged in hostilities with her, never making up for it afterward. He had an inkling this would happen, but the news was still hard for him to swallow.

"So much for taking pity on him…"

Ashiya, who once crossed swords with Olba in Japan, gritted his teeth as he clenched his fists in rage.

"Regent Camio. Who was leading the 'revenge' faction that followed Olba?"

"It was…Barbariccia, aide to Malacoda, General of the Southern Island. *Cheep*."

"I wish you'd stop talking like a Pokéture when we're trying to be serious."

Maou scratched his head distractedly.

"But if we're gonna have this conversation, why out in the open like this? Why not back at Ohguro-ya? Amane's gone by now."

"Didn't you hear Camio? Amane might have killed everyone in his force."

"Yeah, I *heard* that, but…"

"Well, maybe you forgot because she's a total Type A personality, but she's *that* landlord's niece, remember? Maybe she's not our enemy, but don't forget—she's not exactly a normal person, either."

Emi spared nothing in her harsh rebuke.

But this wasn't her usual antagonism writ large. There was something more chiding to it now.

"But even if Amane has some mysterious power we don't know about, something strong enough to defeat Camio and a squad of demons…we can't just leave what's coming up next to her."

"What's coming up next? What do you mean?"

Camio swiveled his head toward the dubious Ashiya.

"The moderates among us wished to prevent our struggle from

speep...spilling out to other realms. Thus, before the human-agitated 'revenge' faction could vent their fury in this world, we decided to stage a covert o*peep*...operation to secure Emilia's holy sword. Olba Meiyer stated only that it was in a land known as Tokyo, in the king-dom known as Japan. Our intention as a result was to conjure a Gate that existed on the realm's far eastern coast, then search westward with the *peep*...proverbial fine-toothed comb."

Which meant that Camio's appearance over Choshi, the eastern-most point in the Kanto region, was a pure coincidence?

"Uh, but this isn't Tokyo, you realize? This is Chiba."

"Yeah, but a lot of buildings and stuff in Chiba are still named 'The Tokyo Something-something,' you know?"

"Shut up, Lucifer."

"It was not sim*peep*-le coincidence. We used an object Olba left behind, claiming it would provide clues to the sword's position. This region reacted to it first."

"Clues to its position?"

That topic seemed like it had come up just recently, somehow.

Before Maou could scour his memory banks, Camio continued.

"But, I am afraid, it is now just as you *peep*...see. We were unable to defend ourselves against the great force that dwells in this realm..."

Camio's beady eyes drifted toward a corner of the box. His way of expressing shame, perhaps. Emi picked up his line of discussion.

"He's saying that the 'revenge' faction's already headed to Japan... To Earth!"

"What?!"

"What did you say?"

"Why didn't you say that *first*?!"

"*Eeep!*"

All three demons verbally expressed their surprise, Maou accen-tuating his shock by absentmindedly dropping the box.

"The...the Gate will open in the middle of the night, based on its size and our pr*eep*vious intelligence. We believe they will also rely upon their numbers to comb this land from its easternmost point forward."

The chicken strutting his way out of the box tucked his feet underneath his wings and sat upon the ground.

"To be frank with you, that woman's *peep*-power was simply inconceivable. I fear there is every chance a similar fate will befall the advancing force..."

And to be even franker, Camio was more or less condemning this third-party force to death, seeing no hope for them against the power of a bumbling beach-toggery owner.

Maou, relying on hearsay for the moment, had trouble picturing Amane as a presence strong enough to vaporize entire armies. But Camio was serious, more so than his naturally frowning beak signaled.

"We may have *peep*...parted company, but Barbariccia was a comrade in our struggle to unify the demonic realms. I do not have the heart to wage hostilities against him...and I cannot sit idly by and watch as his enraged but nonetheless decent and sensible fighters die a fool's death against that woman's might."

"And I really don't care about what happens to you guys..."

Emi retained her strict I'm-different-from-you approach with the demons surrounding her.

"But if Olba's really involved here, I can't ignore that. It doesn't matter to me whether Amane's this superwoman or whatever. Friend or foe, I don't care."

She turned her glare toward Maou.

"If Japan's attacked by this army of demons after my holy sword, then it's *our* job to drive them off. Mine, *and* yours. We're the ones who brought the fight here. We can't just palm this off on Amane."

A powerful light beam swept the skies above Emi as she stood tall.

"I'd, uh...kind of prefer it if Amane's a friend, but... Either way, she and my landlord are still good people. If they weren't around, we'd be panhandling right now."

Maou flashed a lonely smile.

"Emi."

"What."

"...You really believed it, huh?"

"Sorry?"

The question made Emi's face burst into alarm mode. The tone of Maou's voice suggested that he'd planted a story for Camio to tell her the whole time.

"You probably think this is a trap, don't you? All set up by this demon who risked his life trying to rescue me."

"...Oh. That?"

Emi's voice betrayed her blank disappointment.

"Even if you and that chicken trapped me, you think I'd do something about that?" Now she was brimming with confidence, although it still seemed like an act.

She tried to stand straight up, staring down at the demons, but then relaxed herself, thinking better of it...or, maybe, finding the act too idiotic to continue.

"Would you mind not treating me like some stupid woman?"

"Uh?"

Emi winced and brought a hand to her forehead.

"When Camio was talking to me, you know I had Chiho and Alas Ramus in there, too, right?"

"Y...yeah...? So what?"

He thought he knew. Or, maybe, he didn't know at all. So he decided to keep staring instead. Emi turned her back, as if trying to flee him.

"So, look, you're an evil demon, the king of all devils, a poor, dirty bum, my father's killer, the enemy of all mankind, worth nothing more than a piece of space debris to anyone. Anyone! But you know what?"

The anger seemed to come from the heart as her nose and eyelids twitched in supreme annoyance.

"At least to the point that I know you won't tell a lie that stabs Chiho or Alas Ramus in the back... I *trust* in all of you demons! So..."

She shot a look at the three, each blinking helplessly at her, overwhelmed.

"I want you to step up and take responsibility for this! With *me!*"

The shout echoed across the cape.

"...Are you on board, or not?! If you are, forget everything I just said! You piles of space junk!"

She was screaming, to the point where she seemed ready to hurl her sword— and Alas Ramus—at them.

A gust of wind blew through, perhaps hurried along by Emi's miniature sonic boom, and created an awkward silence.

"Uh, I really don't *feel* like you trust me at all, and I'm not really sure 'space junk' works as an insult..."

Maou looked at the night sky, a wide beam of light spinning its way through it, and nodded.

"But thanks. I'm glad you do."

Maybe it was just his imagination, but it seemed like Emi's face loosened just a touch to him.

And after that momentary, almost illusory softening, there was a wail akin to the howl of a cackling hellspawn.

"I *said, forget about it*!!"

Emi swung the Better Half, creating an arc of light that mimicked the lighthouse's leisurely sweep.

"Hey, uh, hey, Alas Ramus work hard, too, okay?"

She almost seemed like a celestial being, standing there like a war maiden, but the bouncy voice from her sword didn't quite match.

It wasn't bad, though.

"...Quite a *peep*—an enigmatic relationship, this."

"You said it. But what'll we do now? 'Cause if we're really going face-to-face with an entire demon squadron, I *really* don't like my chances."

"Yes, well, *peep*, I have a plan. The jeweled sword I *peep*ed along with me..."

The chirping was starting to grate on everyone, but still they all leaned over, lending an open ear to Camio's idea.

Then it happened. At a faraway point over the sea, the light from the tower flickered for a moment.

A rift in the darkness caught it.

"...They're *hee*-eeere."

Urushihara, surprisingly, noticed first.

Although neither Maou, nor Emi, nor Ashiya picked up on it at the time, he was also the first one to spot the Gate that spat Gabriel out into this world.

The group turned toward the direction he was facing. The sight they saw made them doubt their eyes.

In the darkness of the night, there was now a long, horizontal rift in space, extending across the sky.

"Uh, whoa whoa whoa, this is more than just a squadron, guys."

Like a mammoth flock of bats fanning out across the dark, or a group of migratory birds soaring toward some far-off destination, a massive number of shades emerged from the rift.

"Farlight Dazzle."

Urushihara mumbled the words, then focused his eyes on the shadows, still a faint line of mist in the faraway air.

"Camio was right. I don't see Barbariccia, but they're from the Malebranche tribe. Malacoda's servants."

"You can see that from here?"

Urushihara rolled his eyes at Emi, squinting as she surveyed the sea.

"Dude, that's like Holy Magic 101. I'm half angel, and I've been eating Bell's food pretty much daily lately. Her *consecrated* food. Any more questions?"

That went at least halfway toward understanding why Urushihara's wings were white when he dispelled the fog a day ago.

But that wasn't the question to ask right now. Ashiya provided the cue.

"…If they're in Japan, why are they still in demon form?"

"I dunno. Maybe they brought a source with 'em, maybe it's 'cause they left the Gate wide open; something like that?"

Either way, they couldn't tell from here.

The more pressing issue was that, right before Maou's eyes, a huge army of demon warriors was pressing down upon Japan. In their original demon forms, and likely with their original demon strengths.

The Malebranche tribe led by the Great Demon General Malacoda was gifted in what the human race would call necromancy.

In the human world, the art of reviving corpses and spirits to do one's bidding was seen as a taboo, a forbidden and arcane form of magic. But, practically speaking, it was nothing more than charging a corpse with a little demonic power. The necromancer had to fully control every part of this puppet, or else it was of no use at all in battle.

Among the Great Demon Generals working under Satan's rule, Malacoda—leader of the Malebranche, a tribe gifted in the ways of psychological warfare—was the last to pursue a military career.

His tribe were of similar height as the average human, but their batlike wings, and the worryingly long claws that grew from each limb, made them unique among the demons.

"Uhh, I just did a quick head count, but…I think we're lookin' at a thousand or so."

It was almost too many for their needs. And the fact they were visible from Cape Inuboh-saki meant the fishing boats might have already picked up on them.

"The people on the boats out there might be in danger! I'm going on ahead!"

Emi removed an energy-shot bottle from her pocket and hurriedly glugged it down.

Wiping her lips with the back of a hand, Emi focused on her legs as her entire body began to shine in a light-infused aura.

"Here we go, Alas Ramus!"

"'Kay!"

"Heavenly Fleet Feet!"

Before Maou could stop her, Emi flew toward the sea like a shooting star.

The Malebranche must have noticed Emi's vast holy magic. The shadows in the night sky began to waver to and fro, joining in formation.

"Um… Okay, uh, Camio? I'm still waiting for some hot ideas from you? Something about a jeweled sword?"

Maou and Ashiya had only a bare minimum of demonic force left. And even though Urushihara had the basics of holy magic at his disposal, it was nowhere near enough to take on a mob of maniacal gargoyles.

At this rate, they had little option but to watch Emi clash against the Malebranche. It wasn't the most appealing spectator sport they could think of. Presumably they'd die at the end, for one.

"*Peep!* How could it have *peep*ed my mind?! Yes, Lord Satan. The sword I brought with me... If you take it by hand and unsheathe it from its scabbard.........*peep*?"

Camio suddenly noticed that all three demons were looking at him in abject horror.

"Oh, dude, dude."

"My Devil Regent! Such a fundamental error in judgment!"

"L-Lucifer? Er, General of the Eastern Island? *Peep*, why are you...?"

"If we *needed* that thing, frickin' *say so* before we *left, you dumbass!!*"

Maou grabbed at Camio.

"Ah! *Peep!*"

"Don't 'ah' me! You *knew* we were gonna need it the whole time! You want me to sprint all the way over to Ohguro-ya from here to fetch it?! Emi's gonna be *done* by then!"

"*Peep-peep-peep...* Lord Satan...I cannot...*peep*."

"Ugh, we don't even have the time to make yakitori outta you. Yo, Ashiya. You mind running over for me?"

"Y-Yes, my liege!"

Ashiya lowered his body and began to run.

"...Ah!"

Then, after five or so strides, tripped.

Watching a nearly six-foot-tall man try out for the next installment of *Japan's Funniest Viral Videos* caused little more than annoyance to his friends.

"I... These beach sandals... I am not used to them..."

Ashiya understood that much, it seemed, as he brushed himself off underneath the demons' withering stare. Before long, he was off again.

"You all looking for this?"

Then, seeing something dangling in front of him, applied the brakes.

"I *thought* this was a bit too fancy a sword for our little birdie here. But it's kinda more a tool than a weapon, right? A *major* one."

There was the refined, makeup-free face, the flat T-shirt and apron...and the jeweled sword that never lost its luster, even when Camio had lost his form and his armor had shattered to pieces.

"Um...Amane? Ma'am?"

"'Ma'am'? Lord, I hope I don't look *that* old yet!"

Amane Ohguro, the more-or-less proprietor of Ohguro-ya, waved and flashed her usual freewheeling smile.

"You know, I was *wondering*, too, why there was just a little bit of demon force left after I whisked it all away. Well, no wonder! Look at this sword. Take it by its gem-encrusted hilt, unsheathe it from its scabbard..."

Amane unwrapped Camio's cape and slowly removed the sword from its holder.

The blade that appeared was dark red, the color of blood.

"*Et voila!* Look at the demon sword we have here! ...Oof. Just removing it a little bit gives me the willies. What're you gonna use this for, anyway?"

Amane slid the sword back inside its sheath and turned her eyes to Maou.

"Oh, and I'd appreciate it if you didn't go all 'Gee whiz, ma'am, what're you doing here?' on me. No need for all *that* trite nonsense. What I need to know right now is, what are you planning to do with this sword, question mark."

The question was light and airy, like Amane was asking what food needed to be prepped for tomorrow.

Neither Ashiya when he first saw the sword thrust in front of him, nor Urushihara nor Camio nor Maou behind him, bothered to hide their bewilderment. For a moment, everyone hesitated to answer.

Time passed—enough that Emi was just about ready to engage in active warfare with the Malebranche.

"Sadao Maou! Get a grip on yourself!"

Amane scolded the indecisive Maou.

"You let those girls run roughshod over you without saying anything back! And you call yourself a man? What a bum!"

She followed this up by tossing the eerie sword, scabbard and all, at Maou.

"Wah...! Ah, I, um—"

"Bzzt! Wrong answer, you dope! I know we've only known each other two days, but I think I already know what type of guy you are. So go and show me what you're made of already! Show me how you guys take responsibility around here. Go on, take the sword out! And you call yourself..."

All but coerced by Amane's griping, Maou placed a hand on the hilt and removed the sword.

The moment he did, a single pillar of black light shot up to the heavens, dark enough to dispel the lighthouse's lumbering signal from the edge of Cape Inuboh-saki.

"...the Devil King of a faraway world, do you?!"

Buooooooooooooooooonnnnnnnnnnnnn...
Buoooooooooooooooooooooonnnnnnnnnnnnn...
Buooooooooooooooooooooooooonnnnnnnnnnnnnnnnnnnn...

A low scream rang across the Choshi sea, as if keening in horror at the dark beam.

"Are you well, Chiho? How do you feel?"

"Oh, good... Just fine this time, actually."

Chiho and Suzuno stepped out of their inn, into a now-deserted Cape Inuboh-saki. They surveyed the fog that all but cut off their vision.

"...I detect traces of demonic force... But, why...?"

The answer materialized in the mist.

"Well, because whether they're indoors or not, releasing that much demonic power at once would make everyone within earshot of Inuboh go unconscious, is why. I just happened to take a few precautions."

"!!"

Suzuno tensed herself, carefully keeping Chiho behind her.

"Oh, there's no need to be so jumpy. We all ate *yakisoba* from the same griddle, y'know."

It was Amane Ohguro, still in her rough T-shirt.

"I'm not your enemy, I can say that much. They promised me they'd take responsibility for this, so I'm just kinda watching from the side. But don't worry—if they miss any of 'em or start tossing guys out of the ring, so to speak, I'll lend a hand."

Telling someone not to worry following that explanation was asking an awful lot.

According to Emi, a huge brigade of the Devil King's remaining warriors was staging an all-out assault on Choshi.

Could Amane just flick away any of the marauding demons Emi overlooked? It seemed impossible for Suzuno to believe that Amane was anything other than the laid-back beach girl she knew.

"Y'know, human, you really shouldn't underestimate me."

But, as if reading her mind, Amane flashed a supremely confident smile and slapped a hand on her hip.

"!!"

"Agh?!"

Unconsciously, Suzuno and Chiho covered their eyes.

The fog swirled into a tornado, centering itself in the area around Amane.

Her T-shirt and apron; her jeans and sandals; the simple rubber band holding her hair back...

The sort of shopkeeper you'd see in a million places around Japan was now the master of a mist-laden world, surveying her domain across the seas below Cape Inuboh-saki. The power she brandished was neither demonic nor holy, but something wholly unfamiliar... and wholly overwhelming.

"They don't call me Ohguro for nothing. The characters for 'great' and 'black,' you know? If you doubt me, I could always take all these interlopers into our world and blow them to the edge of the universe in the blink of an eye. How's that sound?"

Like it was all scripted for the stage, the beam from the lighthouse stopped dead just as it illuminated Amane's back.

Chiho and Suzuno shut their eyes. The light from the first-order Fresnel lens was too much for them to bear.

But for just a single fleeting moment, they thought they saw another ring of light behind her, one separate and distinct from the white glare that framed her body.

"Well. Anyway. Just take a load off and wait, okay? Besides..."

The afterimage disappeared as quickly as it came, and by the time Chiho and Suzuno recovered their eyesight, all that remained was a personable beach-house proprietor.

"Once Maou and the rest get back, I might just have something I can talk to you about."

"Amane..."

"Now, I've got something Maou and that little birdie asked me to do. See you later!"

With that, she gave them a friendly wave and disappeared into the mist.

Ahead of her was the Inuboh-saki Lighthouse.

With another roar from the dragon, Chiho and Suzuno saw her gazing sharply into the sea of fog.

✳

"Mommy! Knife!"

Thanks to her Idea Link with Alas Ramus, Emi deflected an attack on her left with her Cloth of the Dispeller shield without having to look.

"Fork!"

The wave of surging claws from the right was quickly deflected with her Better Half.

A Malebranche warrior, by himself, was not the most formidable of fighters.

But Malacoda, their leader, and his necromancy could conjure up some tricky moves, and—

"!!"

For example, the warrior who just appeared in front of her detached into several pieces the moment it came into sight.

It was a simple illusory feint, but Emi, fighting a very literal 1-vs.-1,000 battle by herself, had no time to guess whether the sight was real or not.

The moment she raised her shield to block the onrush of body parts:

"Fork!"

Alas Ramus's warning rang out.

She didn't notice the looming ball of demonic energy in time to dodge it. "Heavenly Mirror Beam!"

She reacted instinctively to the threat.

"Grahh!"

But, thanks to having her concentration distracted by the two separate attackers, she was caught in her own beam of light.

Staggering in midair, Emi found a dozen or so Malebranche closing in on her.

"Whoa, what're you... Let go! Ugh... Yah! Don't touch me there!"

If another demonic energy ball struck while she was restrained in midair, there would be no way to block it. Emi gritted her teeth.

"Shock wave of Light!!"

The holy magic triggered from the pit of her stomach. It was a powerful, power-exhausting move, one where holy magic gushed forth from her body and tossed the Malebranche away like rag dolls. But as they flew off in all directions, one of their claws grazed Emi's forehead.

A line of blood ran down—and in an even worse turn of events, seeped into her right eye, blocking her vision.

"Mommy, you okay?!"

There was no time to answer Alas Ramus's cry. It'd be harder than ever to fight now.

"Ugh! This is enough of a pain in the ass as it is!"

That was because this horde was using a battle strategy Emi had never encountered before.

"Knife!"

To dispatch the Malebranche approaching from the left, Emi used:

"Air Rush!"

Neither holy magic nor her sword, but a martial-arts move.

Her holy magic–infused fist smashed into the Malebranche's claw, crushing it to fine particles. The beast wailed and retreated back.

"Thanks for that one, Albert!"

Clenching her left fist once more, Emi rained strikes down upon the Malebranche attempting a frontal body tackle.

"Air Strike Assault!!"

The wind struck by Emi's fist formed projectiles that flew toward her attacker.

Some hit it in the stomach, others on the top of his head. It flitted away, not fully in control of its faculties.

The Malebranche who dodged the wind bullets fired energy balls of their own in retaliation. Emi vaporized them all with a sword slash, then:

"*Hrah!*"

She launched a frontal kick on the chin of the lead Malebranche, leaving the ones behind him wide open for a flurry of Air Rush strikes.

"This is…harder than I thought…it'd be…!"

Emi had only known how to fight with weapons before Albert taught her martial arts.

Before Ente Isla's Northern Island was conquered by Adramelech, commander of the Devil King's forces in the region, it was home to the famous Mountain Corps, a team of elite soldiers whose varied martial and holy magic skills were passed down from generation to generation.

By the time Emi met Albert, his Corps was scattered to the winds, himself dividing his time between training and woodcutting. But as a talented fighting monk, he was well-versed in all types of techniques, including sword combat.

"*The Northern Island's packed with all kinds of tribes and warlords and the like, y'see? So when we fight, we fight like this. That way, we keep it civil. Keep it from getting worse. That's how it's always been.*"

But that didn't seem to apply to Emi's quest. She thought it only worked against human opponents, the idea of fighting without killing.

<"Stay back!">

Just then, a shadowy voice boomed across the Malebranche army. In a flash, the incessant attack stopped.

<"Human girl... You are no ordinary fighter.">

It was a Malebranche, one larger than the rest of the horde.

The leader of this rabble, no doubt. He wore an eyepatch, a rare show of vanity for a demon, and the single long fang arcing from one side of his mouth made him even more conspicuous.

"Thanks for the compliment. I don't want to waste energy on an Idea Link, so I'll stick to human language."

<"Twelve hundred of our Malebranche braves...and we have never sustained a single death... No regular human could fight this way. Could you be...?">

As he spoke, the Malebranche leader raised his right hand.

In it was a cheap-looking trinket, like a little girl's pendant, made of colorful glass.

The glass suddenly shone a dull purple, then emitted a beam of light straight for Emi.

"Purple light... Is that...!"

"Mommy! Yeffod! Behind the shiny thing! Yeffod!!"

The voice of Alas Ramus, fused into her sword, told Emi that it was no mistake. Then the Malebranche leader, in customary demon fashion, laughed a hearty, evil laugh.

<"Krah-hah-hah-hah! I never expected to find you so quickly. So you are the bearer of the holy sword, the Hero Emilia Justina?!">

The leader's eyes twinkled, the demonic energy bubbling across his entire body.

<"If you bear the strength to overcome the Devil King Satan and four of his generals, then I must devote my entire soul to this battle! And when I defeat you, the holy sword shall be mine!">

"...No point hiding it."

Emi, quite the actor herself, beamed confidently as she thrust her Better Half into the air. "Release yourself, my force, and rid the world of evil!!"

The shout itself was enough to blow the Malebranche away.

The hordes feebly struggled to flee, their eyes too weak to take in the golden aura that enveloped her.

"I want the whole force to retreat, or else somebody's getting hurt."

Her hair was a blue-tinged silver, her eyes scarlet red. Her Cloth of the Dispeller was now fully formed, instantly healing her wounds.

"For the first time since I came to Japan, my holy blade has reached its second level...and it slices through a lot more than bread, you know."

The Better Half had evolved. Grown...*better*.

Once a thin, single-handed rapier, the holy sword was now wider, its hilt extended, the wings and Yesod-fragment jewel on it glowing brighter than before.

<"It is true! The scourge of the Devil King's force! The Hero of the Holy Sword! Emilia!!">

The Malebranche leader loomed face-to-face with Emilia, not betraying a single trace of fear.

<"I am Ciriatto! The Malebranche has but one chief! For the sake of our departed Malacoda's will, for the sake of the future of our New Devil King's Army, I alone shall wrest the holy sword from your hands! All of you, stay back!">

As Ciriatto ordered his troops to retreat and stated his name in classic warrior style, Emi brought her Better Half to her face and offered a knight's salute.

"Honestly, I'm discovering way too much about demons lately... But I cannot grant you mercy!"

For a single moment, holy power clashed against demon power above the Pacific Ocean. The Better Half crossed paths with Ciriatto's black, rigid claw.

<"*Gnnh!*">

The sword cleanly severed his right claw, sending it to the ocean below.

"Still up for more?"

<"*Kuh...*">

A single exchange was all it took for Ciriatto to groan in frustration.

He was completely unable to follow the path of Emi's sword with his eyes.

No one would expect a Malebranche chieftain to beat a foe that archangels couldn't defeat, but despite facing these overwhelming odds, the warrior refused to budge.

The holy sword had to be his. *It must reach the hands of the New Devil King's Army, so it may reunite the demon realms and succeed in Ente Isla where the Devil King Satan so regrettably faltered.*

"...You're really not leaving, huh?"

<"I am Ciriatto, sole leader of the Malebranche! No demon who would turn away in fear of defeat deserves the title of New Devil King's Army commander! *Orrrhhhh!!*">

"Whoa! Wait a sec!"

Emilia found herself asking Ciriatto for a time-out.

The demon used his remaining claw to neatly shear off the damaged stump on his other arm.

<"I have no need for such broken, useless weaponry! It will always grow back again!">

"Oh, is that how it works?"

She regretted being impressed by the act.

"But that doesn't mean there's no pain, right? It looks like you're bleeding. You sure you still want to do this? After losing one of your best weapons?"

<"Until my blood dries up and my body is torn asunder!">

A very old-fashioned approach to warfare.

Emilia saw zero value to the idea that a fighter only proves his worth once he falls in battle. But if that was how Ciriatto felt, it was Emilia's job to give the demon the last thing he ever wanted.

"You better not expect me to just up and kill you."

Emilia readied her sword.

"Huh? Really, Mommy?"

Alas Ramus noticed Emilia's change in tactics.

She was deliberately weakening her sword's holy energy. It was reverting to its first level, even after so spectacularly reaching its second. In fact, it was almost at the level of a plain, non-magical, decent-enough sword—just barely enough to keep it materialized.

"It's easier to keep this on an even footing..."

She closed her eyes for a moment. The faces of the demons materialized in her mind.

"...if I don't want you dead!"

<"Have at it!">

Ciriatto himself lowered the evil force in his left arm down to minimal levels, accepting Emilia's invitation. Here there would be no fancy magic, just pure battle technique.

The Hero and the Malebranche leader stared hard into each other's eyes. The area above the sea grew tense.

One concern remained with Emilia: She might be able to defeat Ciriatto without striking the lethal blow. But until that moment arrived, she had no idea whether the other Malebranche would accept it.

There was every chance their leader's death would whip them into a frenzy.

If that happened, the overwhelmingly powerful Emilia would be forced to commit a de facto massacre.

"...I've really lost my edge, haven't I?"

Emilia took a deep breath to put her feelings in order. Her foe was the Malebranche chieftain, the equal of Malacoda...or perhaps more. One mistake could spell her doom. She would have to consider that moment when it came.

No battle horn sounded at the start of this fight, a fight climactic enough that it would likely demolish an entire town if conducted on Ente Isla. Instead, the combatants stared each other down, snarling...only to suddenly lift their heads upward.

Buoooooooooooooooonnnnnnnnnnnn...
Buoooooooooooooooooooooonnnnnnnnnnnn...
Buooooooooooooooooooooooooonnnnnnnnnnnnnnnnnnnnn...

The roar of an ancient dragon ruled the skies.

If that was all it was, Emilia and Ciriatto would have immediately clashed afterward.

But the roar summoned the ruler of the white mist that loomed above the water. Emilia turned around. There was nothing but pure white around herself and the Malebranche.

<"?!">

Inside this world of white, a single point of darkness—a large, black *something*—approached.

Its presence alone made the fog split apart, forming a path like harried attendants laying a red carpet for their king.

"'Ciriatto'? I remember that name. One of the Malebranche chieftains beneath Malacoda, I trust."

The enormous shadow appeared behind Emilia's back.

"But what is the meaning of this? I have heard nothing of this so-called New Devil King's Army. Who would ever dare to call himself Devil King and rebuild the royal force...without me?"

<"Who...are...?!">

The demon's questioning voice cracked apart, his neck choked by some unseen hand before he could complete the cry.

"You have my full permission. Close his mouth... Crush the throat of this insolent Malebranche pretender to the throne."

Another sheer black form, making itself known next to the first, enormous shade, pointed an arm at Ciriatto.

The man—gnarled, forked tail; screeching, grating voice; skin devoid of blood—was racked with anger.

Before these two sudden threats, the Malebranche army tried its best to fall back. They did not go far.

"You promised a fight, and now you're running without so much as an apology? Pathetic. Too pathetic."

Another new voice. A young one, his voice like a frigid blade of ice. The Malebranche near the Gate turned to face it.

He was a small figure, no different from any human.

But behind him, his wings, darker than any clouded night or inky blackness, kept the Malebranche away from their escape hatch.

"Ugh... If you're gonna show up, do it earlier than this. I feel like an idiot getting so worked up now."

The force of light addressed the force of twisted darkness, as if discussing what to have for breakfast.

"Ha-ha! Sorry. I'm a little out of practice."

The gigantic shade toward the rear slowly sidled up next to Emilia.

<"What...*ngh*...are you...">

Ciriatto finally gurgled out the question. As if in reply, a deep, booming voice echoed across the misty realm.

"Silence! Malebranche warriors! Who do you think you behold?!"

"*Pfft!*"

Emilia snickered at the line. It reminded her of too many of her samurai dramas.

But it was still enough to make the helplessly struggling Ciriatto freeze in place.

Before his eyes, a dark avian warrior soared up into the void with a light flapping of his wings.

<"Ah...D-Devil Regent...Camio...">

Ciriatto stared agape at Camio's form.

"You! Dare you bare thy fangs at thy master, deluded by the sweet temptations of humankind?"

<"'M-Master'...?">

In his torment, Ciriatto turned his anguished eyes to the enormous shadow Camio pointed at.

He wore an avian warrior's cloak, his massive torso accentuated by his jeweled sword, shining a vibrant dark red. His feet were hoofed. One horn was shattered. And his eyes could strike fear into the hearts of all that live and ever lived.

<"Ah...no... No...?!">

"Malebranche warriors! Bow before your master: Satan, the Devil King!"

The raspy-voiced man's flair for drama made Emi snort to herself again. "Uh, are you guys doing that on purpose?"

<"T-The Devil King?!">

<"His Demonic Highness?!">

Twelve hundred Malebranche vanguard fighters found themselves awash in a wave of wonder and confusion, the phrase "Devil King" traveling like wildfire across their lips.

"Oh, great, they're playing the scared-peasants role perfectly, too, huh?"

<"Is that the leader of the Eastern Island invasion force... The Great Demon General Alciel?">

<"Wh-Why is the Devil Regent here...? Was Lord Satan not felled in battle?">

Shock continued to reign among the Malebranche, as:

"Uh, dude, hello? I'm here? You're ignoring me? Oh, you're *totally* ignoring me!"

Lucifer's temper tantrum as he blocked the demon army's escape made the Malebranche in the rear guard turn around. After a beat, they noticed him.

<"The fallen general...">

<"Lord Lucifer, the Fallen General?!">

"I *really* don't remember letting anyone call me that, but... Is *that* the kind of respect Malacoda's troops gave me? Huh?!"

Pushed back by Lucifer's anger, several Malebranche attempted to flee into the rest of the horde.

"Alciel, let 'im go."

A relaxed word or two from Satan was all it took for Alciel to pull back his outstretched arm.

Ciriatto, released from his choke hold, panted for breath.

It was so sudden that he floated in the air, bolt upright, trying to regain his bearings.

His eyes turned left and right. The Hero Emilia. The Devil Regent Camio. Two Great Demon Generals, Alciel and Lucifer.

And last, but not least:

<"F-Forgive me for my foolishness, my Devil King!!">

Slowly, he fell to his knees at Satan's feet.

The rest of the Malebranche humbly followed.

"Ciriatto. Chief of the Malebranche."

The voice of the demonic monolith rumbled.

<"Y-Yes!">

"I do not recall permitting anyone besides Camio to lead my people. What have you been doing in my absence?"

<"That... I...!">

Ciriatto hung his head downward. Satan's response was surprisingly gentle.

"Come. Raise your head. If you have something to say for yourself, let me hear it."

<"I, I thank you, my liege... We, the Malebranche, under the leadership of Barbariccia, were not merely lured here by a human's honey-tinged words! We fight for the sake of peace in the demon realms, so that we may obtain the holy sword before those that threaten our homeland—">

"Peace in the demon realms?"

Ciriatto spotted Emilia at the edge of his vision, Better Half at the ready.

<"Our leader, Barbariccia, merely pretended to agree to the human's plan. He wished to bring the sword under full control of our—">

"How *shallow* of you!"

Another rage-laden voice interrupted Ciriatto.

<"L-Lord Alciel?!">

"You were lured here by a single human being—Olba Meiyer, companion to the Hero. If the Malebranche chieftains conferred with one another, they could have easily extracted the necessary information from the human, killed him, and afforded yourself ample time to act. But why did that not happen? Why did you not seek Camio's royal assent?!"

<"B-Because...">

"Don't bully him, Alciel."

Out of the blue, Ciriatto found an unlikely ally in the Devil King himself.

"They aren't stupid enough not to consider that. That's what Barbariccia probably wanted to do in the first place. But Olba wasn't that easily taken, and he wasn't alone in this. Is that what it was?"

<"...I have no way of expressing my sorrow!">

Ciriatto turned his anguished face toward Satan.

"Ciriatto."

<"*Ngh…*">

Then he turned it toward Emilia.

"That purple stone you had… Can I see it?"

<"The purple stone…? This?">

The keyword made Satan and his generals twitch slightly as well.

The item in Ciriatto's hand was a pendant—decorated with a colorless, translucent jewel, not a purple one.

Despite what Emilia assumed at first, the pendant itself was no Yesod fragment. The jewel was just a jewel. But something to its shine jogged her memory.

"A Link Crystal…"

An object that allowed anyone to converse via Idea Link from any distance. In a vague sort of way, the cell phones of Ente Isla.

"That purple light earlier… Was that from someone on the other side of the Crystal?"

Not long ago, Emilia stormed the Devil's Castle on Isla Centurum with her companions, seeking to slay the Devil King who now floated in front of her. She had no way of knowing it at the time, but her holy sword reacted with the seed of Alas Ramus planted near the throne room, providing a "guiding light" to her nemesis.

Emilia thought the glow to her sword was meant to lead her to Satan, but the light was simply the twin Yesod fragments pulling at each other.

<"All I know is that the sword lies in the direction the light points… Even if this jewel is connected to someplace, I have no idea where.">

"…Would you swear it? On my name?"

Satan's face was doubtful as he asked. But Ciriatto stood firm.

<"By the name of my ruler, Lord Satan, I am telling the truth.">

Ciriatto turned his pained face away; Satan, looking down at him, looked far more serene.

"Good. …By the way, the Gate you flew out of… Where is it connected to? Is it a two-way portal?"

<"The…Gate?">

"No, uh, I'd kinda like to kick you guys back to the other side, but

I'd feel kind of crappy about it if you came back empty-handed and got punished for it, so..."

<"My liege, I...er...">

Ciriatto's eyes twinkled in disbelief at his king's sudden mood shift.

"Chill out, guys." Lucifer smiled in the most insincere way possible. "The Devil King's not out to give you all thirty lashes or anything. Those of you who tried taking on the Hero... Uh, think of it as one of those life lessons, you know? And get well soon!"

Ciriatto nodded lifelessly.

"If you want to return to the demon realm...or if that was your intention...we will not stop you. Camio, I order you not to persecute the 'revenge' faction of my armies when they return. My realm is in your hands."

"Yes, my liege."

Camio fell to a deferential knee.

"Right. Ciriatto. I'm gonna take all you guys back where you need to be. It'll kinda be a bumpy ride, but deal with it, okay? Camio'll follow after you."

<"Bumpy...?">

"And once you're back home, give everyone a message for me. Tell them that the Devil King Satan is very much alive."

"Hey! What are you... Aiigh!"

Emilia feared Satan was using Ciriatto to drum up morale in the demon realms. But before she could speak up, she shrieked as Satan restrained her by the shoulders.

Feeling Satan's solid hands through her Cloth of the Dispeller, she froze, goose bumps erupting across her body.

Ignoring this, Satan issued an order as deafening as the crashing waves beneath him.

"And tell them also that one of the holy swords is already in my grasp! Tell my people that Satan is in another world, amassing his powers to bring peace back to the demon realms. Use that to quell their disquiet. Ciriatto, I hereby appoint you as Camio's assistant. Until I return, you must lead my people, and unite my realm!"

The command of Devil King Satan, supreme leader of every demon that breathes (whether oxygen, fire, or poison gas), echoed across the foggy Pacific.

At that moment, Ciriatto was joined on his knees by his Malebranche tribe, along with Alciel, Camio, even Lucifer. It was a moment of homage, of united respect.

Satan surveyed the scene before him and nodded, satisfied.

"Very good. Anyway, all passengers, prepare for departure!"

<"Huhh? *Brnngh!!*">

Confusion ruled among the mist.

Ciriatto, still kneeling in front of Satan, was suddenly enveloped by a cocoon-like fog. He was illuminated by a sweeping beam of light, then vanished with a pained scream.

The sight made the Malebranche erupt in confused horror.

"All right, it's crowded out in the back, so everybody form a line, all right? Don't worry… Apparently it doesn't hurt, so…"

Using the skills he learned manning the shaved-ice machine, Lucifer calmed the crowd as he assembled the Malebranche into two neat lines. As if waiting for this moment, the light swept through again.

Each of the Malebranche, wrapped in a cigar-like casing of mist, screamed their best Ciriatto-like scream before vanishing, one after another.

"Y'know, I can't help but notice some hesitation here. Maybe they're screaming 'cause they hit the ground at light speed on the other side? I dunno."

Satan's anxious observation dissipated into the now Malebranche-free empty space.

"Well, Ciriatto's still a Malebranche chieftain. He's not gonna die that easy."

"Yeah, but at light speed? I dunno if *I'd* survive that."

"Let the sinners pay for their foolish sins. We need to close that enormous Gate now."

Alciel, usually silent in demon form unless it was necessary to speak, flew toward the Gate the Malebranche had come through.

Camio followed behind, Lucifer hurriedly attempting to catch up. And behind him:

"...Get your hand off my shoulder! I'll *kill* you!!"

An explosion of outraged holy energy chased after Lucifer.

Behind her, Satan fluttered along, eyes teared up as the bridge of his nose blushed a deep red.

"Look at how big this Gate is. Who could have...?"

As they approached, Emilia found herself shivering at the sheer scope of the portal.

Over a thousand Malebranche fighters, their chief included, had passed through this Gate. Yet it still maintained its form. It was unheard of.

Since the Malebranche appeared from this Gate, there was no way to go through it from the Earth end. But if there was, it looked strong enough to easily accommodate Satan and Emilia at full force.

An almost-unthinkable quantity of demonic force flowed from the void, offering a suggestion as to how the Malebranche had retained their forms.

"It's definitely a demon-power Gate, but...even if Barbariccia was a gifted underling of Malacoda's, he's still a rank-and-file Malebranche. Could he have opened a Gate so large?"

"Didn't have to be just him. Olba's with him, yeah? I guess he's pretty good at this stuff too, so maybe it was a team job..."

"Ridiculous, Lucifer. This Gate has retained its arcing shape even after allowing all those Malebranche through. This could never be work of a lone human and a lone demon."

"You know, just once I'd like to be called *Lord* Lucifer by you guys..."

Emilia gracefully poked her way into the demons' conversation:

"But the Devil King could've done this up easy back in his glory days, no? He made one robust enough to toss the archangel Sariel in."

"Uh, Satan's right here, lady."

"Mm. So?"

Satan smiled a bit. The sight of the Hero pondering over this issue with the demons seemed oddly comedic.

"...What's so funny? Stop making that creepy face at me. I'll *cut* you, and I mean it this time."

"Oooh, sorry, sorry. But anyway! That's not the thing here."

Satan waved his arms in an attempt to regain control over the conversation. Already his body language was back to human form.

"...Don't you see? There's only one way you can open a Gate, like, anywhere and anytime you want."

"...?"

Alciel, Lucifer, and Emilia all tilted their heads in unison. Satan couldn't help smiling again.

"Right, Camio?"

"Sir."

Satan turned to Camio, loyally attending to his side.

"It always winds up like this, doesn't it? It always has."

"Very true, my liege. And even the Hero is no exception, you are saying?"

"...I don't know what you're mumbling about, but I am *seriously* looking to cut someone right now, all right?"

"Now is not the time for that, Emilia. I need your power, too. We have to close the rift." Alciel's voice was a monotone as he chided her, his hands arching up toward the dimensional tear in space.

"...I have been doing *so* many favors for you guys..." Lining up next to Alciel, Emilia pointed her Better Half at the schism.

"Don't blame me if this goes wacky. You got any complaints, bring 'em to Satan." Lucifer, already looking to avoid any and all responsibility, settled down across from Emilia and next to Alciel.

"And you wonder why I refuse to treat you with respect. Your travels have changed you but little." Camio, voicing what everyone was thinking, brought his own talon to the void.

"Well, like it or not, you're all in the same boat now. Jeez. Who knows *what* kinda crap I'd be in if I was alone." With these few parting words, Satan held the jeweled sword in his right hand.

Given that it was fitted for Camio, the sword looked like a fancy letter opener when wielded by the larger-than-life Satan.

And yet:

"Ahh, this sure brings me back."

Bringing the blade of the sword to his eyes, Satan muttered softly enough that his words stayed only with himself. The blade began to glow stronger, redder, and darker. The demonic power within it resonated with Satan's.

"I was really this strong, huh? Man."

As she lent a disinterested ear to the demons' conversation, Emilia sharpened her wits as she leered at the dimensional rift. "...All right. I'm gonna cut the force keeping this Gate intact away from the local space. After that, it's up to you guys. Push the leaking demonic force back and close up the scar."

"Cut the force away? You can do that?"

Emilia's eyes, and nothing else, turned toward Satan.

The Better Half glowing in her hands all but evoked the image of the small child inside, eyes sparkling, chest puffed up proudly.

"I'm *saying*...that I can."

"Huh. Well, *that's* gonna keep me up at night."

Leaving the snickering Satan behind, Emilia tore off.

Like a shot of lightning piercing a lake of dark sludge, she made a beeline straight at the eerie Gate, then let off two bolts of purple-tinged lightning.

The moment they reached the rift, the horizon between the Gate and normal space began to waver.

"Now!"

"Right! Shut 'er down!!"

Following Emilia's signal, the four great demons thrust their force at the Gate en masse.

The border wavered, the stable part of the rift growing increasingly smaller and smaller.

If the foghorn sounded like the roaring of an ancient dragon, the cacophony emitted by the shrinking Gate would have been the dying wail of a slavering, chaotic beast, smote by the lightning of some mythical god. It was not of this world, and it was enough to even set the King of All Demons' ears on edge.

The fog began to swarm toward the shrinking Gate.
The dragon roared, as if prodded by the demons' force.
And then...

✳

"The sea... It's calmed down."
Suzuno and Chiho heard the dragon-roar from the deserted Cape
Inuboh-saki.

Buooooooooooooooooonnnnnnnnnnnn...
Buoooooooooooooooooooooonnnnnnnnnnnnn...
Buooooooooooooooooooooooooonnnnnnnnnnnnnnnnnnnnnnn...

The scream of an ancient god, a lone survivor in his world calling
out for his long-fallen companions, echoed loud and long across the
Inuboh seas.
"Suzuno! The fog!"
The fog began to disappear just as rapidly as it formed, as if the
foghorn scared it off.
"Is it over?"
"Looks a fair bit like it."
Amane appeared once more from the dissipating fog.
She still acted the part of a cheerful shop runner. Not even a smidgen
of the dignified forcefulness she revealed in the fog earlier remained.
"I took those scary guys and the little birdie back to the world they
belonged in. Looks like Maou and crew boarded up that big ol' pit
trap, too. Thing is, though..."
She turned back toward the ocean and ruefully scratched her
cheek.
"They kinda took a little too much time. I bet they used up all their
power in the process. Kind of too far to see, but they probably fell in
the water. You know if they can swim at all? 'Cause they got a pretty
long haul ahead of 'em."

Amane grinned as she sized up Suzuno and Chiho.

"Huhh?!"

It all ended in the middle of the night, but by the time the horizon began to brighten and the sun began to hide the starlight, neither Emi, nor Maou, nor Ashiya, nor Urushihara were back.

All Chiho could do was scan the dark seas for a sign of them, her eyes all but ready to erupt in tears, and all Suzuno could do was pray that Emi's holy energy wouldn't disappear from her senses.

Inuboh-saki Lighthouse loomed above, as it always did, a sentry of light guiding early-morning voyagers to safety.

There was a pathway underneath the bluff the lighthouse was built upon, letting tourists walk right up to the shoreline.

Just as the sun was about to poke its way above the horizon, underneath the cape bluff:

"Yusa! Maou!"

"Alciel! Lucifer! You're alive?!"

The Hero Emilia, hair still a blue-tinged silver, was washed ashore, soaked to the core. Sadao Maou, Shirou Ashiya, and Hanzou Urushihara were right next to her.

"*Huff...! Huff...huff...* C-Chiho... Bell... Um... Um, it's pretty much over..."

Gasping for air, Emilia transformed out of Hero mode before their eyes, returning to her regular Emi Yusa form.

"Chi-Sis! Suzu-Sis!"

Then another, smaller figure appeared.

"Alas Ramus!"

"Guess what? Guess what? Mommy and Daddy and tweety-tweet and Al-Cell and Looshifer, and, and, *guess what!*"

Alas Ramus could only barely contain her excitement.

"It was, *booooom*, then *baaaaam*, and then we all went *zoooooom*, then *oomph!*"

"......"

"......"

Her commentary wasn't much help.

"Then it was all light, then tweety-tweet went home!"

"'Tweety-tweet'... Camio went back to the demon realm?"

Chiho tried to ask Maou, but between the important business of lying on the beach and breathing shallowly, he wasn't in the mood for conversation.

"The sword...and Camio went back. Then the fog lifted."

Emi, her breath a bit more collected, began to move her lips.

"And right when it did, they all turned human again. Like, six hundred feet above sea level!"

"Oh."

"Ooh, I just *wish* I could've recorded their screaming when they all fell in the water. It was poetry in motion. I mean, if they knew *that* would happen, they shoulda at least retained enough demon force to fly back."

Emi wasn't one to talk. The exhaustion was written on her face. She might have retained her demi-angel form through the whole ordeal, but dragging three grown men through the rugged Choshi waves couldn't have been an easy swim.

"...They *really, really* owe me now. Don't these demons ever...*plan* anything?"

"Mommy's all wet! You okeh? You'll get a cold!"

"I'm fine. How about you?"

"I'm okeh!"

It was the first real battle the holy sword had seen since its fusion with Alas Ramus, but just as the child said, nothing seemed off with her at all.

"Well, someone was sure a hard worker today, huh? I think you deserve a big reward later on."

"Yay!"

"Well, hello! Talk about a hard day's night, huh?"

Amane chose that moment to stroll down from the top of the path, clapping as she took a glance at every waterlogged rat on the shore in order. They knew she wasn't any normal human being by now, but on the more important question—*Friend, or foe?*—there was still no guessing.

Emi and Suzuno tensed up, making their alarm at her presence clear.

"Oh, whoa, whooooa, why're you picking a fight with me? *I* didn't do anything. Really! I'll tell you everything I can, so, um… Y'know, even if it *is* summer, I can't just leave you guys to dry out down here, so…"

Emi, glaring upward at Amane, could no longer resist the urge.

"Huh-*choo*!!"

The sneeze was like a shotgun.

"…See? You're gonna get a monster cold."

Amane pointed up at the cape.

"How 'bout we all head back to Ohguro-ya? I'll make sure we pump some hot water into the showers for you. Hey, and look!"

She brought a hand to her forehead as she gazed at the ocean.

"What a great morning, huh? The perfect way to end a battle."

The sun was now visible on the horizon. As it shyly peeked out, the beam from Inuboh-kai Lighthouse shut itself off. Shutters gradually closed themselves over the light room on the tip of the tower, covering the first-order Fresnel lens that guarded the Chiba seas.

The most beautiful sunrise in all of Japan, a source of pride for all Choshi locals, unfurled its generous arms of light to the people, demons, and Hero who witnessed the conflict.

✳

By the time the sun made it fully above the horizon, it was already shaping up to be another hot day in Kimigahama Beach.

Despite yesterday's barely controlled chaos, Ohguro-ya, the only beach shop in operation, was preparing to board the treadmill again today.

As Amane put it:

"Whether it's water or javelins coming from the sky, any Japanese worth his salt always keeps the shop doors open!"

Maou had a word or two to say about that. But what the boss says, goes.

The day after she witnessed the three demons in their true forms as they waged cross-dimensional warfare with alien invaders, Amane only needed seven words to shut the three of them up:

"I'm not paying you if you don't."

So there was Maou wiping down the tables, Urushihara filling the kiddie pool with water, Ashiya striving to prepare enough ingredients to cover a crowd as big as yesterday's.

"You know, when I first showed up, Chiho and Kamazuki…well, *my*, they were just *beside* themselves! What on earth have you been saying to them about me?"

"Well, I mean, you were just a total riddle to us, so…"

Maou did his best to make excuses.

Suzuno and Chiho, from the safety of the inn, looked on as Emi and Maou flew off over the sea.

Maou resented Emi at first for leaving Chiho at Kimigahama as the Malebranche loomed in the skies. But as Emi explained:

"If Amane really *did* have some kind of power, I figured she'd find her if things really *did* get that bad."

"Oh, now now, it wasn't just Chiho. There was someone else, remember? What did you think about *her*?"

Suzuno, pouting to herself in a corner of the store, flailed about as Amane made her the topic of conversation.

"I, I was not seeking the aid of anyone! Against the Malebranche, I could fight effectively with one hand as I protected Chiho!"

"Yeah, I mean, Suzuno's strong enough, and… Okay, it's great if she kept Chiho safe. That's all."

"Eeeee!!"

"Your Demonic Highness, have you learned nothing? She was never even made aware of Camio. The odd woman out, the entire time! You have to at least show a little care for—*grrgbbh!*"

Ashiya began lecturing Maou once again, but made the mistake of doing so in full earshot of Suzuno. This time, he was rewarded with a bottle of soy sauce to the back of the head.

"I am not the odd *anything* out! I haven't a care in the world for such nonsense! If *I* were there, I could have rendered a thousand-strong demon army into so much flotsam and jetsam! But Emilia! What of *your* performance?!"

Suzuno frowned a sort of lonely frown as she directed her ire at Emi in the corner.

"I understand you slew *not a single demon*, Emilia! What is the meaning of that?!"

"What? Nothing, really."

Emi, seated in a shady section of the shop, was the only one in a swimsuit.

Her clothing was currently being hurriedly washed after her little overnight swim, but since she had no change of clothes with her, she was forced to rock the beach-gal look the entire day.

"I just... I stopped letting my hate drive me to kill everyone in my way. If I *need* to, then sure. I swear I wouldn't hesitate to take someone's life...but..."

Emi glanced at Maou, currently preoccupied with wiping the tables and chairs.

"If I'm gonna go at it with someone, it's not gonna be fair unless we go back *there* first. I think Ciriatto's a lot stronger than that, too, back home. And I can't bust out my full strength in Japan, either, of course. It's easy to kill someone, but making someone on the other side hate you for it... Well, that's just a pain, you know? This..."

Emi shrugged and held her arms up in the air.

"This ridiculous war we're fighting... I don't want to keep postponing it to the future. When it happens, I want to win. I want to overwhelm them with my power. That's why I didn't kill them."

"Kaahhh... Bright and early in the morning, you girls are going on about killing and maiming and gouging people's eyes out. What happened to the pretty li'l pearls of Japan that showed up a couple days ago?" Amane commented to no one in particular as she filled the cash register with change.

"So...that light was from the lighthouse, right? And you were controlling the fog and everything, Amane? What *was* that, anyway? And that first cyclopean and the beast demonoid... What about them? Are they dead?"

Amane didn't shift an inch at Urushihara's barrage of questions. She paused and sipped from a 5-Honest Energy.

"The children of the Tree of Life belong to the land of Sephirot."

"Huh?"

The word *Sephirot* being tossed around without warning brought everybody to attention.

"They simply returned to the place they needed to be. The light merely showed them the way. ...Well, showed them to the cliff and kind of pushed them off, but you know what I mean. People like those are bad news, you know. We don't need them getting in the way of our business."

After giving that inscrutable answer, Amane looked at Maou.

"You've met my Aunt Mikitty before, right, Maou?"

"Uh, yeah, of course..."

"Did she tell you at all about us?"

"About you... 'Us'? You mean besides how you're relatives?"

"...Aww. Well, never mind. Can't say any more out of *my* mouth." Amane closed the register and wryly shook her head.

"What do you mean, though? That you are more than merely human?"

Amane shook her head again at Ashiya as he wrapped up the day's vegetables and took his knife to the whetstone.

"Welllll... If you want to say we aren't human, then I suppose you could do that, but... Y'know, though, I go in for my physical every year, and nothing ever comes up in the tests. The picture of health!"

"No, er, that wasn't quite what I was asking..."

"Well, it's fine, isn't it? We're all alive, so." With that, Amane strode up to Emi.

"...Um?"

"Aw, look at her sleep."

She brought a hand to Emi's forehead, eyes focused upon hers.

Emi stared right back at her. There was no "sleep" involved.

Maybe Amane knew about Alas Ramus inside of her after all.

"Make sure you don't let that kid down, okay? She deserves that. In fact, she might just be a really, *really* distant relative of mine."

"Uh?"

Before Emi could parse what that meant, Amane removed her hand and turned back around.

"Okay! Are we about ready to open?"

She was speaking to the demons.

"Ooh, guess I came in just at the right time."

Chiho let herself in from the back, Emi's wardrobe in tow.

"It's going to be another hot one today. I only had these hanging out for a little bit, but they're already dry. Here you are, Yusa."

"Oh, thanks, Chiho."

Emi accepted the laundry from Chiho, never taking her eyes off Amane as she did.

"Ah, perfect timing! Right, then."

Then Amane clapped twice to gather everyone's attention.

"I know it's only been a couple days, and I'd like to thank you all very much, but I'm afraid I can't have you work here any longer."

"...Uhm?"

"Uhmm?!!"

None of the demons could manage more than a pained whimper in response.

"I'll figure out how to manage this place well enough, so don't worry about that. Oh, and—hey, Maou and Kamazuki? Aunt Mikitty got the repairs finished in record time, apparently, so your apartment's all ready to go."

"Uh, what are you talking about? I don't get where this is all coming from."

Finally swallowing Amane's out-of-left-field announcement, Maou felt his face turn white as the morning sun hit it.

"Did I tell you about the moren-yassa? I forget."

"Moren-yassa?"

He did vaguely remember something about that during that beachside evening with the fireworks.

The moren-yassa, the seafaring ghosts that stalked the Choshi seas.

"Well, that story's true, you know. The details are kind of off a little, but..."

"Er?"

"But, *yeahhh*, I figured there had to be something up with you guys since Aunt Mikitty recommended you and everything. But, Lordy, you guys are just too much for my customers! Especially you, Maou and Ashiya. Why, you could mess up the entire energy balance on this beach, you know?"

"...Uh, umm, Amane, I'm sorry to interrupt you and all, but..."

Chiho, her face just as white as Maou's for some reason, stepped up to the plate. She pointed a shaky finger at a corner of the shop opposite from Emi's seat.

"Is...is that a child's shadow over there?"

"...Whoopsie."

Amane took a look, then turned her face toward the ceiling.

None of the demons, nor Emi or Suzuno, had noticed any kind of shadow over there.

The shadow suddenly turned upward, as if realizing it was now the center of attention.

"...!!!!"

Emi let out a silent shriek and leaped out of her chair.

The shadow had no face. Or, to be exact, it really was nothing more than a dark shade against the wall.

It looked like the matte-black silhouette of a child, and as everyone stared at it, frozen in fear, it dashed off toward the beach.

"M-M-M-My, my, my l-lieeeege..."

They all had the shock of their lives yet again as Ashiya pointed outside.

The sea, and the beach itself, was teeming.

Not with beachgoers.

With what seemed like hundreds and hundreds of shadows, just like the one that darted out of the shop.

Kimigahama, bright and sunny in the late-summer morning, was now playing host to a large conference of black silhouettes.

Every one of them was person shaped. Some even had inner tubes and beach balls in hand, all just as jet-black as themselves. There were even a few enjoying what looked like an early lunch.

But it was all shadows. Just a massive crowd of shadows.

"A-Ama, ma, ma, ma, *Amane*, what's *that*?!"

The vision came on so suddenly, so without warning, that everyone fell into a panic, not knowing how to cope.

What were these silhouettes? They didn't seem hostile, but they were definitely *not* the crowd they had been selling soft drinks and curry to yesterday.

"Well, it's partly you guys' fault, is what it is."

Amane, completely unfazed, waved a hand at the crowd of shades, as if greeting her neighbors down the street.

"Wh-Wh-Wh-What do you *mean*?!"

Maou, keeping the dazed Chiho protected, all but shouted at Amane.

"Well, think about it. Demonic force, and holy energy. Have you ever considered what those *are*, really?"

"Wh-What are you...?"

"They say there's something special to a beautiful sunrise, right? A kind of energy you can't find anywhere else. There are moren-yassa, all right, but they aren't the spirits of the drowned or anything. This is a holy sanctuary, one of the few on Earth where a soul can go to cleanse itself. The season only runs from mid-July to mid-August, pretty much, but this is where they kick back and take a load off. And me and my dad... We hold the fort, so to speak. We fight to protect the souls of the dead that show up here. But, y'know..."

Amane gave Maou an uncharacteristically disapproving frown.

"Your demonic and holy forces could only exist in a world that was on the brink of collapse anyway. And yesterday, when you shot all that energy over kingdom come... It threw off the all-but-perfect balance we had going in this sanctuary. They have the chance to take on human form while they're here, but now they've just about lost it. So that's why I'm afraid I can't keep you on any longer."

"On the brink of collapse? Wh-What do you mean?"

Amane flashed a suggestive smile at Suzuno's question.

"Here on planet Earth, you know... There're a lot of forces, and mysteries, you'd never be aware of. From long, loooooong ago. Long before there were gods, even."

She showed a politician's knack for vagueness in the reply, but Amane gave them no chance to fire back.

"So! Now that we're clear on *that*... Again, sorry about this, folks. You definitely filled the place up, so I'll be giving you all a bonus for that. My dad always taught me that I need to reward people when they go the extra mile, so don't worry about that."

Amane raised an arm and snapped her fingers.

Buooooooooooooooooonnnnnnnnnnnn...
Buoooooooooooooooooooooonnnnnnnnnnnnn...
Buooooooooooooooooooooooooonnnnnnnnnnnnnnnnnnnn...

The foghorn went off.

Along with it, the fog rolled back on to the beach from some unknown spot, like a ninja firing off the all-time mother of smoke bombs.

Between the ocean gales and flying sand, Maou could barely keep his eyes open as he heard Amane speak.

"Call me the 'Binah' of Earth."

She was standing right in front of them a moment ago, but with her voice muffled and thrown by the wind and fog, it was hard to tell where she was any longer.

"Search for the Da'at of your world, and bring the world back to what it should be. I'm sure that's what my Aunt Mikitty's waiting for."

And that was the end.

The moment after the foghorn fell silent, the fog was driven away by an explosive blast.

Then, when they opened their eyes, Kimigahama, the strange shades frolicking in it, and the Ohguro-ya sundry shop were all gone.

In place of the bright, wide beach, there was a path lining a concrete levee, anti-erosion tetrapods piled up on the shoreline. It was the same sight Chiho saw among the waves the first day in Choshi, on the van to Ohguro-ya. The water was shallow, lined with reefs, and wholly unsuitable for wading.

Maou, Ashiya, and Urushihara; Emi, Chiho, and Suzuno; and all of their luggage were lined up neatly on the weed-lined walkway.

"Wha...wha...wha..."

Maou's voice trembled.

"Where the hell *are* we?!!"

His scream charged deep into the sea before dissipating out on the horizon.

It couldn't have been in response to that, but it was then that he noticed something fluttering in the air: what looked like red pieces of paper. They could easily be counted, because each settled to the ground at a corresponding person's feet.

"M-Maou, is that...?"

Chiho showed one of the envelopes to him.

"Our...bonus?"

✳

Even with all the travel and prep costs, a 50,000-yen bonus per demon for about two and a half days of work wasn't too shabby at all.

Counting the 10,000 yen Emi and Chiho received, and the 20,000 Suzuno earned for her sand-castle mastery, Amane blew most of yesterday's profit on these envelopes.

Even after all the bizarre events of the past forty-eight hours or so, the King of All Demons still had serious concern over whether Ohguro-ya could remain going.

"I...assume this is not counterfeit? It will not dissolve in water, or the like?"

After that gathering of shades enjoying the beach, no one could blame Suzuno for her suspicions.

Like an evil cartoon magnate, each one of them carefully observed every millimeter of the bills. Then:

"…Let's just go home."

No one offered any dissent.

There was nothing along the walkway to hide behind, forcing Emi to put her dry clothes back on over her swimsuit.

The Inuboh-saki Inn and lighthouse in the distance looked the same as it always did these past two days. But if you asked any of the passersby about a public beach around here, there was no doubt they'd all shake their heads.

Maou's landlord vanished from Tokyo after taking a similarly suggestive attitude with them, leaving a boundless number of doubts up in the air. And, much in the same way, if they tried looking for any trace of Ohguro-ya and Amane right now, they'd almost certainly come up empty.

They tried calling Amane's cell phone, just in case—more out of curiosity than anything—but it always came up as not available or outside of service range.

"Your Demonic Highness. I found this among our luggage."

Maou ran his eyes down the large piece of paper Ashiya handed him.

"…Man. This is too much. Does she take *anything* seriously, or what?"

It was a handwritten guide to Choshi's best tourist sites.

✳

The ocean spread out 330 degrees around them. The altitude gave them the ability to view all of Choshi in one glance.

"Dude, big whoop. We were flying higher than this just a—*ow!*"

Maou, shutting Urushihara down before he could ruin the mood further, climbed the stairs to a viewing platform in the middle of the observation deck.

"…Damn. This is huge."

His vantage point gave him a 360-degree panoramic view of Choshi and the ocean surrounding it, inspiring him to stretch his body out and take in the heady wind.

The deck had the somewhat unwieldy name of "The Observatory That Makes the Earth Look Round."

It was really more the roof of a building than an observatory, but the site, atop one of the taller hills near Inuboh rail station, was one of the most well-known sightseeing spots in all of Choshi.

The gang's intention was to clamber into the Choshi Electric Railway car and get the hell out of there, but they were cursed by bad timing—the train pulled out of the station just as they arrived.

The next one wasn't due for over half an hour, so they climbed up here rather than spend the time staring into space on the platform. They were rewarded with a view that outclassed all expectations.

The sun was beating down hard on them, but the cloudless sky allowed them to examine Choshi unobstructed, from edge to edge.

Inuboh-saki Lighthouse seemed pretty big from nearby, but up here, it looked about as tall as a stoplight.

"If I may, Your Demonic Highness, this is nothing. A mere speck. Hardly anything worthy of your praise. You are destined to seize Ente Isla one day. Do not fool Emilia into believing *this* view is enough to satisfy you."

"Yeah, Ashiya. Someday. Right *now*, though, we had to rely on a bunch of other people just to keep Choshi safe."

"That is...perhaps the case, yes."

"Plus, if I didn't have you, and Urushihara, and Malacoda and Adramelech, and Camio for that matter, I wouldn't even be ruling the demon realms. You all used to be enemies to me once upon a time, remember? And then you joined me to support my cause."

Maou put a hand on Ashiya's shoulder.

"That's how humans work, too, don't you think?"

"...Indeed. Perhaps you are correct."

"Eesh. I thought that keen observation would amaze you a little more than that."

"I am quite used to your fanciful turns of speech at this point, my liege."

Something about Ashiya's finely honed rejoinder irked Maou.

"Well, I mean, look at all this. Doesn't it make you wonder what the hell we were wasting our time with, sometimes? I mean, they make *electricity* with those things."

He pointed at the wind turbines looming over Byoubugaura.

"There's zero magic power on Earth, and they still built that Skytree-type thing over there. That's taller than my old Devil's Castle!"

"It is called Choshi Port Tower, Your Demonic Highness, according to the map. The Devil's Castle was quite a bit taller."

"And despite that, they have crap like the Choshi Electric Railway. Taking all those clunky old locomotives and building something new out of them. A new culture. There's no way I could ever annihilate this species. Don't you just want to gather them all up and rule over them instead?"

"It is a nice thought, my liege, but first we must find a way to give you consistent access to your demonic force."

Ashiya grinned helplessly at Maou, his eyes shimmering with childlike ambition. Emi chose the moment to speak up.

"Say, how'd you find enough power to return to demon form anyway?"

This wasn't like the previous times. Choshi wasn't blighted by some disaster that filled the locals with enough negative energy to power the transformation.

"Oh, that? Well, you remember the sword Camio brought along, right? Turns out it's made from that horn of mine you lopped off."

"…Huh?"

Emi let her jaw hang open.

"Hey, don't blame me. Blame Olba. He collected all the horn fragments and had a sword forged from 'em, but there was so much demonic force in it, they couldn't find anyone to wield the thing. I guess he brought it to Camio as kind of a bargaining chip. But that's not the problem right now. *This* is."

Maou took something out of his shorts pocket and tossed it at Emi.

It was small, the size of a marble, and it glistened a purple shade in the sun.

"Is this…?!"

"I found it with all the other bling engraved on the scabbard. Remember what Camio said? The clue Olba relied on to track down the holy sword? That's probably it."

"Who…made that sword set, though?"

"Well, I doubt Olba carried that sword around without the scabbard. I didn't hear anything about it, but I'm pretty sure he had the blade and scabbard as a set, so… Kinda makes it easier to picture what kind of bastards are backing him up, huh?"

"Ah…yes. My internal investigations did reveal a supply of your horn's fragments in Olba's private office… But how could one forge those into a blade?"

"Hell if I know."

It was nothing Suzuno could ignore. The whole reason she found Japan was because she had tracked the path Olba took after examining the horn fragments.

And even now, Olba's name wielded considerable power among Church officials on Ente Isla's Western Island.

What drove him to *do* all of that, however? She still couldn't even guess.

"If I had to imagine, this Yesod fragment was stuck on there to try and offset the demonic power in my horn. Kind of a safety valve to keep my force from leaking out of the sword…although it still leaked out enough that it kept Camio and that cyclopean in their demon forms on Earth. Not that I know why he'd give this fragment up so easily, even though he's going nuts looking for your holy sword."

Emi peered at the purple Yesod fragment in her hand.

"But anyway, it's not much use to me. Let Alas Ramus have it. Maybe it'll make you stronger or something, huh?"

"Th-Thank you… Wait, *no* thank you! Are you serious?!" Emi shook her head, desperately trying to keep her gratitude from slipping through for all to see. "You realize you're not kidding, right? This is seriously gonna amplify my power. Just merging with Alas Ramus let me beat an archangel!"

"Oh, you don't want it?"

Maou snorted indignantly.

"Don't kid yourself, girl. Just a few bits from my horn that you so kindly shattered to pieces was enough to transform both myself and three other top-level demons. If I ever get my *full* strength back, I'm taking over this entire planet. You included."

"What?!" It was Chiho who picked up on his declaration first. "So you'll really do it, Maou? You're going to conquer the world? Really?!"

There was something about the way Chiho used the term "conquer the world" that seemed to drain it of all meaning as it dissolved into the air.

Emi was nonplussed, her face red with shame.

"I... Oh, *now* what're you going on about?"

"Emilia, it is not too late. We could search for Amane right now, have her transport the Devil King and his cohorts back to the world, and slay them there. Yes. We should do it at once. Come."

Suzuno's invitation sounded more like an incantation, emanating from her dark, brooding visage.

"My liege, if you could restrain yourself... There are people nearby."

"Dude, you are seriously embarrassing me right now, Maou. It's too hot for that crap. Can we go? I don't wanna get sunburned."

To the wrong pair of ears, Maou might just have sounded like someone making a serious threat. Ashiya fretted to himself about it, while Urushihara actively jeered—making sure he was a safe distance away first.

"I...I have never been so humiliated in my life!"

Emi's face burned with rage. She looked ready to pounce upon Maou at any moment.

But even she was prudent enough not to break out her holy sword.

It was a childish and altogether immature argument between human and demon, and soon, it was absorbed into the cloudless summer sky and disappeared.

EPILOGUE

The great city of Noza Quartus, located on the north side of Isla Centurum in the middle of Ente Isla, was both the seat of the local government as it rebuilt the island and home of the Federated Order of the Five Continents, the international brotherhood of soldiers charged with protecting it.

The news that reached the Noza Quartus administration in the early morning threw the government representatives and Order commanders—so used to the current peace that reigned across the land that they were already focused on their old political infighting and border squabbles—into a paroxysm of chaos and despair.

Efzahan, the mighty empire that spread out across the whole of the Eastern Island, had sent a declaration of war to the knightly orders of the Northern, Western, and Southern Islands, each stamped with the seal of the unifying Azure Emperor who led the nation.

The communiqué declared the empire's intention to stage a military takeover of the Central Continent.

Controlling all of the Eastern Island as it did, Efzahan enjoyed the largest territory and population of any country in the world. But this size was thanks to the swallowing up of multiple neighboring countries over the years, creating a near-constant cycle of internal strife and political instability.

Since the empire was already well-known for starting, then retreating from, small naval skirmishes at its borders with the Northern and Southern Islands, the idea of Efzahan declaring war on the rest of the world seemed less than credible in terms of international diplomacy.

But that wasn't all. News was spreading like wildfire among the Federated Order that among the armies stationed along Efzahan's borders with its neighboring islands and the Central Continent, there were some demons sighted in their ranks.

It spelled the end of the Order itself. All the Eastern Island knights stationed in Noza Quartus were recalled back to their homeland, and soon, almost every local army was calling upon its native soldiers to return and defend their homelands for what was anticipated to come.

To the Central Continent, laid bare on the ground and with little to no warpower of its own, it was an extremely precarious state of affairs.

The text of the Azure Emperor's declaration was unsparing in its cruelty.

It offered no chance at peace or reconciliation. Only by swearing deference to the Great Efzahanian Empire or providing suitable tribute to its ruler would the Central Continent be allowed to retain any form of autonomy.

The "suitable tribute," in this case, made it difficult for the Continent and its three allies to work as a cohesive team.

War-weary representatives from the North and South, memories of the Devil King's invasion fresh in their minds, strongly criticized the Western Island for retaining exclusive control over this "tribute." The Western Island, in turn, could not present a unified front, tensions between the influential Church and the Holy Empire of Saint Aile finally brimming to the surface.

Thus, the peace that reigned over Ente Isla was, for the first time in over two years, gravely imperiled.

The "tribute" that Efzahan demanded:

The Better Half.

THE AUTHOR, THE AFTERWORD, AND YOU!

Back when I was a kid, at the Chiba seaside town of Onjuku for a family vacation, a firework shot off by some people on the beach changed direction in the wind and hit me directly on the head, causing severe burns.

I managed to avoid permanent scarring, thanks to the lady at the inn and her timely first aid, but for a while after that, I couldn't bring myself to use any fire spells in the RPGs I played. It may not seem like that big a deal written in words like this, but to a child's frame of mind, it was pretty traumatic. I went bald in the spot where it hit for a while, too.

So when you're playing with fireworks, make sure you follow the rules and clean up afterward. The More You Know.

Telling a *Devil* story in the area where the Devil King and Hero "worked" together in this volume was actually a goal of mine since the initial brainstorming phase for the series.

This area is the site of no less than two actual miracles.

The first is a natural miracle—out of anyplace in Honshu, the largest of the islands that make up Japan, this is the spot where the sun rises first every day (unless you're up on a high mountain or off on one of Japan's more remote islands).

The sunrise as viewed from Inuboh-saki, the easternmost point in Chiba, really is too beautiful to put into words. It's almost a mystery, how nature can create such a supreme and overpowering work of art on such a regular basis.

The second miracle is a human-engineered one—the way that an entire region and its industry was rescued by a timely opportunity, a local souvenir, a gathering of people, and a *senbei* cracker.

The story of the Choshi Electric Railway—one where the concerted efforts and training of many people allowed them to connect with the rest of Japan via the net and keep on operating, keeping themselves alive without having to rely on charity or external support—is kind of an ideal, I think, in terms of people working hard and being economically rewarded for it.

Like the classic grandmother out in the country, I thought that the Devil King and his cohorts might learn a thing or two working out in the sticks. But it's doubtful that either the Hero or her nemesis learned anything that constructive. They were too busy giving their all in this unfamiliar place, flailing about as they tried to carve a path to the future for themselves. That's how the story turned out.

I'd like to take this opportunity to express my heartfelt sorrow for Urushihara's rantings and Ashiya's occasional (unintentional) slip of the tongue. If anyone at the Choshi Electric Railway or NASA's Apollo program are offended, they have every right to be. My bad.

I'd also like to note that, in real life, Shiosai Park in Kimigahama isn't open for swimming due to high waves and rip currents. You won't find any beach to play on there, and there's no hyperdimensional snack bar either, so don't visit expecting either of those.

With this volume, *The Devil is a Part-Timer!* is now enjoying its first full year in publication. I simply must thank my editor (Mr. A), my illustrator (029), everyone at ASCII Media Works, the proofers, the printers, the distributors, the bookstores, and, most important, the people holding this book in their hands right now. I'd like to wrap up this afterword by saying, with every fiber of my body and soul: Thank you.